Larkwood Academy

WHISPERS

JAYCE CARTER

Totally Bound Publishing books by Jayce Carter

The Omega's Alphas
Owned by the Alphas
Shared by the Alphas
Saved by the Alphas
Protected by Her Alphas
Caught by Her Alphas
Tamed by the Alphas
Claimed by the Alphas
Exposed by Her Alphas
Trained by the Alphas
Reclaimed by Her Alphas

Ready or Not
Fake It 'til You Make It
Opposites Attract
Third Time Lucky
Enemies Closer

Grave Concerns
Grave Robbing and Other Hobbies
Hell Raising and Other Pastimes
Saving the World and Other Bad Ideas

Dark Sanctuary
Bound by Fear
Trapped by Doubt
Buried by Despair

Nemesis
The Corpse Princess
The Resurrected Queen

Larkwood Academy
Silenced
Whispers

Collections
Sun, Sea and Sinful Delights

WHISPERS

Dedication

To my penis keychain — thanks for discouraging strangers from talking to me.

Chapter One

I never missed my voice more than when Deacon touched me, when I opened my mouth and wanted to moan his name.

Sure, there were other times it annoyed me — when I wanted to tell someone off, when I wanted to explain myself, when I just wanted to *be heard.* Those times irked, but the loss never bothered me as much as when Deacon teased his lips over my breast, when the lack of noise from me made it feel incomplete.

Not that Deacon seemed to mind — or perhaps it was better to say he could make up for it easily. He might not have been the most vocal man in his normal life, but that all changed in bed.

I looked around for a moment, noting the quiet corner of a shed in the yard where we'd tucked ourselves away. *Maybe bed is a stretch…*

We couldn't risk people catching on to us, which had left us finding out-of-the-way spots like this for our little rendezvous. Neither of us wanted to turn into a weakness for the other.

"I missed you," Deacon whispered in his low, rough voice against my skin, his breath warm and rapid.

I loved these moments, how he lost that composure he usually had, how he seemed like anyone else. Normally Deacon was bigger than life, a guard at Larkwood Academy who even the other guards feared and distrusted.

In these moments, though, he wasn't any of that. He was just *mine*.

I set my hand on the back of his neck and brought him closer, pulled him to my body until I could use my lips to try to tell him the things I couldn't say with my kiss.

He groaned against my lips, then grabbed my thigh to pull it around him. My ass pressed against the small table I sat on, but I didn't care about anything. Not splinters, not discomfort, nothing but drowning myself in these rare moments of happiness.

I'd lived at Larkwood for months and had mostly accepted the brutality that made up my world now, but that made these moments even more important. When Deacon touched me, when he growled into my ear, it made the rest of the ugliness of my life drift away.

He sank his cock into me, and I dug my nails into his back. It always gave me this wonderful burn when he took me, when I could feel entirely filled by him.

So I lost myself in him, in his strength, in the rough whispered praise he offered. Too soon, it ended. Too quickly, I wiped off and pulled my sweats back on, brushing my hair with my fingers to appear presentable. We never had much time, never got to indulge in the quiet happiness normal people could when they enjoyed languid motions and gentle kisses through the night.

Deacon buttoned his pants, his expression having shifted back to the usual closed-off one he showed to everyone else. No doubt that was one reason I so cherished the times we had, because they were the only chances I got to really see him.

"You need to be more careful," he muttered.

I turned toward him, furrowing my brows.

The zipper of his pants was loud in the quiet shed. "You've got guards watching you. Warden put out a memo to keep a close eye on you. You think they don't know you've been meeting up with those delinquents you seem to think are friends?"

I pressed my lips together and narrowed my eyes. Of course Deacon didn't care for the other connections I'd made—he considered all the shades dangerous, so he saw any other resident as a risk to me.

What he didn't understand was that *everything* was a risk to me. The whole damned world seemed to want to take me apart, to pull me to pieces until nothing was left.

He came forward and set his hand on the back of my neck, angling my face so I looked right into those bright purple eyes of his. Those eyes had ushered me into my new life at one time, but they meant so much more to me now. "I don't want to lose you, Hera. You can't trust anyone, can't let your guard down. Whatever they're talking you into, it'll get you killed."

I set my hand on his chest and pushed. He didn't move because of the pressure I applied, but because he chose to. I could have used my powers, my ability to control sound waves, but I tried my hardest to keep that hidden. I'd finally gotten to where I didn't do it on accident, so I kept it on a tight leash. While he'd witnessed that skill, he had no idea of the extent of it.

"Nothing to say?" Anger flashed across his features, but I didn't fear him. I knew him too well already, knew he'd never hurt me, at least not on purpose. Sure, he was a guard at the very place holding me captive, but he did all he could to protect me.

"No one makes me do anything," I signed to him.

"You're too naïve," he snapped. "You think I don't know they're trouble? That they're looking for some magical way out? Look, this place has stood for a long damned time, and no level-one shade has ever escaped. A lot of them have died trying, though. I don't care how good a *friend* you think they are, they'll let you take the fall if it benefits them at all."

Deacon's words were callous but not unexpected.

We'd done this for weeks, ever since I'd left solitary after being caught breaking into a file room. Deacon was smart enough to know I was up to something, but pushing too much might just end up making me a bigger target. It had driven a wedge between us, one that hurt more than I liked to admit.

I hated having to separate my life, to keep things from all the people around me, but I didn't have a choice.

Deacon couldn't find out about the plans I had with Wade, Knox and Brax, and the three of them couldn't know the extent of my relationship with Deacon.

Though I had a feeling all the men in my life had made wrong guesses about one another. It was in the looks, in the aggression they all showed when talking about each other. No doubt each of them assumed I was sleeping with all the others in my life.

Which wasn't true.

Though…not because of lack of effort on my part.

It just turned out romance was as foreign a concept to me as the economics of other countries and how football worked. Getting people into bed was much more difficult than I'd have ever imagined. I recalled all the times I'd heard as a teenager how boys were animals who only wanted one thing, how I had to be careful as a woman or I'd get taken advantage of.

Yet most of these men were not taking advantage of me in the way I wanted them to, no matter how I tried to tempt them.

Not that telling them that would matter. Deception was a way of life here at Larkwood, and we *all* had our secrets.

"Don't fight with me. We don't have long."

"I'm not trying to fight," he assured me, despite the aggressive tone of voice that he used almost exclusively for fighting. "I just worry about you. I'm afraid I'll open my email and see your name on the North Tower list. I don't want that."

To be fair, neither did I. Despite the fact that the North Tower seemed my only real escape option, I wasn't ready to face that horror just yet. I needed a better plan, more information—anything to give me an edge.

But it wasn't as if I could admit any of that to Deacon. If he discovered any plan for escape I had, he'd just ruin it to protect me.

So I had to keep that all close to my chest and play dumb. *"You don't need to worry about me."*

He made a soft sound low in his throat, as if he couldn't believe what an idiot I was. "Of course I do. You're trouble, Hera, and you attract trouble like a fucking magnet. Don't forget, I was the one who saved you that night when you changed. I saw it all. I know exactly how much you need someone worrying about you."

I dropped my gaze at the painful reminder. If it wasn't for him, I'd have died on that parking structure floor. I'd have bled out because of the man who had slit my throat, the one who had taken my voice.

Instead, Deacon had heard my scream, had come and saved me.

Then he'd brought me to Larkwood…

It was a complicated relationship.

He reached forward again, but he didn't touch my cheek. Instead, he touched the scar at my throat, the whole reason I couldn't speak. "You almost died. *This* happened because the world didn't like what you were. I saved you that time, but I'm terrified I won't be able to the next, that you'll do something stupid and end up in a situation I can't do anything about." His words were so soft, so sad that they took me aback.

I forced myself to stare into his eyes, to witness the pain and fear there. For all Deacon's faults — and there were a lot of them — he wasn't a bad man. He wanted the best for me.

The problem?

We didn't agree on what was best. He wanted me alive even if it meant losing everything else. I wanted freedom, even if it meant risking my life for it.

It was an impasse I didn't know how to fix.

"I don't want to see you get finished off because you want to escape," he whispered.

I forced my hand up so I could sign back. *"I'm not planning anything."*

* * * *

"So, what's the plan for our escape?"

Knox let out a laugh as he read what I had signed. "You really don't beat around the bush, do you?"

12

I shrugged before reaching into his fridge for a water. It was odd to think that weeks before, I'd been so nervous in his place, so afraid of doing anything wrong, of upsetting him.

Now I treated his space as if it were my own, and each time I did? He smiled a little wider.

I held one water out to him, but he shook his head. It gave me the chance to look at him for a moment, surprised as ever by just how handsome he was.

He had a body that could have tempted me even if he hadn't been the kind man he was. He was lean but strong, and he kept his hair so short it was basically buzzed off. He had on a T-shirt, and while that wasn't normally the type of outfit to swoon over, he made even it look amazing.

Then again, that was partly due to the general sensuality he had, all thanks to his incubus side. He was essentially a walking billboard offering sex, and while he and I had never fully gone there, it didn't make me immune to noticing.

Hell, maybe that denial made me even more aware.

"How's Deacon?"

I let out an obvious sigh along with an eye roll for good measure. *"Why do you ask?"*

"You're way too casual with him." Knox shook his head, the same argument I'd had with him a few times. I'd had the same fight with Brax as well, though my fights with him were more yelling — at least from him — and always ended up with us having angry sex. Wade didn't bitch, but his snarky comments suggested he didn't approve.

Knox at least acted nice when we argued.

"It's nothing to worry about."

"You say that because you don't know the real him. If he gets wind of anything, he'll turn you right in."

"He wouldn't do that."

Knox didn't know Deacon like I did. Sure, I wasn't rushing to tell Deacon everything—that would have been stupid. But I was fully capable of spending time with him without blurting out every last thing on my mind.

Not being able to speak helps.

Knox set his hand on my cheek, his palm warm and teasing. He stroked his thumb against my skin. "That you still have some of that innocence after being here is amazing. I just don't want to see it get you killed because you trusted the wrong person."

His words melted some of my annoyance. I understood his worry, especially because if I made the wrong choice. If I trusted the wrong person and we got caught, Knox and his brother could easily pay the price for it.

Even with that, though, I couldn't just *not* spend time with Deacon. Sure, things would end when I escaped, because what sort of future did we have? That should have made it easier to let go now, before I got too attached, but the opposite seemed true.

I just couldn't imagine ending it sooner than I had to.

Knox offered a half-hearted smile, as if I were an idiot climbing too high into a tree, and he knew I'd fall and break something. "You are impossible." He leaned in and brushed his soft lips against mine, the touch gentle and sweet.

And it did what his innocent touches *always* did to me. A rush of sensation, like drowning and suddenly being able to breathe all at once. It was his power, that incubus part of him hungry and wanting to feed.

But he'd refused to feed from me or to touch me almost at all. I'd been able to touch him, to focus on him, but he never reciprocated. It wasn't selfishness but fear.

As soon as it happened, he pulled back and shook his head hard, as though to clear it.

"It's okay," I told him the way I always did, even when his rejection hurt, even when it didn't feel okay at all.

"It's not."

I missed the warmth of his hand when he took it away, when we stood there with this distance between us that I had no idea how to fix. Understanding the reason for it didn't change the hurt. No matter what I did, he didn't trust himself, didn't trust that other part of him, didn't want it near me.

And there wasn't a thing I could do about that.

Instead of letting him see just how much it hurt, I turned away and brought the water bottle to my lips, trying to let the cold liquid cool my flushed cheeks and slow my racing heart.

"Hera," Knox started to say, but the opening of his front door saved me.

Sort of…

Not sure if the angry face of a berserker who I'm pretty sure hates me counts as being saved.

"Have you found anything yet?" Brax asked, his tone annoyed.

Was he ever *not* annoyed, though? Maybe, when around others. I had no idea if it was just me or if he was always unpleasant.

Judging from his glare my way, I'd say it was a mixture.

"Nothing yet."

Knox translated for me, since Brax seemed the only person unable—or more likely unwilling—to learn American Sign Language. When it was just the two of us, I used my writing pad, but when others were around, they translated.

"So what good are you? You had this big idea about wanting to escape but then you get nothing over the last month? Fuck, I hate people who are all talk."

And, as usual, I rose to the occasion when it came to his anger. Funny that back when I'd first met him, he'd terrified me. Now? Now I didn't give a fuck about his little hissy fits. If he hadn't killed me yet, he probably wouldn't.

Most likely…

I was pretty sure…

"I'm sorry that I'm not doing enough for you. What exactly was it you've done? Because I'm pretty sure I figured out about the North Tower and the two projects they're doing there."

Brax narrowed his blue eyes into a murderous glare as Knox translated. It was funny how similar the twins looked—everything but their eye color. Physically, they were identical, despite their behavior being nothing alike. At the end, he let out a huff. "Well, don't get sloppy. If you fuck up, we all go down, and I'm not about to let that happen."

I lifted my eyebrow to stare back. What was the point in arguing? Brax only heard what he wanted to hear, and having Knox translate everything made it all take longer.

"Be careful," Knox offered, his voice even gentler than before, as if trying to make up for the attitude of his twin.

Then again, the two were always looking out for each other. Brax tried to protect Knox and Knox made excuses for Brax's horrible behavior.

When I didn't respond, Knox went on. "After getting thrown in solitary, you're bound to be watched more closely. I know Brax is pushing you, but don't do anything risky."

Brax opened his mouth as if to argue that point but snapped his lips together before he could. He let out an angry sound and the edges of his face sharpened the way they always did when his temper got away from him. Berserkers weren't known for their control and calm. Instead of saying anything else, he turned on his heel and stormed out, slamming the door behind him, his exit as dramatic and quick as his entrance had been.

Knox sighed, his gaze pinned to the door as if he could still watch his brother through it. "I swear, his temper is worse than ever…"

It seemed the same to me. The only reason he'd gotten annoyed was because he wanted me to do whatever it took, no matter the danger to me, and that it was a dick-thing to say frustrated him.

"You don't understand him," Knox said.

"Stop defending him."

"That's never going to happen." Knox gave me a sad smile. "He's not the easiest to get along with, but there's more to him than anyone realizes. Don't take the things he says at face value."

I took another drink of water, mostly to give us a way to end the conversation. I knew what Brax was like, had experienced his brand of asshole behavior plenty of times. The last thing I needed was for Brax's bad behavior to sour my relationship with Knox.

It was all rather precarious already.

Knox glanced behind him at the clock on the wall. "You had your work detail this morning, right?"

"I have an evaluation in about an hour."

He pressed his lips together, and I knew he was getting ready to lecture me yet again. This time, about Kit.

But what did all these warnings matter? I couldn't just *not* see Kit, since the adjunct professor handled not only teaching lessons but also most of the evaluations. It wasn't like I had an option to not go.

Besides, we hadn't had one since solitary, since I'd gotten caught with files from a restricted room. After spending the time being punished, I'd had my work details increased for two weeks. That made this the first eval since that had all happened.

Which meant I'd probably get an earful from him as well.

Why was it that everyone thought I needed their advice? That everyone saw me as some helpless creature who others had to tell how to behave?

Well, I did get caught when I tried to work on my own…

I cut off his lecture by tossing the now-empty water bottle into the recycling bin under Knox's sink. *"I'll be careful, I promise."*

Knox let out a long breath, catching my arm before I walked out. When he tugged me back and pressed his lips to mine in a kiss that stole all my annoyance away, I worried I'd lose myself. Kissing him was like looking over a cliff and down at a body of water. It tempted me to jump, made me want to dive in no matter how deep or dangerous.

As quickly as it happened, however, he let me go, stealing away that warmth. It was like shoving me away from the edge of that cliff. He swallowed hard, his green eyes bright as he stared at me, as if he wanted me to understand something.

What, though?

Maybe he didn't know, either. Maybe it was just hopeless, pointless desire, a drive to have something that wasn't possible.

Whatever it was, he stepped backward, fleeing as he so often did to his room, leaving me there confused and surprisingly cold.

Which felt like a good representation of whatever I had with Knox.

Chapter Two

I rushed into the room listed on my schedule out of breath, a glance at the clock telling me I'd just made it in time.

Lateness didn't go over well at Larkwood, and that hadn't bothered me when I'd first arrived. At first, just moving from my room to class or work had seemed easy enough. The longer I spent here, however, the more filled my days became and the easier it was to end up late.

Especially now that the guards kept a much closer eye on me.

"Cutting it close, aren't you?" Kit's voice made me turn to find him standing in the room already. Of course he was there early — that was so like Kit.

He wore a suit, looking like any other instructor there. At least, he would if it weren't for his entirely black eyes and the cuff on his wrist like all the other shades there.

And there was the fact that I'd glimpsed what he really looked like, and that sight never quite left me. I recalled the deer skull, the large antlers, the thin, elongated limbs, the terrifyingly deep voice that called through an endless, empty darkness.

I shivered, unable to help it each time I remembered what I'd seen.

When he hadn't moved, I swallowed and signed a response to him. *"The guards searched me."*

Kit nodded, leaning against a desk along the wall of the room. "You should expect that. You made a nuisance of yourself, and the Warden took notice. Now you're being watched closely."

"Lucky me."

"Well, if you don't like that much scrutiny, perhaps you shouldn't get caught with files you shouldn't have."

Which told me Kit knew exactly what had happened. Not that I thought it would have been some secret. Word traveled fast through Larkwood, and Kit had an ability to access information others wouldn't.

"Does this mean I get yet another lecture?"

He didn't glare—no, not Kit. He wasn't the type to sink to something like that. While I didn't know him that well, he was forever calm from what I'd seen.

Instead, he crossed his arms and tilted his head. "Who has been lecturing you, songbird?"

The nickname burned as it always did, like some joke everyone else found hilarious. Given I'd had my voice stolen, calling me 'songbird' just seemed cruel.

But I'd taken the advice I'd gotten to claim it as my own, to not fight against it. Not that it had helped yet. The name still sucked.

"No one," I signed because it wasn't like I could tell him that the other shades who were helping me come up with an escape plan liked to complain to me about, well, everything.

"You are a terrible liar," he said but didn't press the issue further. "It's been a few weeks since we've had an evaluation. Have you been practicing on your own?"

I nodded. I took time each evening to work on controlling my powers, on how to twist sound waves to my advantage, how to block out sounds I didn't need or want. It wasn't easy, and the bags under my eyes spoke volumes about how much I'd sacrificed to work on it.

However, after getting thrown in solitary, after learning what I had, I realized how much I needed those powers. I couldn't face off against Larkwood and the Warden if I had no skills of my own.

"Good," Kit said. "Let's work on that. I want to see what you've managed."

I peered around the room and frowned.

"We're not going outside for this," he said. "You've proven you're capable of causing large-scale destruction with your powers, but that isn't always useful. It's just as important to learn to control it on a small scale." At my look, he sighed softly. "Blowing doors off a frame is effective, but sometimes it's a better idea to just unlock a door."

That made me go still at the fact that he was *far* too close to the truth.

"You really are extremely easy to read, you know? You need to learn how to school your features better. I have no idea how you've lasted as long as you have without getting into more trouble." Even with that, he didn't press, didn't try to get me to admit anything.

Whether that was because he didn't feel it necessary since he already knew, or whether he just didn't care, I wasn't sure. Kit was forever an enigma.

He nodded toward a table in the middle of the room and the items set on it. There was a stack of small boxes and an apple on top. "I want you to knock the apple off without disturbing the boxes."

"Are you kidding me? I can't do that!"

"Yes, you can." Kit didn't move or tell me it was all a joke like I wanted him to.

Opening a lock was one thing—that was about replicating something I'd heard before. This would be trying to harness and hone a wave down to a very narrow effect…

Still, he seemed unwilling to back down, which meant I had little choice.

"I scheduled your evaluation on this floor since there aren't any guards here and no one else should be in the area. Don't worry."

Easy for him to say. He wouldn't pay the price if I did it wrong. What if I didn't manage it and ended up blowing the side of the building off? Pretty sure the Warden wouldn't take that too lightly…

With no way to get out of it, I took a deep breath and tilted my head to ease the tension in my neck. After giving myself as much procrastination time as I thought I could get away with, I lifted my hands. There had been a time when I'd first done this when I'd needed to snap my fingers to create the initial sound, but after my practice?

I'd realized that there was *always* sound around me. The world was never truly silent, which meant I didn't have to create sound first to use it. In the room at that moment was the subtle creak of the building, the breathing of Kit and me, even the beating of our hearts.

I lowered my guards, let the sounds melt into me, felt them moving over my skin like a caress welcoming me home. I so rarely did this, so rarely gave myself over to it, and it reminded me why.

It was dangerous. It pulled me in deeper, made me want to lose everything to just the sounds.

"Don't dive too deep," Kit said, his voice lower than usual, rougher.

Right. Focus. I stopped letting myself enjoy the sensation so much and put my attention to the task at hand. I stopped trying to take something from the room and instead snapped my fingers. It helped my power start in one place.

I pushed it forward, toward the apple, but my calculations were all wrong. The apple went flying, but so did the boxes, and even the table they sat on flipped over.

I let out a sigh at the colossal failure. I mean, I hadn't taken out a wall or anything, so that was better than I thought, right?

Kit moved as if he'd expected that. He set the table back up — and he didn't struggle despite the weight — then picked up the boxes. He put it all back the way it had been, finally adding the apple on again. After he returned to his spot, he nodded. "Again."

I lifted my hand and tried it again, ready for a long damned day.

No wonder he'd scheduled the evaluation for the rest of today, and knowing Kit, I wasn't getting out of it until I got it right.

* * * *

Kit

I blinked slowly, trying to ease the exhaustion that hung on me. Four hours of watching Hera fail seemed to be my limit.

Still, I couldn't deny my pride over the fact that she had refused to give up. Each time she didn't manage the task I'd set before her, she'd blow out a hard breath, narrow her eyes, then rest as I set them back up.

She'd thus far managed to knock down the boxes, the table, even the chalkboard from the far wall. All of that happened when she'd attempted to use less power. It again reminded me that the girl possessed far more power than she should have, that she had the potential to be exceedingly dangerous on a level that concerned even me.

"This is impossible," she signed before looking my way with a frown.

"It isn't impossible. You've proven you can use this power, so now you simply have to control it."

"It's easy to say that, but you haven't explained how I'm supposed to do that."

"Because I'm not a siren. I don't know how it feels to control sound waves, to manipulate them. How can I explain something I am not able to do?"

She set her hands on her hips, her chest rising and falling as she breathed hard. No doubt I'd pushed her about to her limit.

It almost made me feel bad. Or perhaps the better way to put that was that I would have felt bad if I felt much of anything. Since I didn't, it was just a vague sensation that I should have felt bad. Pushing people to their limit wasn't new to me or all that unusual.

It was how a person got results, by pushing others, by seeing what they could do when at the end of their rope. People grew the most when they had no other choice.

However, for the first time, the task really bothered me.

Or perhaps not the first time. I recalled watching Hera get thrown to the dirt repeatedly during another evaluation. I'd felt it then, too.

"So why are you doing this? If you can't actually teach me what do to, what is the whole point of this?" she asked.

"I can't tell you *how* to do it, but I can offer advice and push you to your potential."

"Why, though? You're the one who keeps telling me to keep this secret, to be careful, but then you push me to do more. What's your angle?"

Her question made me want to rub the heel of my hand against my chest, a discomfort there. "You never would have asked me that when you first got here."

She narrowed her eyes.

When she didn't seem willing to respond, I went on and explained. "You trusted people when you came here, and even if you didn't, you never would have actually spoken up against anyone." I paused for a moment, then added on, "Especially me."

"I needed to grow up. I got plenty of reminders about that."

While fair, I didn't care for her explanation. Which was strange… I was usually the first to ensure that new shades understood how dangerous the world was. I'd never tried to hide it, to protect anyone from the truth.

Doing so only ensured they'd end up a victim in the future.

Yet…the fact that some of those soft edges of Hera's had now sharpened caused an ache I was unaccustomed to. For the first time, I wanted her to keep that softness.

I wanted her to fall asleep without the worries of the real world. I wanted to hold back that reality for her, to keep her safe from it.

The last time I'd felt like that…

I shook away the memory, the pain and the horrible lesson that I'd taken to heart from it.

This world crushed the innocent and the naïve. Wanting her to stay that way would only ensure that she ended up the same. It was selfish to desire that when she would pay the price for it.

She lifted an eyebrow, which made me realize I hadn't answered her question.

Some strange part of me wanted to tell her the truth, but I couldn't. Instead, I went with the easy lie, the one anyone would have believed. "Because it's my job. I'm supposed to help evaluate and train shades so they can prove useful."

"If you just wanted me to be useful, you'd have told the Warden about what I can do."

The fact that she could so easily see through my words annoyed me. It was the issue when dealing with creatures like Hera who could read lies in a person's voice. It made interacting with them far more troublesome.

"People without skills don't last long," I said when I realized that offering no answer would create a larger problem than offering a partly true one. "I've been here a very long time, and I've seen what happens to those who lack the ability to protect themselves. I do not want that to happen to you."

Hera let out a sigh before sitting on top of one of the desks in the room. Exhaustion tugged at her, which didn't surprise me. Using their powers took energy and focus for any shade. While the more source a shade had, the more they could use their powers, there was always a toll on the body.

And Hera had been using hers a lot today.

The fact that she could still stand impressed me.

"Does it ever get easier?"

"I'm afraid I'll need a few more nouns to understand your question."

"This. All of it. Being a shade, being here, being afraid of what you can do while also being afraid of losing it. Does it ever become normal?"

"No."

Her shoulders fell at that response. Normally I'd have left it at that, at the simple, obvious answer, but something about her crestfallen expression had me speaking again. "People become stronger and better able to handle the unpleasant parts of life, but it doesn't become easier. I wish I could tell you that now my life is perfect, that I found some secret which erases all the pain in life, but that isn't how it works. Life hurts — every life. Show me the richest, most handsome man in the world and I'll still be able to drag out the hidden pain he holds."

"What's the point, then?"

"I'm no philosopher, songbird. I only know that I won't find any meaning tomorrow if I don't survive today."

She snorted softly, as if she found the answer cryptic.

I hadn't thought so, but others often misunderstood me, often thought I spoke in riddles rather than bluntly. I blamed that misunderstanding on my age. To the young, I no doubt sounded cryptic, like when an adult explains complex issues to a child. They simply lacked enough of the background I had to comprehend it.

"I think you're afraid," I said softly.

She lifted her gaze to mine, her hazel eyes narrowed. *You don't like that, do you?*

"You want to be able to use your powers, but you're afraid that doing so means accepting what you are. This is even more the case when it comes to honing that

28

power down to a precise weapon. You feel you're turning your back on the life you wish to return to. You don't know how you'll fit back into that life if you continue to grow into the siren you are."

She swallowed hard. Even if I hadn't been sure that I'd guessed correctly, that proved it.

"The thing is," I told her, "if you don't learn this, if you don't give in and embrace exactly what you are, you won't survive long enough to get your old life back."

"Do you really think it's possible for me to get my old life back?"

I wanted to lie, to tell her it was, if for no other reason than to selfishly keep her closer, to give her false hope to keep going. Instead, I pushed off from the table I leaned against. "Honestly? No. I've never seen a single shade manage it, and I can't imagine you being the first. Still, the only chance you have is to actually put in the work."

I turned my back on her, walking toward the door. "However, I can tell you that very slim chance dwindles to nothing if you choose to let fear rule you, if you decide to sulk and wish instead of doing anything. People thought you were a rich, useless heiress when you came here, and this behavior only proves them right."

An odd sound struck my ears a heartbeat before a sense of danger made the hairs on the back of my neck stand on edge. Wendigos were not creatures taken down easily, and I was old enough to have well-honed senses.

I twisted, my hand shifting into my true form on instinct, the limb elongating, the fingers lengthening and the claws growing in the blink of an eye.

Something struck the palm of my hand, my body moving to catch it without a clue as to what it was.

Hera sat on the desk, still, her normally passive eyes nearly burning with anger, the sort of sight that should have driven a man backward out of fear.

I looked down into my hand to find the apple, and on the table the boxes sat undisturbed.

I let out a dark chuckle. "The first day I saw you, all but shaking on the floor after dealing with Brax, I was sure you wouldn't last a week. Keep this up, and you might just outlive all of us."

I lifted the apple up, then allowed my powers to draw from it, to pull out everything alive until it withered. I didn't stop until the apple turned to dust in my hand, until the particles blew out of my palm.

The anger that had been on her face turned to fear— which was good, right? I rarely let others see my power, too aware of the negative reactions. Knowing something and seeing it were two very different things. It took witnessing the ability of wendigos to truly grasp their danger.

So why did I do so then? Why was it that when Hera was actually starting to listen, I felt the need to terrify her?

Because I'm more of a coward than she could ever be. It's better she figures out what I really am now, before I risk myself again.

I'd survived Larkwood longer than any other shade, had survived this world longer than nearly any other shade, and yet I did what I did out of fear of what that little muted siren could do to me if I let down my guard.

Fear was a far less risky emotion.

Chapter Three

Hera

I tilted my head back and let the sun streaming through the top-floor windows soak into me.

I remembered going tanning in my old life. The scent of the lotion, the tightness of the goggles, the tingle on my skin as the rays warmed me. I'd stopped and moved to spray-on when the risk of skin cancer became too much for me to allow, but I missed it sometimes.

I never realized how much I'd miss sunlight until I got to Larkwood, though. Few places in the building had windows. I'd wondered at first how they could get away with that due to building codes, then remembered where I was.

Larkwood didn't give a damn about what would happen in the event of a fire. We could all burn, and they'd just rebuild and start over with a fresh batch.

All of that meant the main areas of the building were lit artificially. The slight flicker of the overhead fluorescents was a constant in my life, and it drove me to this floor for the sun.

I wasn't the only one, either.

On the other side of the large open floor sat a few other shades. They didn't approach me, and when I'd arrived, they had actually moved away from my side of the floor. It seemed I was about as welcome as I'd been when I'd first gotten here.

Getting thrown in solitary had lessened the comments from others, but it sure hadn't endeared me to anyone. Worse, those I ended up associating with weren't well liked at all either.

Deacon was a guard, Kit was a teacher and seen as a turncoat, Wade was annoyingly friendly but others were terrified of him, Brax had no issue breaking bones when unhappy and he was unhappy a *lot*, and Knox was only popular because people wanted to sleep with him.

I'd formed some sort of group for myself, but it consisted of outcasts as well.

Which meant the shades who sunbathed as well wanted *nothing* to do with me. I was pretty sure I saw a dryad over there, a look of pure happiness on her face. Then again, if I recalled my shade-types correctly, dryads required sunlight just like plants. No doubt she had some sort of UV light in her room, but it wasn't the same thing.

Beside her was a cat shifter, lounging on the carpet in a sunny spot just like I imagined a house cat would do. It was almost sweet.

"You know, skin cancer is a real thing."

Wade's voice drew a smile from me as it always did. Something about the carefree way he spoke felt as if it made the rest of the world shrink, as if he pushed away the stress just by saying something stupid.

And the things he said were nearly always stupid.

"Windows have UV protection in them to filter out the more harmful rays."

"So no Bahama-mama golden skin for you?"

I shook my head before opening my eyes to find Wade standing beside where I'd stretched out over a few of the seats. *"I just can't get warm sometimes and need to feel the sun."*

He dropped his gaze to his own hands, to the gloves that covered him up past his shirt. I'd seen him without those gloves, but it was rare.

Then again, I'd also both gotten to witness it and had a first-person taste of what he could do if his skin touched another shade. While it hadn't been frightening to me, watching him pull the power from an ifrit who had threatened me never went away. Wade could take down the most powerful shade with nothing more than a brush of his skin.

"Well, with porcelain skin like this, I need to keep it covered." The words were his normal humorous ones, but I caught the waver inside them. He took a seat on the row of chairs just above where my head rested.

I shifted, wincing when my body didn't seem to care for resting on the hard surfaces. Instead of sitting up, however, I scooted toward Wade and set my head on his lap.

"Better."

He let out a nervous laugh. "Aren't you cuddly? You sure this is the sort of thing for public viewing?"

I waved him off and closed my eyes again. A shadow made me snap them open, finding his hand just above me.

He moved slowly, as if giving me the chance to stop him, before he stroked his fingers through my hair. The touch was gentle, sweet.

It was strange, because in some ways it felt the most real of all my relationships. The least complicated. Wade lacked some of the defense mechanisms of the other men in my life.

Still, he spoke as if I wasn't in his lap, as if he weren't stroking my head. "I heard a rumor."

I closed my eyes, and that seemed to give him the courage to keep going, as if me not looking at him or pulling away reassured him that I welcomed his touch.

"Your name is on the list for Medical in a few days."

And there went that relaxation I'd felt.

I had finally healed from my last run-in with Medical, when they'd taken a number of punch biopsies and had drugged me to the point where Deacon had had to carry me back to my room.

I couldn't stop the shiver that ran through me at the idea of returning there, of feeling that helpless again. Larkwood could make any shade feel as if they had no use, as if they were simple property, but nothing had dehumanized me as much as my short stay in Medical, and the drugs had stolen most of those memories from me.

Wade didn't stop his gentle touch. "I wasn't even sure if I should say anything. It's not like there's much that can be done, so I didn't know if me telling you would be better, if you worrying about it for days would be better."

"I can't do anything if I don't know," I assured him.

He made a soft sound that neither agreed nor disagreed, as if just to acknowledge that he'd heard me.

"I'm surprised they're taking you again so quickly. Medical rarely gives a damn about shades. Most only go there a time or two, and some never do after initial testing."

"They said my source numbers are unprecedented. I knew it was coming."

"I wonder why yours are so high…" He spoke with a distant tone, as if not addressing me at all. Then again, Wade was the type to talk to himself. "I've heard rumors about people working on a way to create stronger shades."

"Why?"

"Because they probably want to weaponize us, and the stronger a shade is, the more useful. Plus, scientists always want to push the limits of what's possible. Sometimes by creating something that shouldn't exist, they discover secrets they hadn't known before."

I shook my head. *"I wasn't put into some lab before I changed. I'd remember that."*

"Maybe," he said softly, telling me he didn't agree but didn't know either. "But the fact remains that if they want to do that, understanding how your body tolerated the extremely high levels along with looking into how it happened might get them closer to their goal." His hand paused for a moment before his voice dropped. "What was Medical like?"

"You've never been?"

"No. They did my intake tests, though I don't recall much of that. Since then, they'll do yearly blood draws, but they don't bring me to Medical for that. They just draw the blood and deliver it there. I've heard it's…bad."

"They drugged me, so I don't remember most of it. I remember pain, though. I remember struggling and crying and they didn't give a damn." I grabbed the hem of my shirt and lifted it, showing the almost fully healed mark on my hip. *"They took a bunch of samples. I had six of them taken, but I'd assume they took others that didn't leave marks."*

Just saying that made me swallow hard. What I remembered was terrible, but not nearly as bad as what I *didn't* know. They most likely took other samples — swabs from my cheeks, blood samples, hair samples, even ones from places on my body that I shuddered to consider too closely. That others had done that to me, that I'd had no say and no memory even, was so much worse than the pain of the exams.

It felt like another way to remind me that I wasn't my own person, that I had no rights, that even my body wasn't mine.

Wade made a soft, comforting sound as he ran his fingers through my hair. "Maybe it's best not to remember everything. There are a few types of shades who can't be drugged, who remember everything, and from what I've seen? That isn't any better."

I was about to argue with him until his words fully sank in.

"What sort of shades can't be drugged?"

"I'm not sure of all the types. Vampires, some shifters when in their other form, phantoms. I'm sure there are others, but no one makes a list of them." He paused, then asked with more than a little suspicion, "Why?"

I pulled up and off his lap, my mind moving as I tried to come up with a plan. *"No reason,"* I signed quickly before getting to my feet. *"I'll talk to you later."*

I caught the sound of him groaning as I rushed off, as if he knew I had some bad idea planned but also knew he couldn't stop me.

Which was fair.

I needed to go see a certain grumpy guard and get his help.

And I was *sure* he wouldn't be happy about it.

* * * *

Deacon

Having Hera in my room always made me nervous.

It was a stupid response, one that didn't fit at all with our surroundings. Hell, we'd had sex multiple times, so why did I turn into some young man inviting a girl over for the first time just because she was in my place?

Because you're a romantic idiot.

Hard to argue with that.

She had something in her hand, and I narrowed my eyes at it.

"What's that?"

She held it out to me without answering.

It wasn't as if Hera was likely to turn on me at this point, so I took the item and peeked into the paper bag.

A box of animal crackers sat inside, making me frown. It was an odd gift, and I wasn't sure I understood. "What's this about?"

"You like them, don't you?"

"I guess." I set the bag on the counter, unsure what to say back other than a quiet, "Thanks."

She tilted her head, as if trying to work something out. After a moment, her hands started to move. *"You don't remember?"*

"Remember what?"

She pressed her lips together, then shook her head. *"It doesn't matter."*

I wanted to ask more, but let it go. Hera didn't usually seek me out, and whenever she had, it hadn't ever been for anything good. I focused on that. "What is it you want?"

"Can't I come just because I want to see you?"

I didn't bother to call her out for that but lifted my eyebrow instead.

She sighed. *"I need some information."*

"What are you scheming this time?"

"Nothing."

I snorted at the obvious lie.

"I know I'm on the list for Medical soon."

Those words sent a chill through me. I recalled the last time, when I'd carried her back to her room, when she'd been drugged up and innocent and vulnerable. Why would they call her back again so soon? They were interested in how they could use her, but even with that, it seemed odd timing.

I wanted to tell her I could fix that, that I could get her out of it, but the words wouldn't come out. They weren't true. Instead, I had to be honest. "I have no access or control over Medical's choices."

"I'm not asking for that."

"Then what?"

"I heard the drugs don't work on some shades."

I sat on the couch and nodded at the spot beside me for Hera. "Yeah, there are a few."

"I need to know what types and how it works."

"Why?"

She took the spot I'd indicated and faced me, so close her knee brushed me as she sat sideways. *"Not being conscious last time was the worst part. I don't want that, don't want to have to question what happened, to feel that out of control."*

I understood that, but I didn't like it. "I told you before that remembering isn't all it's chalked up to be."

"That's easy for you to say — you do remember. I keep wondering what else they might have done and not knowing keeps me up at night. I just don't want them to be able to steal my thoughts. Larkwood has already stolen everything else

from me, but I don't want them to have my mind, too. It's all I get, and I want to keep it."

I rubbed my temple as I blew out a long, slow breath. I wanted to tell her no for so many damned reasons. I wanted to say it because it was dangerous, because remembering it all would do nothing but cause her harm, because I didn't want her to carry that pain.

However, staring at her, at her earnest eyes and the pain that rested there, meant I couldn't just blow off her request.

Powerlessness was a hell of a motivator, and the last thing I wanted was her going around and searching for a shade on her own.

"There's only one shade in level 1 who might be able to help," I told her.

"Who?"

I didn't answer her question directly, wanting to discuss it first. "Being able to counter drugs is one thing, but a shade who can transfer that ability to another is way rarer. If you do this, though, you'll remember everything they do. You'll have to carry that with you. Are you sure it's worth it?"

She nodded. *"I'm sure. I need this, especially because I have no idea how often they'll call me."*

Given that they'd done so twice already in so short a time period, she wasn't wrong. Still...

I tried to think of another option, to figure out a way for her to get what she seemed to want without the risk of what she'd suggested.

But...nothing came to mind. The reality was that if she wanted to do this, if she was dead-set on finding a way—and she sure seemed to be—she'd figure out something. Which meant she'd be in far more danger if I did nothing.

"Please," she signed, then set her hand on my knee.

The touch was innocent compared to the other things we'd done, yet it poured ice through my veins. I went back to Layla, back to the last time I'd thought a relationship could work out, to how she'd used our connections and my feelings for her to get what she'd wanted from me.

And I'd been the fool who hadn't realized it.

I jerked away from Hera, my face hardening. "I thought I made it clear — I don't trade favors like that."

She furrowed her eyebrows then dropped her gaze to where her hand still hung, now in mid-air since I'd moved. She didn't respond right away, and all I could think about was how stupid I'd felt after Layla, how much I'd cursed my own blindness at the truth that I was nothing but a tool for her to use when I'd thought we were…more.

Hera pressed her lips together, then stood. She headed toward the door, something that threw me.

The few times I'd tried to turn Layla down, back when I'd questioned the things she'd said, she'd always put on the charm. She had smiled, fluttered her lashes and done anything to reel me in.

Hera did none of that.

I caught her by the door, wrapping my hand around her arm to pull her to a stop before she could escape into my office. "Don't just run away."

She yanked free of my grasp, and her hands flew so fast it took a moment for me to understand what she was trying to tell me. It seemed she'd gotten much better with her sign language than I'd realized. *"I don't trade anything for favors."*

"So what do you call this?" I gestured between us. "Because it seems like you're here wanting me to go out on a limb to help you, and when I'm not sure, you put your hand on my knee. I've told you before, I won't pay for sex like that."

The anger burned on her face, but on the edges of it? Hurt. It nearly made me want to take it all back, to apologize to her for the misunderstanding, but I couldn't move.

"I have enough of my own neuroses to deal with. I can't be responsible for yours, too." Her gaze moved past me and to the animal crackers on the counter. Breath escaped her nose in a silent chuckle before she shook her head. It was a sad sound, as if just seeing them hurt, which I didn't get at all.

The sound made me freeze, so when she reached for the door again, I let her go. What was the point of trying to keep her there? So we could fight more?

I didn't need that anymore, and I'd spent far too much time arguing with her recently. The girl was keeping a hell of a lot of secrets and I didn't like any of them. I wanted to keep her safe but I couldn't do a damned thing.

I wanted to tell her she'd never have to go to Medical again, that I'd keep her off the Warden's radar, that I'd make her life what she wanted it to be. Wasn't that what all men wanted? To be some stupid hero for the woman they loved? Someone who could keep her safe?

Yet I couldn't do any of that. I couldn't keep her safe from Larkwood, from the other shades, from the whole damned world that seemed determined to hurt her. I'd never felt so powerless before.

My gaze moved over to the animal crackers, some strange nagging in my mind, an old memory I hadn't thought about in a long damned time.

I remembered being a kid, living in the North Tower, having all of nothing. There had been a scientist, one of the few who seemed to give a damn about us kids. She'd brought in a box of animal crackers and given them to me, telling me 'Happy Birthday' despite me not understanding what that meant.

I tried to think about whether or not I'd written that in my journal, if that was how she'd figured it out. No, I didn't think so. She must have seen it sometime, read it from my voice, then had gone out of her way to get them.

Items like that didn't come cheap, and I had no idea what she'd had to trade to get them. Still, she'd done it, and for what?

To bribe me?

No, that wasn't it. If she'd wanted to use it as a favor, she'd have explained why she did it, how they were important, would have wanted to capitalize on the gift for her own ends. Instead, she'd said nothing. She'd accepted that I might not understand it, that I might not care, but she'd gotten them because she'd wanted to.

I rubbed my head, frustration eating away at me as I realized again that she wasn't Layla, that I'd snapped at her for no good reason, that'd I'd made an already difficult situation even harder on her.

Which meant I had to make it up to her yet again…

Chapter Four

Hera

I pulled my shirt over my head, then styled my hair into a ponytail. Today was the day—my appointment with Medical—and I'd gotten no closer to my idea of blocking the drugs. I'd asked Wade again, but neither he, Knox nor Brax knew anything.

And I hadn't spoken to Deacon since our fight.

His words still stung, digging in even though I'd told myself to stop thinking about it. I hadn't been kidding when I'd said that he needed to deal with his own issues, that he couldn't take them out on me, but that didn't stop the pain in my chest at the way he'd looked at me.

He'd stared at me as if I were some creature trying to drag him down to hell.

He hadn't even realized why the animal crackers were important. I'd taken on extra shifts from another shade to get those crackers, and he hadn't given a damn.

A knock on the door made me turn that way, frowning. Was it time already? I'd thought my schedule had Medical near noon, but maybe they'd moved it up?

I went to the door and pulled it open, startled to find Kit standing there.

"Are you going to invite me in?" Kit asked as if showing up without notice were the most normal thing in the world.

I nodded, the reaction probably based more on my upbringing than my actual desires. Inviting someone in was normal, it was expected of me, and my mother's voice in my head told me to be gracious.

Of course, it wasn't until he was actually inside my apartment that I realized just how uncomfortable it was.

Kit didn't match with the rest of my space. He was perfectly dressed and proper, whereas my place was tiny and messy. I suddenly wished I'd taken time to pick up the water bottles from the table, to straighten it all.

Which was stupid.

I wasn't trying to impress him.

Wait, why is he here at all?

Kit turned back toward me and folded his hands at the small of his back. His black eyes were as unnerving as they always were, especially because I couldn't read him well. "Deacon sent me."

Deacon? I frowned as I tried to piece together what he meant.

Kit nodded as if he'd read it on my face. "I understand you're wanting a resistance to the drugs Medical uses."

It felt like a trap, so I didn't nod right away. Trusting Deacon was one thing—trusting Kit was another. Even with Deacon, I never told him the entire truth, so the idea of letting Kit in on anything felt way too dangerous.

"You can do that?" I asked to be safe.

He nodded with one quick jerk of his head. "Yes."

"How?"

"Wendigos are immune to most powers and nearly all medications and drugs. We can't even get drunk."

"And you can lend me that ability?"

"Yes and no. I can't just hand it over, and it won't work the way it does for me. The medications they give will still affect you, just to a much lesser degree. It means you will likely feel what they do in addition to remembering it all."

I swallowed at the way the memory came back to me, the last time I'd been there, the flashes of panic.

"Think carefully about this," Kit said, his voice lowering. "Once you make this choice, you can't take it back. You will go to Medical today, and you may find it is much better to allow them to drug you. Once you are there, however, you will have no choice but to endure the process. If I had to have surgery, I'd rather not be awake during it. There is no benefit to recalling the entire thing."

Of course there was. I needed information and I could only get that if people talked when they didn't think I could hear. Why was the Warden interested in me? What did they want from me? I had no other way to find out the truth. No matter how horrible it sounded, I didn't have another option.

"I'm sure," I said.

He nodded even though he didn't appear pleased. "Come and sit."

I didn't follow at first, but eventually forced my feet to move. I sat on the couch where Kit had indicated. He set a hand on my arm to turn me so I faced away from him before he sat behind me, my back to him.

Which was so much more terrifying than I'd expected. How hadn't I realized how scary Kit was? Somehow, having him at my back where I couldn't watch him brought up so many feelings I wasn't sure how to categorize.

"Relax." He sat so close that his breath blew strands of my hair around. It felt like him whispering into my ear, something intimate and personal.

And it made me wonder when the hell I'd started to feel *this* way about him.

"Your heart is racing."

I wanted to blame him for that, but with my back toward him, I couldn't sign a response.

His fingers dragged across the nape of my neck, his touch unbearably gentle. The warmth of his fingers shocked me. After feeling the coldness and darkness inside him, I found it hard to believe he was so warm. "As I said, the effect won't be complete. It won't work as it does for me."

I nodded, shivering hard when he touched the neckline of my shirt. The touch felt personal, like the start of something between lovers. Given that Kit and I had never acted that way, I had no idea how to handle it.

"This will have two parts. The first is that I'll need to infect you with my toxin."

"*Infect?*" I signed it without thinking before going to turn toward him, to ask him just what the hell he was talking about.

The word infect was a very bad word. Few people used it in a positive way.

He grasped my shoulder to keep me still and faced away from him. "Just listen to me. Wendigos resist most poisons and illnesses because we can consume everything living. Medications rarely work for much of the same reason. We have toxin on our claws, so when we bind others to us, they will not be easily felled. So by introducing a small amount into you, it should lessen the reaction to any drugs."

"Will I turn into what you are?"

"No. Shades can't transform into anything else once changed. The toxin will remain inside you until your own source destroys it—usually after a few days. In addition, I'll use a command to help ease the pain that the drugs will no longer block without causing you any memory loss."

"Command?"

He sighed, as if my questions annoyed him. Well, that was really too bad, given he was talking about somehow infecting me with something that consumed living material. I felt like that earned me all the questions I wanted to ask.

"You saw it with the dragon shifter before. My voice can command living creatures and force their compliance. In addition, you should be aware it will create a bond between us."

"Bond? What does that mean?"

"It is as I said. Between using my toxin and commanding you, you will become bound to me."

"So you'll be able to control me?"

"I could do that anytime I wish already. I do not require a bond to force your compliance. However, in this case, you should notice little of a bond. It is a skill intended to allow my kind to rule over others. It may cause you to think about me more, perhaps even to be a little more fond of me." His tone almost made it seem as if he'd just made a joke, but that was so unlike him I struggled to believe it. "It can allow us to speak telepathically and sense one another. It has the added benefit of ensuring other similar shades will not be able to bind you to them, and may offer some protection from others."

"What's in it for you?"

He didn't respond at first, as if considering his answer. When he did speak, his voice was quiet. "I have cared about little since coming here. No, that isn't right. It was well before Larkwood when I stopped caring. However, for some reason, I do not want to see you harmed. You are foolish enough to do as you please on your own, so I feel…drawn to help you so you do not end up hurt."

I dragged my tongue over my bottom lip, nerves getting the better of me.

"We can still opt not to do this." His voice was so soft and his body so close that the goosebumps on my skin had nothing to do with fear. "You can still back out. I will release you and walk out of your room. Nothing will change."

As soon as he said that, my questions and worries all disappeared, because I only had one option. I needed to do this, so the risks, the reasons it was dangerous, none of that mattered.

"Nod if you want me to continue."

I nodded.

He exhaled, the noise sounding as if he'd hoped I'd back out.

Too bad.

He pulled me backward and wrapped an arm around my waist. It pinned me to his chest and forced me to recognize he was far stronger than I'd realized. It was probably because of the way he dressed, but I'd assumed he was thin and weak. That was clearly not the case.

And my heart sped all the more, my body reacting to his closeness on an instinctual level.

He grasped my wrist to trap my arm across my body, then used his other hand to touch the crook of my elbow. When he spoke, his lips brushed my ear. "My toxin is in my claws, so I'll need to change."

His hand, the one that touched my arm, shifted. I'd seen it before, but it never failed to startle me.

He looked nothing like a human when he changed, instead resembling some sort of ancient evil creature, some nature god. His entire body shifted behind me, which made me think he'd pinned me there so I didn't have to look at him.

I was oddly thankful for it right then. Just seeing his shifted, clawed hand was freaky enough. I couldn't imagine allowing him so close to me fully changed. Worse, his body was so much larger now, making me feel like a tiny, trapped creature.

"I'm going to inject a small amount into the crook of each elbow. It may make you sick at first as it works through your bloodstream, but it shouldn't hurt much as I do it. I'll make it as quick as possible."

I nodded, then closed my eyes so I didn't have to watch.

The pain was quick, as he'd promised, and it made me snap my eyes open out of instinct. I saw the long white claws there, and the sharp tip had punctured into the crook of my elbow. It didn't go in far, not nearly as much as a syringe would. When he withdrew, a dot of blood puddled on top of the skin.

He repeated the motion on the other side, and this time, I watched. He struck fast, clearly comfortable with the claws and easily able to use them with precision.

"All done," he whispered when he pulled his claw away.

The moment he released me, I yanked back and got to my feet. I rubbed at the crook of each elbow, trying to ease the sting.

Except, the sting wouldn't go away. It increased, shifting until it turned into burning. Instead of rubbing, I scratched at the spot on each arm.

Hands wrapped around my wrists, and they were the still shifted ones that had just done this to me. All the passion I'd felt a moment before had withered, and when I looked up into the true face of Kit, I fell into his black eyes.

Where on a human face they seemed odd, they fit perfectly against the white bone that made up his entire head. The antlers reached up, making him even taller, though he didn't stand up straight. He bent forward, which made me wonder just how tall he was in this form if he rose to his full height.

"Relax," he said, his voice forcing my compliance.

I took a deep breath then let it shudder from my body.

"I know the spots hurt. They will burn for a short while, but the discomfort will go away within ten minutes. After that, you'll have a headache and feel nauseous, but that will also go away within the hour. You should feel fine by the time of your appointment."

I nodded, trying to ignore how fire crept through my veins, searing me. It was so strong, as if it would turn me to ash right there. I recalled the apple, the way it had disintegrated to nothing in Kit's hand just days before. Had he tricked me? Would that happen to me?

He must have noticed the fear on my face, because he shook his head. "It won't hurt you. If I wanted to harm you, I could do so at any time. I wouldn't need to trick you like this."

Even though he told me that, I struggled to believe it. Panic beat at me, reminding me of the pain when that man had slit my throat, when I'd realized just how powerless I could be.

He let out a sigh, then dropped lower so his face was just in front of mine, so I couldn't look away from those bottomless eyes of his. His voice changed as well, taking on the tone I'd heard just before he'd killed that dragon shifter. "Relax, Hera."

My body obeyed. Some part of me knew I should fight it, that there was no reason to trust him. I didn't want to give in, to give any more of myself to others, but I couldn't. His voice and his eyes had some endless void inside them, something dark and deep enough to drown me and never let me surface again.

"If you panic now, the guards will suspect something when they arrive. You need to take deep breaths and relax."

The fresh air that filled my lungs as I listened to him was nice and made me realize I hadn't been breathing deeply enough. It was as if my conscious mind and my body obeyed him, relaxing and breathing slowly, but another part of me rebelled, silent and trapped.

This was his power? It made me want to tremble, to wonder how a shade could be this strong, why

Larkwood would choose to keep him alive and here after knowing what he was capable of?

The thought shamed me, especially after what I'd suffered because of others' fear, but that didn't change how I felt.

"I'm not going to do anything bad to you," Kit whispered, his voice losing that command, as if he wanted to ensure I really heard him. "I could force you to believe me, command you to believe and trust me. I could demand that you will do whatever I want, that you will do nothing foolish or dangerous. I could ensure I never lost you. It would be so easy to turn you into my own mindless, safe puppet who would be only mine forever. I won't do that, however." He didn't add on what I was sure he was thinking — *I'm not like that.*

Before I had to think about it much, his voice took on the other tone, the terrifying one I couldn't ignore. "You will resist the effects of the medications they give you. Your head will remain clear, but you will feel no pain."

I nodded even if he didn't ask me to, even if he didn't want a response.

He breathed in deeply, the sound odd since he didn't have a flesh and blood face, didn't have a mouth or nostrils. He nodded, then pulled back and released me.

When he turned his head away, I collapsed to the floor. It was as if he had held me up by his eyes alone, as if that had been all that kept me on my feet. With the string cut, I couldn't hold myself up anymore.

He turned his back on me, his body twisting until he returned to his normal size, until his shape reverted to his human form. Why he'd turned his back I didn't know—it wasn't as if I hadn't just been face-to-face with what he really was.

Still, when he faced me again, I shrank back. I couldn't help it—I'd assumed his powers wouldn't work on me. It was an arrogant thought, perhaps, but since I didn't seem to struggle with Knox's incubus powers as others did, I'd thought perhaps Kit wouldn't be able to control me, especially since he used his voice and sound was the seat of my power.

However, he'd proven me wrong. I had been helpless against Kit's voice. If he'd commanded me to do *anything* in that moment, I'd have done it. That fact terrified me, the reality that when it came to Kit, I had no control. I had to trust that he'd never turn on me, that he'd never use it against me, because I had no defense.

When I moved away, he came no closer. I couldn't read his expression, especially because I worked hard to not look him in the eyes. I didn't want to be caught again.

He let out a long sigh that at least sounded normal. Not that I would believe it. Kit had just proven he was *anything* but normal.

"Be careful," he said, his voice strangely soft. "I did what I could, but make no mistake—Medical is dangerous. You'll be on your own there." He crouched so he was in front of me, and I had nowhere to retreat to since I'd backed up to the couch. He caught my chin, and I flinched as if those claws would dig into me. They didn't—his hands were human. "I expect you to be cautious, Hera. I do not want to find out you got yourself killed. Understood?"

I nodded, probably just to end the conversation, my gaze locked over his shoulder so I didn't risk meeting his eyes.

He ran his thumb over my chin then released me and left without another word.

I'd woken this morning expecting Medical to be the most terrifying part of my day, and yet Kit had shown up and proven me wrong.

I was pretty sure he was far more dangerous than anything else at Larkwood.

* * * *

"You had a visitor this morning?" Deacon asked as his gaze dropped to my arm.

After our last fight, I hadn't spoken to him, but it seemed he had still looked out for me.

Which was something I wasn't ready to deal with. After the exhausting morning and the upcoming Medical trip, I lacked the energy to talk out whatever mess Deacon had tangled up in his head.

I had enough of my own problems.

I nodded.

"Good. It seem to work?"

I shrugged. The pain had gone away, just as he'd said it would, but I had no idea if it would actually work once they injected the drugs into me. It was like testing a parachute. I'd only know for sure after I jumped.

He hit the button for the Medical floor, then stood back, his gaze on the elevator door as if trying not to look at me.

I suddenly missed Wade. Everything was so simple with him. It seemed I was growing extremely frustrated with men who had so many hang-ups, with the idea that it was my job to fix them all.

"The schedule looks like you'll stay in Medical overnight. I'll be back tomorrow morning to pick you up again."

I didn't respond, since I wasn't sure what else to say.

"Hera," he started, but before he said anything else, he shut his mouth.

So, it seemed neither of us was willing to actually voice what ran around in our heads.

Fine by me. I've got bigger fish to fry right now.

The elevator doors opened and I found myself faced with the same hallway as the last time. Whereas I'd managed not to stress yet, and I'd ignored the panic and fear that still clutched me from the last time, when faced with that hallway, it prowled closer.

Deacon took a step off the elevator, then paused when I didn't follow. He turned toward me, his dark eyebrows drawn toward each other. "Hera?" he asked.

I blinked slowly, my gaze locked past him and down the hall.

He sighed, then came closer. He dropped his voice lower, probably so no one would hear. "It's time to go. I know you don't want to, I know you're scared, but you need to pull it together."

A part of me wanted to yell at him, to ask him *why* I was expected to just pull everything together. Didn't people get the chance to break down? Especially after all I'd been through, didn't I deserve that?

But what was the point? He wasn't wrong. It was like trying to tread water in the middle of the ocean. Yeah, it was unfair to have to, but if a person was there, they had no other options.

"Look at me," Deacon said, his voice nearly a whisper.

I forced myself to look into his purple eyes, to stare right at him. He said nothing, just peered back as if he could transfer some of his strength to me.

It made me take a deep breath and steel myself for what I had to do. If I lost my nerve, if I fought, Deacon would have no choice but to haul me there. Even if he didn't, another guard would. Doing all that would only make things worse for myself when I arrived at Medical.

A quick nod from him said he knew I'd gathered myself, that I was ready to face reality head-on.

When he turned and started to walk off the elevator, I followed him. We went down the hallway to the door we'd gone through before. It all seemed eerily familiar, especially when I actually entered that pass-off location.

"So we get another shot at the siren?" the other guard asked as he entered the hand-off location.

Deacon said nothing, but his jaw twitched as if he had to control his temper.

That nearly made me smile, because he was angry on my behalf. It was a time when some of my own annoyance with him slid away. This life was hard and the more I lived it, the more I realized no one got out of it without some heavy scars.

"The schedule says she'll be done at nine in the morning. I'll be back then," Deacon said.

"We'll contact you," the guard responded. "Given her results last time, this could take longer. I'd hate to waste your time and make you wait. I'm sure you're *very* busy." The guard smirked back, as if amused by the interaction.

Which was funny, since the *last time* he'd faced off against Deacon, the win had clearly gone to Deacon. Perhaps he just didn't think Deacon would risk doing that again.

"She has work and classes tomorrow. I've already changed the schedule, because if you keep her up all night, she won't be any use tomorrow. However, if it's longer than that, she'll need to have her schedule for the next few days cleared. These are things I need to be aware of."

"And you'll become aware—when we tell you." The guard said nothing else, as if that should answer everything.

Deacon closed his hand into a fist but remained silent. He was as backed into a corner as I was.

"You can leave," the guard said, dismissing Deacon as if he were a pest.

Deacon hesitated for a moment, but then let out a soft sound of frustration. When he turned toward me, I could see the pain in his eyes. I offered him a slight smile, the most I could do, an attempt to tell him not to worry. It didn't seem to help, and the heavy fall of his footsteps echoed down the hall as he left.

The guard crooked his fingers to me, as if beckoning over a pet. "Come here, siren."

I followed the demand no matter how badly I didn't want to. Pissing him off wouldn't help me. When I got closer, he caught my chin and forced my face to his.

"I heard you caused a lot of problems a few weeks ago. I have to admit, I wasn't expecting that. You seemed like such a good girl while you were here last time. Were you faking it, or were you somehow not at fault for what happened?" He rubbed his finger along my chin, a touch I normally adored if others did it, but he only made me sick from it. "You were probably tricked into it. You seem like a woman who could be easily swayed by sweet lies. Who put you up to it? What did they tell you to get you to do it? Did they threaten you? Or are you more of a carrot than stick, girl? Someone who risked that much because some big strong man swore up and down that he loved you?" He let out a cruel laugh, as if amused by that idea.

I didn't bother to respond. Even if I could, even if he understood ASL or if I had my writing pad, it wasn't as if he gave a fuck about what I had to say.

He brushed his thumb over my lip before a static sound left the radio at his waist, followed by a voice. "This isn't the time for you to play with subjects. Hurry up and bring the siren here." The voice was familiar, and I had to guess it had been the main doctor. While my memories of him were fuzzy, I had to admit, I wanted to thank him for the interruption.

The guard pulled his hand away, then darted his gaze up to the corner of the room, to a camera positioned there. He pressed his lips together, then grabbed his radio. "On our way, Sir."

With that, he gripped my arm in a tight hold and all but yanked me through the pass-off area, into what I could only describe as hell.

Chapter Five

Wade

Watching Deacon sulk on the top floor weirded me out. The guard was normally too busy scowling to have an emotion deeper than hunger or mild annoyance.

It wasn't hard to figure out what bothered him, of course.

I sure as hell felt it, too.

Hera was in Medical. She'd been there a few hours already, and that was bound to bother anyone, to drive them to frustration.

Dealing with someone being in danger, trying to protect them, trying to help them, those were all normal. However, knowing someone was suffering and knowing there wasn't a damned thing to be done about it was pure agony.

I wasn't sure if I sat beside him because I gave a damn or because he was one of the few who would understand what I felt.

He glanced over, gaze suspicious, his purple eyes as unnerving as ever.

It wasn't due to them being purple, not exactly. It was more that I *knew* they were that color from source, as if I could see that magical, terrible power swirling inside him through his eyes. As someone who could steal that, who *wanted* to steal that power from most people, it beckoned to me.

Not that I could take his. I'd tried, and probably because his body never took to it right, because he'd never changed into a shade, it was like trying to gather water with my hands, except my fingers couldn't close to create a cup.

"Any idea when she'll be back?" I sat back on the seat beside him.

"They said nine in the morning, but who knows if that's true?"

At least he hadn't pretended to have no idea what I meant.

"She's tough. She'll be fine."

Deacon made a soft, unhappy sound, as if I were naïve for thinking such a thing.

And maybe I was. Maybe I thought she'd be fine because that was easier on me, because it let me relax and not just rehash the horrible things she suffered through.

"You're moving better."

He didn't respond to my comment.

"I remember after she got sent to solitary—no one saw you for a few days. When I did get a glimpse of you, you weren't walking too well."

"Is there a reason for this little trip down memory lane?"

I shrugged. "Just making conversation."

"Well, don't. We aren't friends, and I don't want to become friends with you."

I pressed a hand to my chest. "Ouch. Do you know how much that pains me? Not all of us are emotionless cogs like you. Words hurt, Deacon."

He didn't rise to the barb, didn't even roll his eyes.

Am I losing my touch?

The day I couldn't even annoy Deacon into a reaction was the day I knew I'd started my downslide.

"I heard the Warden has been all over her ass since the incident." When he didn't respond, I pushed. "Just us boys here right now—no reason to act shy."

Deacon let out a long breath, as if I tried his patience. Finally, he answered, though he kept his gaze straight forward. "Yeah. She's kept Hera on close watch. She did before, too, but this is different."

"Hera did break into a locked filing room. That sort of thing can make the Warden testy."

Deacon shook his head after a moment. "No, this is more. If she was just annoyed, she'd have punished Hera then let it go. Instead, it's like…it's like Hera is a bug the Warden is interested in. She wants to see what she'll do next."

I frowned. Gaining the interest of the Warden wasn't good for anyone. I'd met the woman a time or two— once when I'd first arrived, since voids were uncommon—and she sent shivers up my spine.

Then again, that was the type of person needed when dealing with an academy full of creatures who wanted to kill her, and worse, who had every ability to do so if they got the chance.

Still, it being unexpected didn't change that it was bad, that it was asking for trouble.

The last thing Hera needed when planning an escape with us was being shadowed by the person in charge.

"Any idea why she's so interested?"

"Hera's numbers are off the chart. Maybe that's why?"

I shook my head. "There are other high-level shades, and she's only sent Hera to Medical twice. If she really wanted to use those skills, she'd send Hera to the North Tower for special training."

Deacon swung his head toward me, his eyes narrowed. "You know about special training?"

"Information is a lot easier to get than people think. If there's one thing to trust in Larkwood, it's that nothing stays a secret." Besides, they'd wanted to put me into special training when I'd first arrived.

I still recalled the brief attempt at that, back when they'd known little about voids, when they'd thought I'd be able to do things they wanted me to do. It had quickly turned out that I was far less useful than they'd expected. Voids needed to get up close and personal with targets, and we were pretty vulnerable until then.

Still, they hadn't wanted to kill me as they normally did those who failed special training, since a void had some use, so they'd thrown me back into general population.

"You're right," Deacon said softly. "If Warden just wanted to use her powers or test them, she could do something more than using Kit to train her. And if she wanted information on the high source levels, the North Tower has far better science labs than Medical does."

"Which means the Warden wants Hera *here* for some reason, and not in the North Tower." I ran my fingers through my hair, trying to push the curly locks from my eyes.

Deacon nodded. "That's about as much as I can figure." He lifted his arm to glance at his watch, the anxiety clear.

"You sure you're good for her?" I asked.

"I'm sure that isn't your business."

"She's my friend."

"Just a friend?" Deacon turned toward me, one dark eyebrow raised. "Don't forget, I'm good at spotting lies."

I gestured at myself, using all the self-deprecating humor I could muster to drive home my point. "Look at me—do you really think I'm dumb enough to think I have a shot? She's got a lot bigger game than me on her hook."

It wasn't entirely true, but it wasn't false, either.

He turned away from me again, gazing forward at the far wall. "She's like a drug. Doesn't matter how bad we might be for each other, I can't quit her."

Boy, did that sound familiar…

Hera was dangerous and associating with her was a huge risk—for everyone. She was reckless, headstrong and far too tempting. Just look at how her presence had caused chaos in Larkwood.

She'd caused problems between Knox and Brax, she'd gotten me sent to solitary, she'd gotten herself thrown in solitary and Deacon followed her around like a puppy.

A dangerous, lethal, muscular puppy with a bad attitude, at least.

And yet no matter how much I knew that, I couldn't seem to keep my distance. Hell, I didn't *want* to keep my distance.

So I got what he meant.

"So you're ready to pay the price?"

Deacon nodded.

"No matter what the price might be?"

At least at that, he paused. He leaned forward, setting his forearms on his knees. "I don't know, honestly. I know that every damned time I think I'm done with her, that I tell myself this is going nowhere good, I'm drawn back in. I can't say I want to pay a price, but I don't think I can avoid it." He let out a soft laugh that held no happiness. "She's like driving toward a cliff. I know I'm going to go over it, but I can't take my foot off the gas."

I snorted softly. "Well, that seems like the most accurate description I've ever heard of her. Wouldn't suggest you repeat it to her, though. I have a feeling Hera wouldn't take too kindly to it."

Deacon finally let out a laugh, quiet and not entirely pleased as it was. "That's for sure. Nice as this conversation has been, I'd better get back to work."

He started to walk away, not waiting for my response, but I couldn't quite let it go. Curiosity always got me.

"You took the blame, didn't you?"

He froze, not turning back toward me. "No idea what you're talking about."

Still, I pressed the topic. "When Hera got caught breaking into that filing room, when she got sent to solitary, you took the blame, didn't you? That's why you were gone, why you weren't moving too well afterward, wasn't it?"

"Seems like a pretty stupid thing to do." He didn't deny it but didn't admit it either.

He didn't need to, though. It had been my strong guess before, but after seeing him react, he'd solidified it.

"It seemed strange that for such a large infraction, for such a large security risk, she'd get off so easily. Solitary sucks, but they really let it go after that. That never sat right with me. It's because you took the brunt of the punishment, didn't you?"

He finally turned back toward me, though his gaze remained on the floor. "It was my fault. I showed her that room—on accident, but still, I did that. I didn't realize she was going to try anything, didn't anticipate it like I should have. It was my fault."

"Just not noticing it wouldn't have gotten you in that sort of trouble. You told them something else."

He crossed his arms, making me doubt he'd keep speaking. Amazingly enough, he went on. "I told the Warden I'd brought her in there because she was having a hard time accepting her position here. I lied and said I'd shown her the files as a way to get her to realize she had nowhere else to go, that no one left this place. I said I hadn't expected her to steal anything, so I'd left her there to think about it. Then they wouldn't look too hard at how she'd gotten in."

"And you took the punishment in her place. That's a lot more noble than I'd have expected from you."

Deacon pointed a finger at me, his gaze lifting to mine. "Not a word to Hera—we clear?"

I lifted my hands as if frightened by his obvious threat. "My lips are sealed. Last thing I want is to either endear you to her any more or make her suffer when she feels guilty about it. Still, seems you were right. She really is a cliff for you, isn't she?"

Deacon nodded but paused before turning away again. "She is. I'm pretty sure I'm going to barrel right over the side of it, but fuck, what sort of masochist am I that I'm sort of looking forward to it? Change is change, and maybe that sort of change is worth the impact."

With that, he turned, leaving me there in the room with only his words left.

No matter what happened with Larkwood, with the escape, with any of it, one thing was damned clear.

For better or worse, Hera had changed all our lives, and there was no going back.

* * * *

Hera

I couldn't believe it, but Kit's little trick seemed to work. A nurse had injected drugs into the crook of my elbow, but whereas the last time it had quickly worked through my system and stolen my thoughts and memory, this time it didn't.

Well, I couldn't say it did nothing.

My thoughts weren't as sharp, the world was a bit fuzzy, but it wasn't anywhere near what it had been before. It seemed more like the nice buzz that happened from a girly drink or two, compared to downing shot after shot of whiskey until a person blacked out.

Kit's command had helped, making the pain not go away but at least become a lesser issue. I knew the tests hurt, but my brain didn't react or process it as pain.

I hadn't understood why that had been necessary, but now I did. When they'd taken another small biopsy from my shoulder blade, the sharp circular blade punching into my skin, the tug as it pulled the sample away, there was no way I could have pretended not to react if I'd felt it all.

"Her numbers are still high," the doctor mumbled. He tended to speak to himself when no one else was around — or even when others were around sometimes. He seemed more interested in his own opinions rather than actually discussing anything with anyone else.

I pretended not to hear him, as I'd done the entire time. They seemed to expect me to be awake but so out of it that I'd do little more than shift around and whimper. I had no idea how much time had passed, though I'd moved between sitting on an exam table and being strapped down to it. They had worried little about guards, probably because they assumed I'd been so drugged that I was hardly a threat. The only time they strapped me down was when they needed me still, like when they were taking the biopsies.

It had struck me as far more routine than I'd expected. I'd thought the worst things when I couldn't recall the last time, had feared what could have happened. Instead, it felt more like a run-of-the mill physical.

The typing of the doctor at his computer felt like white noise, and as time dragged on, as I had nothing else to think about or do, exhaustion got the best of me. I drifted off as I lay on the exam table, lulled to sleep by the monotony of it all.

I dreamed as I slept, which was common, though the type of dream differed. Usually my dreams were frantic, a mess of switching from one thing to another based on what I'd heard. My dreams seemed to be less about my brain sorting out what had happened during the day and had changed to reaching into the sounds that surrounded me. It meant I'd pick up noises and glimpse bits of the person's life and their memories.

This time was different. My dream lacked the frenzied movement and instead focused on a single scene.

In the darkness, I saw Kit. He appeared human in my mind, even though I knew the real him beneath that façade. I had been face-to-face with what he really was, had tasted the power of his voice.

When I saw visions based on sound, it normally made me a spectator to whatever happened. They never noticed me because it wasn't real. The images would move around before me, but I could never interact at all.

This felt...different.

His black eyes lifted and met mine, but they didn't flit away. Instead, they locked on me and remained.

"Can you see me?" I asked.

Kit flashed his normal smile, the reserved one he used that was perhaps amused but not thrilled. "Of course."

"How?"

"Because of my voice, my toxin, we're connected. It is the bond between us. I did warn you this may happen."

"So you're really here? This isn't some weird dream?"

He shrugged. "It is a dream, in a way. Not many are able to connect so directly with me. It seems, yet again, you are special."

"Lucky me." That was when it hit me, when I froze for a moment. "Am I speaking?"

His smile widened in amusement. "Yes, and you have a lovely voice. It is even more of a shame that it was stolen from you." At my look, he sighed. "You were silenced by destroying your voice box. This isn't your actual body, however, thus there is no reason for you to be unable to speak like this. It means that at least during these times, you will have no trouble speaking."

The idea that I could talk, that I could communicate as I'd done before, almost made me giddy. I didn't have to write things down, didn't have to use sign language and hope the person I needed to communicate with understood it. I didn't have to keep my hands empty or ensure the other person looked at me. I could just open my mouth and say the things I wanted to say.

How had I taken that for granted for so long? It seemed we never knew what we had until we'd lost it. Hell, a stinging in my eyes made me worried I'd make a fool of myself.

And while Kit made me nervous, while I wasn't sure how to handle him, him being the only person I could talk to meant I'd push past any discomfort I had. What was a little soul-shaking terror between conversational buddies?

"How is Medical?" he asked with a softer voice, as if afraid to bring it up.

"Not bad. Your little trick seems to have worked."

"I'm glad. I've never tried it with a siren, so I had no idea if it would actually allow you to resist the drugs."

"And you just failed to mention that?" I didn't bother to hide my annoyance at how he'd left that out.

"What was the point in telling you? You would only worry and have nothing you could do to change it. Shades are all different—what works with one may not work with another, and even in a single type, the levels of source change how they react." He paused, then let out a soft chuckle. "I didn't intend for this to turn into a lecture."

"Everything turns into a lecture with you."

"I rarely speak to anyone outside of my professional obligations. I suppose I'm used to turning the conversation to those topics."

I frowned at that. "You don't ever talk to anyone else?"

"Not really. And before you choose to pity me for that, have you ever considered having a personal conversation with me?"

Which was pretty much fair. "I guess not," I admitted.

It was then I realized something else. When I heard voices in real life, I felt more from it. I got flashes of their thoughts, of their pasts if I didn't work hard to avoid them. This time, however, there was none of that.

It felt like having a conversation in my old life. It unnerved me, since I'd grown used to that extra information, but it also relaxed me in an odd way.

"Is the command blocking the pain?" he asked.

"Mostly. I'm still aware of it, but it doesn't really hurt. It's like taking a muscle relaxer for my back — I feel tightness, and I know it should hurt, but somehow it doesn't."

"That's good. Do you want to explain to me why you wanted to be conscious for this?"

I could have tried to lie to him, but I didn't see a point. Besides, I'd never been a great liar. "No, I don't."

He made a soft sound, one that said he didn't appreciate my response. Still, he didn't push the issue. "I was surprised Deacon showed up asking for help. I've known that man as long as he's worked at

Larkwood, and I've never seen him ask anyone for help."

"And just what did your help cost?"

"Normally, it would have fetched a rather high price."

"Why not this time?"

"He said it was for you."

That made me pause and narrow my eyes. "Why would that matter?"

"I'm not sure, but it seemed to matter, as I asked for nothing in return."

The words struck me as honest, even though I couldn't use my powers to be sure.

"Does this last as long as I'm asleep?"

"I can't answer that. As I said, it is different with each shade."

"But it has happened before?"

Kit nodded and took a seat. It felt as if the world grew, as if I could recognize more around me. We were in a room of some sort. It reminded me of Deacon's room a bit, but everything was kept far neater. There was a living room with a large sectional couch, then a dining table farther out. The farther from Kit I looked, however, the less I could make out the details.

It was then I realized my steps made no sound.

"Are you asleep also?" I asked.

"No. I'm awake."

"Then how can you talk to me like this?"

He tilted his head as he stared back at me. "Because I can see you. You're sleeping, which allows our connection to grow to the point of contact. No one else would be able to see you or hear you if they came in. They would only see me speaking to empty space."

"What if you went to sleep?"

"I don't sleep, so I wouldn't know."

"You never sleep?"

"No. I don't require any."

I thought back to everything I'd seen from him, everything I'd heard. "You're different from any other shade here."

"Yes."

The way he answered my question without elaborating annoyed me. "Why?"

"Because there are always different types of everything. A house cat and a lion may both be felines, but they are certainly different. There are many types of shades, most who share many of the same traits, but not all."

"So you're telling me that you're a lion and we are cats?"

His smile widened, and it felt more genuine than before. Then again, this was as personal a conversation as we'd ever had. "That sounds egotistical, doesn't it? The reality is that there are a few Elder shades, as you might say. They are changed more than others, and they retain less of their former human selves. They often age much more slowly, or some not at all. Some lose their human emotions, or even occasionally their memories, as if everything they were was wiped clear when they changed."

"And that's what you are?"

"Not all. I have my memories—or rather, I did. They've faded through the years and no longer resemble who I am now. They are like hearing stories about yourself as a baby—you might know the stories are true, but you have no connection to the person they are about. You do not remember them or how you felt during them."

"Do you age?"

"It doesn't appear so. I am the oldest known shade here—perhaps elsewhere as well. I don't know about shades at other academies."

"Just how old are you?"

"Very old. I don't know the exact age—I wasn't brought to Larkwood at first. In fact, there was no Larkwood when I changed. I spent years on my own, learning to control my powers, trying to figure out what I was, trying to find more like myself. I had no idea what exactly I was until Larkwood. I can thank them for that if nothing else—they at least gave me a name."

"So there have been others like you?"

"A few. The more powerful a creature is, the rarer. Larkwood has never had another wendigo, and I have never met another, but there have been others at other academies. It meant I was rather trial and error when it came to how they would deal with me."

I tried to imagine how it would feel to be that powerful, to be immortal. I couldn't fathom it. "Why haven't I heard that? I thought all shades aged like normal?"

"The government prefers people to think that. They like to hide whatever will not serve a purpose for them, at least until they can find a way to use it."

"You told me before that Larkwood wants everyone to be useful. I've seen what you're capable of—why don't they use you more?"

"I'm too well-kept a secret to allow me to leave. Besides, while they give me some level of freedom here, I believe they know I could be too dangerous if they allowed me outside of here. Larkwood is a well-made cage. They do not trust me enough to allow me out of that cage. Instead, they bring tasks for me here."

The room faded around me, losing its definition.

"It seems you are waking. Be cautious, Hera, you have no idea just how many things wait in the shadows for the unaware."

With that, the world collapsed around me. The sound of a voice brought me to, back to the exam table in Medical. My back was toward the room—I must have rolled over in my sleep.

"Her numbers are stable?" I didn't recognize that voice, but I didn't want to turn, to try to see them, because that might clue them in that I wasn't as medicated as they'd thought.

"Yes. I'd thought they might go down after a while. Occasionally, a shade can have a burst of source levels when they first change that then stabilize to an average range. I've never seen them stay elevated this long, which leads me to think they won't go down." I recognized that voice as the doctor.

"Will that have any lasting complications?"

"I can't answer that. It's something we've never seen before. These levels are still many times higher than another other known shade. What that means in terms of her abilities or longevity, I can't answer. I'd suggest we keep her under close scrutiny and continue testing in the meantime. If she were to have offspring, it's possible the high source count could impact the pregnancy or even produce something entirely unknown."

"She has been sterilized, so she shouldn't fall pregnant. Any male shades are likewise unable to father children. I'll send out a note to all guards who interact with her about how relationships between shades and guards are prohibited. She has seemed to get rather close to a number of males from what I've heard. Of course, in the future it might be beneficial to pair her with a shade and see what happens. I'd suggest an Elder—possibly Kit. I'd think that could produce a very interesting result."

That made my cheeks warm, the fact that they seemed so aware of my personal life. Worse, the idea of sleeping with Kit, of them talking about it so casually made my heart race.

"Your interest isn't just because of her unusual numbers, is it?"

"What do you mean?"

"Numbers this high suggest she was exposed to pure source for a long time. I see no way this could have happened naturally without anyone noticing. If I had to guess, I'd say she was somehow exposed on purpose."

"That is an interesting hypothesis," the other voice said. "But it's also one I wouldn't suggest repeating too casually."

The doctor didn't seem afraid, however, as he went on. "I'm not planning on it. The truth is that we need more information about shades, and we need the ability to test on the shades we have. Otherwise, how are we supposed to stay safe?"

"I've heard people say such things before," the woman said. "However, it's still not the sort of thing that should be mentioned in general company, given that experimentation on shades is still considered in the legally questionable area."

I kept still even as I wanted to roll over and glare at their words, at them discussing using shades as lab rats as if we weren't really alive.

"I've heard such ideas are more welcome in some places — such as the North Tower." The doctor said that with a conspiratorial tone, as if in on something with the other voice.

"I like your drive. Perhaps we'll discuss your future sometime soon. I believe your skills could benefit the North Tower. There are a number of projects there that could use fresh eyes, that have stagnated for too long due to a lack of imagination."

"I look forward to that," the doctor said. "I think I'd be a good fit."

"We'll see." The unknown person walked toward the exam table, her footsteps clicking against the tile floor, telling me she wore heels. "Given the trouble this siren has been, I've had people suggesting she go to the North Tower immediately."

"No doubt she could help the projects you have there."

"Perhaps," the woman said. "Though, it's hard to be sure. The most important projects there both require things she has yet to show. I suspect she is more useful here for the time being. If she proves uncontrollable, if she becomes too troublesome or shows powers or skills that would further our specific research, then that decision will be reevaluated. Sometimes the best tools are the least likely."

A shiver ran through me, as if I could feel her gaze on me. Her voice told me she stood just beside me, staring down at me as if I were a specimen to her. I sensed no care, as if I meant nothing beyond how she could use me.

It wasn't uncommon to feel that here, but I wasn't sure it had ever felt so demeaning, so dangerous.

"I'll finish the testing and send her back," the doctor said.

"Good. Ensure you send the report directly to me as soon as you have it finished."

"Yes, Warden."

Warden?

Well, that answered one thing…there was no doubt the Warden knew about me, and judging by that conversation?

She was rather invested in me, though I had no idea why.

The only thing I was sure of was that, whatever the reason, it wasn't anything that would be good for me…

Chapter Six

Brax

Seeing Hera calmed the beast inside me. It had prowled since I'd heard she'd gone to Medical.

The marks from the last time, the round wounds that some fucking butcher pretending to be a nurse had placed on her, had burned themselves into my memory.

It had driven up my temper, but I'd had to keep a close hold to avoid any fights. Someone only had to glance my way before the aching in my jaw from my fangs wanting to drop started up, before my blood sped and pounded through my veins.

She'd remained at Medical for nearly twenty-four hours, which was an unheard-of length. Thinking about what could have happened riled up my other side, but now that I spotted her brown hair in the hallway just outside of her room, I pulled in my first deep breath since she'd gone.

The moment I'd spotted Deacon around, I'd headed to her room to check in. If he was lurking about, it meant he'd already taken her back to her room.

I advanced on Hera, inhaling through my nose to draw her scent deep into me. Mixed with hers was antiseptic and dried blood.

The blood set off that anger again, but seeing her upright helped cage it.

She faced her door as if she wanted to go in but couldn't manage it.

"Hera?" I asked, but she didn't respond. I repeated her name, but with no more luck. It was as if something had her trapped, like she'd fallen into a trance.

I set my hand on her arm, trying to draw her attention. Normally, Hera was downright giddy over touch. Her normal reaction said she'd spent most of her life in a good place, the way she all but purred when I touched her.

That wasn't what happened this time, though.

Instead, Hera yanked away, a look of pure terror on her features when she turned to face me, slamming her back against her door.

I liked to push people, to test boundaries. When things didn't go as I wanted, when others got in my way, I went harder. It was a fucking miracle that when faced with the terror in her expression, I drew back.

Hera had shown flashes of fear before, but *never* like this, and never directed at me.

She ran her tongue along her bottom lip, then shuddered softly. After another moment, she mouthed *"sorry"* then opened the door to her room with trembling hands and went in.

She didn't invite me in, but I didn't wait for an invitation either. We didn't have the sort of relationship where either of us asked for anything from the other. That sort of bullshit was for people like her and Knox, or her and Wade.

Us? We were far too twisted for that.

I closed her door behind me. "You okay?"

She nodded, then reached for one of her writing pads. She didn't use them often — really only with me — so she didn't always have them with her.

"Did you need something?"

I peered at the oddly polite words. "I wanted to check on you. Didn't know I needed a reason to see you."

"I'm not up for..." She paused, her finger hovering above the writing pad as if searching for the right words. Finally, she sighed and kept writing. *"Whatever this is."*

Whatever this is? The way she dismissed our relationship annoyed me. Funny that she soothed my berserker and yet, at the same time, could piss me off like no other.

That was the point, maybe. She pissed me off as a person, as a human, but not as a berserker. Hell, she might be the only one who could do that anymore.

"What is this? Just a reaction from being in Medical?" That didn't feel quite right, though. She'd been to Medical before and hadn't acted so jumpy.

Hera shook her head. *"Nothing. I'm just tired."*

She moved slowly, as if in pain, and a reminder of the last time had me sighing. "Did they do more biopsies? Is that it?"

She didn't respond right away, then nodded slowly, as if she hadn't wanted to admit it. But why? It wasn't as if I didn't already know, as though I hadn't seen them before.

"Show me."

That seemed to wake her up, and she shook her head quickly.

"What are you, shy? It's not like there's an inch on your body I haven't seen, haven't touched, including the marks from last time. Stop acting like we're fucking strangers."

She bit softly at her bottom lip, and the anxiety on her face confused me. It didn't look like her at all and none of it made any damn sense.

Finally, she grasped the hem of her loose T-shirt and pulled it up. More marks rested on her, similar to last time. Bruises covered the insides of her arms. Either they'd used a syringe many times or they'd done a shitty job locating a vein.

Still, it wasn't anything different from the last time, so why was it hitting her this hard?

I wasn't the sort to think through things, especially when it came to feelings, but I did my best. Maybe it was that it was her second time? Maybe she recognized her future for the time being involved this, rather than it being a one-time thing. That could throw even the strongest of people.

I took a seat beside her on the couch but tried to keep my gaze off her. My eyes could be a bit intense when I stared at people, and I didn't need to freak her out anymore. "I'm sorry. I've never gotten sent there so I can't say much, but I'm sure it sucks."

I nearly groaned at my clumsy words, wishing suddenly she had Knox there instead of me. He was better with words, better with comfort. He understood women, knew how to get them to relax, how to talk to them.

Never had my shortcomings frustrated me more than at this moment...

She shrugged softly, picked up her writing pad, then wrote.

She held it out to me, and I reached for it. Our fingers touched, just a brush of them. When it happened, instead of hardly noting the innocent contact as she'd have done before, Hera yanked away as she had in the hallway.

It was like the touch had burned her, as if it terrified her. I'd thought earlier was an issue with surprising her, but clearly it went deep.

"What the fuck?" I asked without trying to reach for her again. "What is wrong?" Before she could say what I knew she would, I added on, "And don't you dare tell me it's nothing. If it was *nothing* you wouldn't be jumping away from me like you're afraid."

She sighed and picked up the writing pad from the floor. She hit the Erase button, then wrote again. *"I guess Medical bothered me more than I realized."*

"But why? You've been through it before."

"I couldn't remember last time."

"No one remembers much of Medical—that's why they drug us."

She didn't write anything else, her gaze on the floor.

And maybe I was stupid, but it took way too long for that to come together, for me to understand what she was saying without saying it.

"You remember it, don't you?"

She nodded.

"How? The drugs work on you, or you'd have remembered the first time."

She wrote quickly. *"Kit."*

That made me groan. Of course Kit had been a part of this, and that made me suspect Deacon had as well. I hated that she had anything to do with either of them. They were dangerous and couldn't be trusted.

It was only a matter of time before they fucked her over for their own benefit. Or, hell, judging from how she jumped away from me and shook, maybe they already had.

"And Kit managed something that made it so you resisted them?"

She nodded.

I didn't even need to ask why she'd done it—I knew Hera well enough to guess.

"You wanted to see if you could overhear anything useful, didn't you?"

Another nod.

"I know I've pushed you hard, said we need to come up with a usable plan, but I didn't mean you needed to do *that*. For fuck's sake, what do you take me for?"

Her shoulders drooped, and I cursed myself. She wasn't feeling great already—I really was the asshole everyone called me for snapping at her now.

"Sorry," I muttered. "So, did you hear anything important?"

She erased what she'd had before and wrote, then turned the pad toward me. *"They implied I didn't turn into a shade naturally, that someone turned me into this. The Warden was there, too. She's really interested in me."*

And there went my temper again. The Warden was bad news, and she rarely took an interest in any specific shade. When she did, however, it never ended well. The shade rarely made it long before going to the North Tower.

"Is that it?"

"The Warden said I wasn't useful for either of their main projects there, so I'm more useful here than in the North Tower for now."

"Useful here? How the hell can you be useful here?" I frowned, trying to make it make sense. "They aren't using your skills for anything like interrogations or missions. Hell, they don't even know what you can do, so how are you useful at all?"

"Gee, thanks." Who knew two words on a pad could contain that much sarcasm?

"I'm not trying to insult you. I'm just trying to figure out what's going on. If the Warden thinks you have a use, we need to know what it is, because it's really fucking important."

She let out a long breath, then nodded as if accepting the truth. After another moment, she leaned toward me and set her head on my shoulder.

The touch was strange. In fact, I nearly jumped away as she had earlier, and wasn't that fucked up? I could have sex with her, could fight with her, but something like this, something almost sweet, made me uneasy.

Still, I couldn't bring myself to push her away. Instead, I sat there, my body rigid and unsure. "What's this?" I asked in a low voice.

She wrote on the pad, which sat on her lap so she didn't need to turn or move it for me to read. *"I can stop if you want."*

"Didn't ask you to stop—just figured with how you were reacting, this wasn't a great idea..." I paused, then all but whispered the rest, "especially with me."

"I just need to relax, to feel like I can close my eyes for a minute."

"And you feel like that with me?"

She didn't nod, but maybe we were more alike than different. Neither of us wanted to admit there was anything but anger and sex between us. Even still, she closed her eyes and before I knew it, she'd drifted off.

I let her rest, and after I was sure she'd fully fallen asleep, I lifted her carefully. She fit against my chest so perfectly, her body lighter than I'd expected. I was so used to dealing with fighters, with larger people with incredible strength, that it felt strange to hold her.

Her body was so much softer, so much more fragile than I'd realized. We'd had sex, so I'd seen this body, felt it, but holding her when she wasn't even awake was different. It felt like an odd trust between us that I never would have expected.

I tucked her into bed, pulling the covers over her. She rolled toward me, all but curling around my hand as if, even when asleep, she didn't want to let me go.

And why did that melt me? Why was it that I didn't want to go, that feeling needed like this, feeling trusted, I struggled to go?

I let out a sigh and gently pulled my hand free. She needed rest, and I needed to deal with Kit.

We all had our places…

* * * *

Kit

Brax heading my way with that look in his eyes signaled trouble. If I were just anyone, just a young shade living my life, I'd have turned in the other direction and run just as fast as I could.

I wasn't young, though, and while Brax was no doubt a formidable enemy, he didn't frighten me.

Nothing did, not anymore. Whether that was due to my being sure I could handle anything or that I just didn't care, I didn't know. Perhaps I was too far gone, too different to feel such things anymore.

However, we couldn't have the conversation I was sure he wanted to have here, in the middle of a common area. I gestured for Brax to follow, and it seemed he had the good sense left inside him to do so.

We remained silent as we went down the hallway and to a large room made for evaluations. I had access to it whenever I needed, and assuming Brax lost control of his berserker rage, it was best to be somewhere we could avoid any real damage.

I shut the door behind him after he stormed past me. The edges of his face had sharpened, a sure sign he struggled to control himself.

Ah, to be young like that, to feel things so deeply.

"I assume you're here about Hera?"

His blue eyes brightened, telling me I'd guessed right. Then again, it wasn't a hard shot to take. We didn't have many things in common, many things to put that sort of anger on his face. "Why would you do that?"

"She asked for help. Given how you trail after her, I would assume you'd understand why I might agree."

"If she wanted to do something stupid and dangerous, I wouldn't help."

"She had good reasons for what she wanted. It was her choice in the end."

"Hera doesn't know how this world works. She still lives in some fancy little corner of it. You know better, though, you've been here long enough to *know* how this works. Do you just get off on the idea that she got to be awake and aware while she was tortured by those fucking assholes in Medical? Is it just some twisted kink for you?"

A sting in my chest surprised me. *Is that upset? Guilt?*

"Maybe it wasn't even about her—maybe you just wanted to trick her into that bond," he went on. "She wouldn't ever consider shit with you without it."

That was a fair point.

It would have been dishonest to claim I hadn't craved that connection, that I hadn't wanted to feel her bound to me. Despite us not communicating beyond that one dream, I still felt her on the other side of that connection.

"I'm not the sort of man to make choices for other people. If she wanted that, who was I to deny her?"

Brax walked up and wrapped his fingers in the front of my shirt, his face having shifted, his body larger so he was taller than I was. "She's jumping and flinching at every fucking thing, and for what? She got nothing out of that, but now she's got scars in her head in addition to those on her body. That's your fucking fault. I should put a few scars on you to make it even, to pay you back."

I didn't bother to knock him away. What was the point? It was like swatting at a fly—it took energy, but since the fly couldn't harm me, why waste my time? "You can try, but in what way would that help her at all? I would think, if you were so concerned about her, you would be with her rather than here."

"She isn't alone."

"Really? So you left her to someone else? You always struck me as the primal, possessive type."

"Don't act like you know shit about me."

"I know you are exceedingly reckless. The only chance you might have against me would be if you fully changed, if you gave yourself over entirely to your berserker, but you aren't about to do that, are you?"

He pressed his lips together, the muscles beneath his skin shifting as they still grew and changed. After a moment, he yanked away.

Well, at least he wasn't as stupid as I'd first thought.

He pointed a finger at me, the nail sharpened to a lethal point. "Stay the fuck away from Hera."

"That isn't up to me, and it isn't up to you, either. If you believe she is someone you can control, who you can lock up, then you truly are just as foolish as everyone says."

He narrowed his shining eyes. "If you hurt her or betray her, I don't care what you are, I *will* put an end to you." He didn't wait for a response—probably because he knew it would only further our little argument—before he left the room. He slammed the door behind him so hard, it shook the walls.

After he'd left, I stared at the door, lost in thought, in the words he'd said, the things I wanted to deny but couldn't.

Maybe he was right.

Maybe it had been a bad choice to help her, to get involved, to bind her to me. While that bond would lessen over time without contact, it would never fully go away.

Even if I scolded myself for my unusually rash decision, I didn't regret it. Even now, I *felt* her. It wasn't telepathy, not even a real emotional sense, but I knew she rested at the end of that thread, she lived, even had a sense of her distance from me. Or perhaps it was better to say I felt my own poison inside her, calling back to me.

Had I caused her pain? Had I endangered her? Had I harmed her?

I couldn't deny any of those things, yet I couldn't bring myself to want to take it back, either.

I hadn't felt attached to anyone or anything in so long. I had drifted aimlessly through life for decades. I wanted this connection, even if it ended up destroying us both.

* * * *

Hera

Everything hurt when I woke, and for a moment, I considered just going back to sleep. Sure, I'd slept for a long damned time, and I wasn't tired anymore, but the idea of dragging myself from bed felt impossible.

I rolled over and pulled the blanket around me tighter, wanting to ignore the world. I had nothing to do all week. Deacon must have called in some good favors, because he'd gotten me out of both work and classes for the next five days.

I sighed as I recalled how I'd leaned against Brax, how I'd flinched when he'd touched me, and that made me want to hide even more. He must have put me into my bed after I'd fallen asleep.

The last thing I wanted was to wake up and see him there, not after he got a glimpse of my breakdown, not with the volatility of our relationship.

A heavenly scent floated through the blanket, and I frowned. A sound from the kitchen further caught my attention, made me sit up and stare toward the closed door.

Was someone cooking food in my kitchen?

Part of me considered going right the fuck back to sleep anyway. I didn't want to deal with whoever had broken in. Let the world fall to chaos as long as I could stay wrapped up in my blanket.

Then my stomach rumbled, and I doubted I could sleep well like that. It seemed the mysterious chef in my kitchen had figured out the perfect lure draw me from my room. I pulled my hair into a bun again, then went into the bathroom long enough to brush my teeth. I didn't feel like showering. The idea of stripping down and getting into the water felt like far too much work just to eat.

It meant when I walked out of the bedroom to find Wade in my kitchen, I probably should have felt self-conscious. My messy hair and rumpled clothing should have embarrassed me, but they didn't.

Not with Wade, especially. His presence relaxed me and rarely made me feel pressured at all.

"I knew eggs and bacon would tempt you."

I frowned at that. I didn't have a stove—none of us did. When I peered past him, I spotted a hot plate plugged in and set on the counter. He had a large pan on top with slices of bacon and over easy eggs there.

"A hot plate like this is worth its weight in gold." Wait gestured at a barstool with his spatula.

"What are you doing here?" I signed.

"When you're upset or overwhelmed, you make a blanket igloo and stop showering and hide from the world. The best way to your heart is food." He paused, as if thinking. "Well, you'd also be won over with the heads of your enemies, but that seems more like a Brax sort of gift."

Wade's words eased me, making me feel as if things would work out. He could make the entire world a little less overwhelming, like if he could laugh through it, so could I.

He used the spatula to scoot the bacon from the pan and onto a waiting plate, then slid the eggs after it. With a flourish, he pushed the plate over toward me. He immediately went about cleaning up while I picked at the food.

Even though my stomach had growled moments ago, actually eating proved more difficult.

"Your appetite is probably off because of Kit's toxin," Wade said.

I lifted my gaze to find him not looking at me as he scrubbed the pan. How was it that he could know what I was doing even when he wasn't looking at me? Despite his attitude as a man who took nothing seriously, his skills of observation impressed me.

"Wendigos don't eat normal food, so their toxin can cause issues with eating for a few days. The high fat and high protein of a good bacon and eggs breakfast should help, though, so try to eat some of it."

I didn't argue with him—I didn't really see a point in that—so I ate slowly.

He cleaned the whole kitchen without complaint, and I had to admit, he was better at such chores than I was. Then again, he'd lived here at Larkwood for a long time, taking care of himself. It made me want to learn some of the tasks from him.

The thought of me standing in the kitchen as he taught me to cook sounded amazing. It seemed so normal, so domestic. I pictured him laughing about my knife work before explaining how to know when something was done cooking.

Once he finished, he pulled one of the stools from my side of the kitchen island to his. He'd probably done it so he wouldn't be as close, to make me feel better.

I once again set down the fork. *"Did Brax ask you to come?"*

He offered me a sheepish grin. "Guilty. Brax stopped by and said you could use my charming personality to cheer you up. Lord knows that Brax's company leaves something to be desired." Even as he said that, his voice held an odd fondness, as if he mocked Brax but didn't truly hate the man.

I didn't respond and picked up the fork again to take another bite.

"You know, you should have told us what you were planning." Wade's gaze hardened, as if he'd made his jokes but now needed me to understand. "If we knew, we'd have been here to support you afterward."

That sounded all fine and well, but they would have complained about my plan at best — at worst, they would have stopped me.

Though, the way I felt said maybe it would have been right to do so.

Wade let out a rare sigh, the humor of his usual expression sliding away. "You have people who care about you, Hera, people who don't want to see you hurting. We're not just working together for our plan — I'd like to think we're at least friends. You need to learn to lean on us more."

I looked down at my plate to realize I'd eaten the entire meal. I wasn't sure when I'd done it, but Wade had been right. The fat in it settled my stomach, made me feel better. Since I'd finished, I set down my fork so I could actually answer him. *"I knew I needed to do it and didn't want to worry anyone."*

"Well, learn to worry us. You're getting breakfast from me this time—pull this sort of thing again, and I won't be so friendly."

"You're always friendly."

He let out a soft huff. "That's not true—I just show you my best side. I've got a temper like anyone, and it turns out you hiding things sets it off. However, I'm also the quickest to bounce back, which is why I get the job of looking after you."

"Don't you have classes?"

"Nope. Woke up today to find my schedule cleared."

I frowned. Was that Deacon's doing? Had he done it so I wouldn't be alone?

It sounded a lot like Deacon, to go behind my back and do what he thought was right for me without even trying to get credit.

"I think I'm going back to bed."

"Not a chance. You've slept enough. You need to shower, then we're going out."

"I don't feel like it."

"Too bad. You've gotten time to rest, and now you're just hiding. Licking your wounds is one thing, but you won't feel better until you start moving again."

I wanted to tell him to fuck off, but one look at him kept me from doing so, especially because he wasn't wrong.

"Go on, shower time. Nothing like hot water to make a person feel like themselves."

I pushed away from the island as Wade took my plate. The sound of him washing the last dish followed me as I went into the master bath.

The marks didn't bother me anymore, neither the one at my throat nor the others I'd accumulated over my time at Larkwood. They'd done fewer biopsies, so the wounds from the last Medical trip didn't bother me as much, at least not physically, and it made a shower possible.

I stripped down and turned on the water, twisting the handle to hot. I didn't want a long shower, but the idea of burning away anything on me sounded great. I wanted to scrub each place the doctor and nurses had touched me, as if that would somehow reclaim my body for myself.

I just wanted to be my own, to belong to myself, but after my time with Medical, after being trapped here and having to do as I was told, I wasn't sure I could have that again.

Chapter Seven

Wade

I snooped around Hera's room after I'd finished cleaning up, while she showered. I'd even straightened her room and got laundry started for her, including her sheets. Nothing better than clean sheets when a person didn't feel well. The second set was already on, the bed made for whenever she crawled back into it.

I didn't feel guilty about snooping, either. Privacy was some distant concept here at Larkwood, and given I'd spent nearly all my life here, it wasn't one I abided by. It was a stupid social norm people prized far too much. The only privacy a person got was what was in their head.

And even that wasn't entirely secure given telepathic shades.

Still, I'd found nothing too interesting in her room. Hera was fairly upfront as a person, so I hadn't expected to find some huge secret. She just wasn't that type, and her face was too easy to read.

Which left me to leaf through the books she had, most of which I'd suggested to her.

I glanced toward the clock and frowned. It had been an hour, and she *still* wasn't out. Unease prickled at me, and while I wanted to give her the time to get herself together — and the idea of interrupting her in the shower felt like a lot for me — it had been too long.

I went to the door of the master bathroom, hearing the water still running. I knocked and called her name, but nothing came back.

The idea of seeing her naked made me hesitate. We hadn't gone anywhere close to that far yet, and the thought of it rooted me in place. Sure, I *wanted* that, more than I should, enough that it made me uneasy and distrusting of myself. Self-control wasn't exactly a great trait of mine, and when it came to sex, it hadn't been something I'd had to do before as I hadn't had any options. I had no interest in guards, and what shade would allow me to touch them when it made them vulnerable?

But no matter how worried it made me, I couldn't just turn around and avoid her, couldn't leave until I knew she was okay.

I took a deep breath then turned the handle, glad to find it unlocked. I pushed the door open to a room filled with steam.

Hera's naked back greeted me inside the shower. I swallowed hard at the sight, stunned enough to see it all before I lifted my gaze to try to keep it from anything she'd rather keep private.

Though, it wasn't like the memory of her ass didn't play through my head. I held in a groan as I tried to get myself under control.

Don't be a creep. She's clearly struggling, you asshole — don't look at her like this.

I went closer, then called her name again.

This time it got through, because she spun toward me, her eyes wide and her skin a pink that bordered on red from the heat of the water. She blinked slowly, the pain in her hazel eyes so obvious that a blind man could see it.

All the lust drifted away at that, at the way she trembled. Her hands moved, so quick that I struggled at first to keep up and understand. *"I can't stop the sounds. I can't use the tricks to shut it out and everything is so loud. I don't know if it's the toxin or the drugs or what happened with Medical, but it's just all so loud."*

I suspected tears ran down her cheeks, but with the water, I couldn't tell.

And for once, I could do something about it, something only I could do for her. I pushed away my fears and my doubt and pulled my shirt off. I left the sweats on—neither of us needed the complication of her seeing my inevitable reaction to the proximity of her naked body—then stepped into the walk-in shower. I set my hands on her cheeks, rested my forehead against hers, then wrapped my arms around her to pull her against me.

The sensation of her bare breasts against me was a special sort of hell, something that made me crave so many things yet still made me happy on its own.

She let out a shuddering breath as her powers slid into me. Like before, the sensation was gentle, warm, wonderful. It wasn't anything like how it normally felt when I touched people, when their power clawed at me like a wild animal trapped inside of me, when that source I temporary stole ripped my insides apart. With Hera, the power hit differently, softer.

Why? Because it was her? Because of what she was? Maybe because she didn't fight me, because I didn't steal it so much as carried it for her for a while.

She dug her fingers into my back, and I suspected that was a thank you from her. She couldn't sign, not with us up against each other like that, but guessed the motion showed her own gratitude.

"I wish I could do more," I whispered to her. "I wish I could fix this all for you, that I could make things better, but Larkwood isn't the sort of place where anyone can save anyone else."

She shifted and brushed her lips against mine. And boy did that *not* do good things for my already tenuous hold on my desire.

"Maybe that's not a great idea," I whispered instead of responding with a kiss, instead of doing what I really wanted. "You've had a hard couple of days, and believe it or not, I didn't come here for this. I mean, I know seeing me all wet and manly in the shower would make anyone react like that..."

She pulled back far enough to look up and into my eyes, though her body remained against mine, and ended my tirade. I used one of my thumbs to trace over her bottom lip, surprised that she could do this to me.

I'd figured I'd feel so damned awkward around her, given my lack of experience. I'd thought I'd be uncomfortable and unsure. Something about her made that impossible. She shut down the part of me that overthought and worried, like she made it so I could feel some deeper instinct inside me.

"Don't get me wrong. I really want to." I let out a soft groan at how adequate that statement was. "I *really, really* want to. I just don't want you regretting anything or feeling like I took advantage of you. You're the most important thing to me."

The corner of her lips pulled into a smile, as if she were charmed by my words.

Which made me again wonder just how I'd done anything in my life to deserve her. She was too damned pure for this place, too good for any of us.

She pulled away, and I let her go, not wanting to ever force her into anything. She signed to respond. *"I'm not going to regret anything. I want you."*

I groaned and rubbed my hand over my face. "You can't just say things like that—it's not fair."

"You quiet the world for me."

"So we'll hold hands as long as you want, but we don't have to do anything like this."

"Please?" The honesty in her expression undid me.

How could I say no? How could I possibly turn her down when she looked at me like that? When she asked so sweetly?

And it really only had one answer—"Okay."

* * * *

Hera

I crawled into the bed, thankful Wade had changed my sheets. He'd said he needed to dry off, so had sent me ahead of him.

The silence of the world felt like a miracle. After the noise, it was everything to feel it quiet, to feel like the person I used to be. I knew his skill didn't last long when he did it like this rather than using it as a weapon, but even the small reprieve was worth it.

It took a few minutes for the door to open, for Wade to exit.

And I didn't bother to hide my disappointment. He was naked, but he had a towel wrapped around his hips, hiding himself from me.

"You saw me naked. Seems unfair to not get the same."

He chuckled but didn't relent. "Yeah, well, I'm not a man to play fair. I have my sweats hanging up to dry, because I doubt the guards would want me wandering around in my birthday suit." He hesitated for a moment, then got into the bed beside me.

I reached for him, scooting closer, wanting to feel his lean body against mine.

He grasped my wrist to stop me, though, then stared into my eyes. When I stopped, he spoke softly. "I don't want to rush this," he said. "I don't think we need to."

I frowned, because he'd said okay. What exactly did he think *okay* meant?

The smile he offered me had strained edges. "I'm not turning you down. I just want to be upfront. I want to do this right, to make it…special? I don't know exactly, but I know I want to do it right. I don't think we need to go all the way today…"

The phrasing made me pause as it sank in, and I couldn't help it when it made me laugh. Despite making no real sound, the laugher must have been obvious, because Wade pouted.

"Laughing at a man when he's naked is cruel, you know?"

I pulled my hand from him so I could answer. *"It was just cute how you phrased it."*

"Oh, *sure*, that makes it better! You're laughing at my awkwardness and lack of experience. You know what? Fine! We'll have sex right now, and you'll be sorry." He reached for me as if to prove a point.

I swatted his hand and shook my head. *"No! Now I want this romance you're talking about. You can't get out of it."*

"Nope, sorry. You wanted to laugh at me, now you'll be lucky to even get foreplay. You can call me a one-pump-chump and lament later about how terrible it was, and it'll be all your fault because you couldn't control your laughter." His words were brash, but his teasing smile let me know he was playing with me.

And it made me fall for him all the more. Even with Wade nervous, even with him having no experience, he always looked out for me. It was so different from every other relationship in my life, ones where we lived in the moment, where we gave in to whatever we felt because we didn't believe in the future.

Instead, Wade thought about tomorrow. He thought about how we would feel, about what he wanted, what he wanted to give me.

And that was far more attractive than I'd thought. Sure, Brax was all aggression, and Deacon was confident and possessive, and Knox was all experienced seduction, and Kit was—I had no idea how to finish that thought, so I let it go.

But Wade? He was sweet and honest and real.

That had me shifting closer until he gave in to the kiss I knew we both craved. He wasn't as hesitant as he'd been at the start, weeks before when we'd shared our first. He'd grown in confidence since then, so when I stroked my tongue along his bottom lip, he let me in.

He tasted like mint, making me suspect he'd used the mouthwash in my bathroom before coming in here. The little gesture made me want him more, made me appreciate him all the more. He was always thinking about me, never about himself.

I slid my leg over him so I shifted into his lap, then set my hands on his shoulders. I drifted my palms down his chest, finally able to touch him like I'd wanted for a while. His body was lean but firm, with little fat and no large muscles. Only the towel sat between us, and I could easily feel just how interested he was despite the limits he'd set.

He set his hands on my hips, the touch hesitant. The blanket had slid down so nothing covered me, nothing hid me from his view. Then again, he'd already seen me in the shower, so it wasn't as if anything was a secret.

Still, the stroke of his hands was like fire against my heated skin. He moved them down over the outsides of my thighs, the touch light as if he were nervous. I shivered at the sensation while he ran his hands to where my knees spread around his hips, then back up to my waist.

He broke the kiss, but I didn't have time for disappointment. He pressed his lips to my jaw, then to my throat. I let my head drop back, exposing myself to him. The touches slowed until they petered out.

I pulled back, suddenly self-conscious. I didn't feel that often anymore, maybe because Larkwood didn't allow people to put their best side forward. In my old life, I always dressed so well, never let people see me when not perfect, but that wasn't me anymore.

However, as it turned out, being naked and in the lap of a man they loved could make anyone doubt themselves, especially when that man put the brakes on. I peered into his eyes, easily reading the hesitation there, the fear.

I let out a sigh and pulled out of his lap. I couldn't blame him, couldn't get upset with him. If he wasn't ready, he wasn't ready. That didn't change the way he shook my confidence, however.

"Hera," he whispered as I lay down in the bed again. Despite his original plan for us to go out, I no longer had any desire to do that. Everything Wade had held back with that passion between us crushed against me again.

I shook my head and pulled the blanket around him.

I expected him to leave, to want the distance and time to think over it all. Instead, he got beneath the blanket with me and pressed against my back, the warmth of his body like a cruel joke. How could someone be so close yet so far away at the same time?

He ran his fingers through my hair. "I'm sorry. I don't blame you for being frustrated with me, but I just want this to be right. I can't give you what you want, not right now, but I can at least keep the world quiet for you for a while." He pressed his lips to the top of my head before he wrapped his arms around me.

So I let him silence the world for me. Too bad his skills didn't silence the thoughts that crashed around in my head as well.

Chapter Eight

Hera

I frowned as I watched the woman lean into Knox's space and twirl her hair around her finger.

It made me wonder if I looked that way when I talked to him. Did I look that desperate? Was I so obvious?

Probably.

Of course, getting jealous over people hitting on Knox was as stupid as being angry over the sun shining. Nothing would ever change that. As an incubus, Knox drew people to him. All he had to do was exist somewhere and eyes followed him, desire all but drowning those around him.

It didn't hit me as hard, but I still understood.

Which was why when I walked into the pantry area to find Knox standing near the wall with a woman I didn't recognize, my expecting it didn't lessen my annoyance. The woman was pretty, though dressed stuffy. She wasn't a shade, because she had no identification band on her wrist. She also wasn't a guard, since she didn't wear the outfit.

It meant she was staff.

I listened in, wanting to catch their conversation over the rest of the noise in the busy pantry.

"Come on, Knox. You always turn me down," the woman said.

"Because it wouldn't be appropriate, Nisha."

Well, that gave me her name, at least. I hadn't heard it around, but that didn't mean much. I knew the librarian and a few of the people who worked in the various areas such as the pantry, but I hadn't heard of or seen her before.

It meant she likely came from the administration level, and I avoided that area as best I could.

"What do you mean by appropriate? No one cares about fraternization here. It's expected, so everyone turns their back on it."

I closed my hands into fists to calm myself before I did something I shouldn't. I suddenly felt like I understood Brax better, like I knew how he felt when people tried to take advantage of Knox. It wasn't just that he attracted them, but that they tried to use his needs against him, to force him into things he'd made it clear he didn't want.

"I'm not interested," he repeated, crossing his arms over his chest as if to drive the point home.

She stuck her bottom lip out in a sullen pout. "You've been hungry lately, haven't you? I see all the reports, have access to your recent strange requests in exchange for your help recently. Are they to help you deal with your hunger? Why starve? There's no reason to do that to yourself."

A familiar twitch in his cheek told me all I needed to know about Knox's feelings. He wasn't just not interested—he was furious with the proposition. Of course, dealing with guards or staff was a far cry from dealing with other shades. Knox could threaten other shades, but he had to use caution with the humans.

They could make his life a living hell if he didn't tread lightly.

It made my chest tight with worry that he'd give in just because he didn't have a way to avoid it. That was the last thing I wanted for him.

"Incubi are dangerous," he said as a response. It was strange because I'd heard that from him before. There was so much self-loathing in those words, but he still said it to her. "They're even more dangerous to humans. You don't know what you're asking for. If I were too hungry, if I took too much, I could kill you."

She stared into his eyes like some lovestruck teenager, like a girl who had romanticized tragic love stories to the point where she deemed the risk acceptable. "You wouldn't do that, but if it happened? I don't know that I'd care. I can make your life easier here, you know. Being the assistant to the Warden has benefits. What do you want? Whatever it is, I can give it to you."

"If I give you want you want, you mean?" His words came out cold and full of anger. She treated him like an object, like something she could use then discard and she didn't give a damn what he wanted.

"It's a fair trade," she swore. "You'll enjoy it too. You can be well fed and have an easier life. I can keep your name off the search lists, and I can approve requests for you. You can live in luxury if you just agree."

Knox swallowed hard, his gaze darting around as if trapped. She didn't want to take no for an answer, but he didn't want to say yes.

Which was about the point I tired of watching her back him into a corner. I didn't have to think much before I moved, before my temper got the better of me. I lifted my hand and snapped softly, then twisted my fingers to shape the soft sound, thankful for Kit's lessons.

Delicate and precise was rather useful…

I sent the small sound wave toward her, angled down. It struck her shoe, knocking the heel out and causing her to topple backward. She hit the tile floor hard, right on her ass, and everyone turned to stare.

Her cheeks flushed bright red, probably because I'd bet she'd worn those ridiculously high heels and dolled herself up just to tempt Knox—which hadn't even worked—and now she'd fallen on her ass right in front of him and all the shades who she wanted to think she was better than.

She scrambled to her feet, staring down for a moment to find the heel of her shoe knocked off. She picked up the missing part, then mumbled some apology to Knox and rushed off with an unstable gait from her ruined shoe.

I didn't bother to hide my grin at the success. Knox frowned as she left, then turned his head toward me. Our gazes met, and I wasn't sure if it was my grin that let him know I'd been involved. Whatever it was, he narrowed his eyes as though he couldn't figure out how to feel about it.

I shrugged, my way of telling him not to think too hard about it, then turned to stroll out. I'd gone to the pantry to get some items, but I sure wasn't about to stay in there just for some crackers and cereal. I wanted the badass-walk-out moment, the one where I got to be the hero who headed off into the horizon after setting things right.

Or walk off toward the elevator, as it was.

Still, the surprise on Knox's face was worth it, as was the petty thrill of taking that woman down a notch or two for touching him.

So, I could be rather jealous. I was just learning new things about myself right and left.

* * * *

Spending time together with Knox, Brax and Wade never got any less awkward. I almost thought if it did, I might miss this heavy feeling, the way everyone seemed at least slightly uncomfortable.

We were in my place, as always. We met here because the men's places caused territorial issues, but somehow they all felt like they had a right to mine. At the moment, Wade and Brax bickered like children over the last of a bag of cookies I had in the kitchen.

"I could rip your heart from your body," Brax all but snarled.

"After I leave you as a heap on the floor because I've stolen all that fancy power from you?" Wade asked back, his usual smirk on his lips.

All this for a few cookies?

"They're like children," Knox said from his spot beside me, his arms crossed as he watched.

I nodded, because it was true. *"Then again, Brax fights with everyone like this."*

"And Wade acts like a child even if he isn't fighting. I guess they'll never be best friends."

I tried to picture Brax and Wade suddenly getting along. They'd hang out together, watching bad movies, annoying or beating up every other person around. The thought of Wade's sarcastic smirk and Brax's glare had me breaking into a smile.

Yeah, that's never going to happen.

"Still, we'll never get anything done if they keep this up…"

Knox had a point, so I held up one finger to tell him to wait a moment. I went into my bedroom — it didn't so much as faze the other two — and got my secret weapon. On my way back, I tossed each man a new pack of the cookies I'd hidden in my closet.

They easily caught the bags, breaking their little stand-off and both appearing sheepish, as if they'd just realized they were fighting in front of me over desserts.

Still, while neither apologized, they sat down with their cookies like good boys.

At that, I stood in front of them. A nod from Knox said he'd translate for me so Brax understood as well.

"I think I have an idea."

Everyone settled at that. Then again, I hadn't said why I'd wanted them to come over. They probably expected a random check-in, but that wasn't it. I'd spent time hashing out our options about how to proceed, and the longer I sat in Larkwood, the more I knew we had to get moving. We couldn't keep waiting around for some perfect idea to fall into our laps.

I took the large piece of posterboard I'd gotten from Kit a few days prior and set it on the coffee table between the men, then kneeled beside it, pen in hand. Writing things down made me feel better, like I had everything organized and under control even when I obviously didn't.

I wrote on the board between signing, making a list on the side. *"Escaping is going to need a few things. We're going to need to take the security system down."*

Wade nodded. "If we don't take out the alarms and door locks, getting out will be all but impossible."

"Right. So that's one thing. We also need to plan the best exit."

"Options there are roof exit or front door in the main building," Brax said.

"We also need to break off their communications," Knox added in. "If each guard is on their own, if they can't work together, it'll limit what they can to do. Regular staff and guards aren't allowed to bring cell phones with them when working, to limit the risk of a shade getting it, so without their radios or tablets, they can't talk to each other. It would work best if we could throw up a false alarm first, to draw guards there."

I added the points they made onto the board, the steps feeling overwhelming yet somehow better than not having any plan at all.

"We need to knock out the power," Wade said. At my look, he went on. "Security systems are all run by computers and use generators out back. If we sabotage the security features to open doors and locks, that's great, but they have enough back doors in the system to reverse it. Taking down the power will give us time to get out before they can gain control of it all again. It will basically lock all the systems open."

I nodded and added that to the list. We'd spent the last month trying to come up with ideas, with plans, observing everything. Now we needed to get serious.

Brax gestured toward the board. "Let's separate these tasks and assign them. No one can do everything, and it'll take us all to figure it out. We'll each focus on a part of it and come up with a plan, then we'll work the plan out together with all the steps."

Wade tapped on the board. "I'll take the security system. Pretty sure I'm the only one here who knows how to use a computer even, and if I need to get help with coding a virus, I know enough people to get it done quietly."

"I'll take the escape route," Knox said. "I can move around a little easier than the rest of you because people don't mind me being around."

"I'll handle the generators," Brax offered. "A bit of brute strength would work best there, and it doesn't call for much finesse. I'll figure out the best way to approach or get in."

"Guess that leaves me with communication."

"Absolutely not," Brax interrupted as Knox translated for me. "I'll figure that out, too."

I frowned. *"What? Why?"*

Wade let out a sigh and answered for Brax. "Communications is run through the North Tower."

"How do you even know that?"

"It's one of those not well-kept secrets. Larkwood likes to keep areas apart for safety, which is why generators are in one place, security in another, records in another. It makes it harder to attack at once because it requires more people and the more people involved in a plan, the better chance someone slips up and gets caught. Communications has historically been one of the most important things, so it's in the North Tower to keep it safe."

Which meant I'd somehow picked the part of the plan that required me to go to the most dangerous area of Larkwood. It didn't seem like bad luck but rather like some strange twist of fate.

I'd figured the North Tower was going to be an important part of my plan back when it had just been me, but now? It seemed that was my part, like the place was calling me back, like I was always meant to end up there.

I swallowed hard, then stared back at the men. *"I can do it. The Warden's already said they might need to send me there, and she's already watching me. I can't do anything about the security, I don't know the layout or people well enough to figure out an escape route, and I'm more likely to get into the North Tower than the rest of you. This makes sense."*

Knox and Wade pressed their lips together, but neither responded. Brax, however, didn't seem as willing to sit quietly and accept it. "This is bullshit," he muttered.

"It's the right choice, and you know it."

He stood, his hands pulled into fists. "Do you just want to die? If you do, there are a lot less painful ways than getting sent to the North Tower, you know. If this is all just a death wish for you, don't expect any of us to stop you." Even though his words were cruel, I picked up the pain beneath them. He stormed toward the door, pausing before he left. "What the fuck is the point of any of this if you get yourself killed in the North Tower? If you take down the communications and we get out and you're stuck in there? Why the fuck did we do any of it, then?" He didn't wait for an answer, slamming the door behind him.

I sighed as I remained kneeling on the ground. He didn't think I could do it. It hurt, the way they accepted everyone else's tasks, but didn't think I could do my part.

Even after how much I'd grown, how much I'd done to prove myself, I still wasn't trusted.

Life never really changed, did it?

Chapter Nine

Knox

I eyed the security cameras, searching for any exit other than the two I knew of. Neither seemed like a good idea.

The roof was difficult to get to, accessible through an emergency exit on the top floor that led to a set of stairs on the outside of the building. The issue didn't stop after getting through that, though. The exit used a physical key rather than the normal electronic locks, which meant Hera wouldn't be able to bypass it. Brax could break it down, if needed, but given it opened to an outside staircase, we didn't need to risk the security of the actual staircase. Plummeting to our deaths because Brax had loosened screws into the building would be a horrible end to our escape plans.

Even if I could get the key, even if we could get up to the roof, what then? Brax could scale all of anything, but Wade, Hera and I were far less physically capable.

I could survive the fall, especially if well fed, but that still left two stranded.

I started wondering about things like ziplines, rappelling or even hang gliding over the wall.

The moment I started considering how to make a hang glider, I suspected my plan wasn't going well. That had the makings of a hilarious story for Larkwood to tell for years to come. They probably wouldn't even clean up the blood spot from where we landed so they could use it as a cautionary tale for the new shades.

Our other option was the front door. Unfortunately, unless we came up with a really good distraction for the guards, that would be the first place they'd amass in the event of a security breach. No doubt they knew the roof was a hard sell for an escape, so they'd marshal their forces at the most likely exit point.

"What are you even looking for?" The guard currently stationed in the security room asked as he stared at me, nearly pouting.

"I just like seeing the cameras," I lied. "They make me feel like I'm free."

The guard, whose name I didn't bother to learn, let out a soft laugh. "Freedom is a joke. There isn't any real freedom, not for anyone. You can stare at those screens as long as you want, but it doesn't make a difference. As someone who spends day after day here, I can promise you that." He set his hand on mine. "Only thing that can make you feel free are a few moments of pleasure."

The touch made me shudder both due to what I wanted and what I hated. Of course, that didn't surprise me. I'd made my way into the room in the first place with little more than a suggestive smile and a few well-placed words. People looked at me and saw sex, so it didn't take much to make them think they had a chance.

The other part of me, that beast inside me that prowled around and looked so tempting, wanted him. It wanted to taste him, to take from him, to pull sounds of pleasure from him until I was strong and well fed.

I'd have done it before, but a flash of Hera in my head made my stomach clench. I really didn't want to… I didn't want to sully myself like this, to give in to what I knew would cause me to hate myself even more. I wanted to be better for Hera.

"I want to see the sky," I said. "I want to stare up at the stars and stretch out and just watch the night sky."

He slid his hand up my arm before he rose from his seat. He was taller than I was, more muscular. Of course, that didn't mean much when comparing a human to a shade. Even as an incubus, I had more strength than any human. "I wish I could take you out there. I bet you'd look good in the moonlight," he whispered.

The pretty words made me sick. I heard them all the time, people who saw no deeper than my body, than my use to them, than the feelings I could give to them. They never saw who I was, didn't see the bad sides of me, the difficult ones, the ugly parts of me. No, I was just a pretty face and an orgasm dispenser to them.

Even people I cared about saw me as little more. Why did Brax agree to let me do this? Because he knew that it was all I could do, that selling myself for information was the only way I could contribute.

Again, Hera's face flashed in my head, the way she'd rolled me the bottle of water when I'd been starving, the way she'd given me pleasure, something I'd never experienced before.

Why? Why did she have to do that? Why had she made me recognize and face what I really wanted, so now the rest of this felt so much worse?

I sighed softly when the guard's hand drifted below my shirt, when his fingers touched my abs, when they traced the line of my sweats. "I can't get you outside. They track that and only let them out for work."

"What about the roof?" I asked, knowing he was too drunk with lust to think carefully, to guess that my question might be strange or suspicious.

He shook his head. "Only the Warden and her assistant have keys to the roof."

"I was so looking forward to that," I whispered, like a lover pouting.

He groaned before reaching his hand into my sweats. I hated myself all the more for my body reacting, for how when he cupped my groin, I was hard no matter how much I didn't want any of this. I felt no pleasure, no desire, nothing but my incubus, as if it laughed happily over it.

Then again, it didn't give a damn where we fed from. It didn't care how I felt or what I wanted, so long as it could devour, so long as it could get what it craved.

"Maybe I can see," he whispered as he pressed his lips to my throat. "The Warden wouldn't hand one over, but her assistant? She might be willing to…"

That made me frown as I recalled the assistant, Nisha, the woman who had come on to me just the other day.

The day when Hera had knocked her over for me. I still hadn't mentioned it to Hera, not sure how to approach it. I wasn't used to people looking out for me other than Brax. Why had she done that? Why risk herself for me?

It wasn't as if she'd even tasted what I could offer...
That thought almost shamed me. I'd let her get on her
knees for me, had let her give me something that
special, and what had I done for her? I'd turned her
down every time she tried to get closer to me.

The guard scraped his teeth over my pulse to get me
in the mood.

Who was I kidding? He didn't give a damn about
my mood — if I enjoyed it, if I wanted it. He only cared
about getting what he'd come for, only wanted to use
me.

He drowned in lust, and my incubus all but purred,
ready to drop to my knees, to become whatever he
wanted. It was part of what I was, the ability to sense
what my partner craved and to become that.

At the start, I'd had fun as an object of desire, but
now? I hated it. I hated how I shifted and changed. This
man was more submissive, which meant I felt myself
rising to that occasion, to become rougher, more
dominant, to turn into the perfect lover for him.

But I wanted to be *me*. Whoever that was, I didn't
want to throw it away for the whims of someone else.

So instead of giving in, I wrapped my hand around
the man's throat and pushed him backward, against the
wall. He moaned and shuddered at the rough
treatment, his eyes clouded, completely taken over by
my pheromones.

I could have pushed this more, could have bent him
over, could have given him exactly what he wanted and
fed off it all. The image of Hera in my head made me
hesitate.

Instead, I allowed myself to feed from him. The
sexual energy wasn't ripe, wasn't from orgasm, from
that climax of sensation, so it was like eating green

bananas. I could consume it, but it wasn't the same, it wasn't as good, was difficult to get down. I kept pulling it from him until his eyes fluttered closed, until he gasped and groaned in ecstasy and went limp.

I lowered his body to the floor carefully. He'd wake up in a few minutes with no real memory of what had happened, would just assume the sex with me had been so great he'd passed out. I rarely did it this way because it didn't do much to feed me and could even make me sick. In the past, it had always been better to just give in, to gorge myself on the energy no matter how much I hated myself afterward, but I couldn't bring myself to do so today.

I stared down at him, my stomach churning as I recalled the touch of his lips on my skin, his hand on my cock, the un-ripe feeling of his energy twisting inside me.

I wanted to see the person whose face had kept appearing to me. My incubus went quiet at that, as if it didn't like its denied meal or the idea of seeing Hera.

But I couldn't bring myself to do so, not after that man had touched me, not when I'd allowed it, when I felt as if he'd stained me.

I didn't deserve to be anywhere around her.

* * * *

Brax

I stared at the building that housed the generators. Getting outside wasn't that hard for someone like me. I'd done enough tasks for Larkwood to have some favors to call in. It meant when I'd said I wanted some time outside to exercise and run, they'd allowed it.

Deacon watched me, which made the entire thing trickier. No doubt he'd volunteered for the task just to annoy me.

Or, rather, to keep a close eye on me.

The fact that Deacon and Hera had some connection didn't fail to rile up my temper. What she saw in that asshole, I had no idea. He was the enemy. His job and life revolved around keeping us prisoner, so why the hell couldn't she break off whatever they had between them?

Because she's too fucking sweet for her own good. Hera didn't see people for what they really were. She saw the best even when it wasn't there.

Maybe I shouldn't hate that about her, because that fault allowed her to accept me.

Deacon stood far away, having given me the full space behind the main building to exercise. Then again, he probably knew I wouldn't try to escape.

At least not right then…

He knew I had Knox to think about, that I'd never abandon my brother. Hell, Larkwood used that like a card, knowing that so long as my twin remained, I'd never really try to escape.

It meant I had the chance to exercise, and each time I neared the small outside building where the generators sat, I took note of a bit more.

The exercise helped, though. I rarely got the chance to let go, to fall into the full strength of my own body. I usually had to hold back, to ensure I kept myself under control. I ran on a treadmill and lifted weights to leash it as best I could, but that wasn't the same as really pushing my body to its limits outdoors.

The last time I'd been able to go all out, the last time I'd fully given myself over to my berserker had been a mission a year prior, when they'd dropped me off somewhere—I had no idea where because they didn't give me information I didn't need—and immediately had taken a bullet to my shoulder.

Talk about a way to release my other side. Between the bullet and the drugs they'd pumped into me to hype up my adrenaline, I'd turned almost instantly. I still recalled sitting in the plane on the way back, covered in blood, a smile on my lips. No matter how much I hated losing control, it still gave me a sense of peace, like tension leaving me.

I shook my head and focused on my task rather than anything else.

I easily picked up the hum of the generators from inside. I stopped just beside the door and hid my interest by dropping to the dirt to do pushups.

I peered toward the building as I worked out, spotting the lock on the door. It was one like those in the building, which meant it opened with a properly programmed wristband that had access. So long as Wade could handle security, the door would unlock and the cameras would go down. That would mean I could enter the building without worrying about calling more guards there until I took out all the generators.

"You're spending more time looking around than exercising." Deacon's voice came from closer than I expected, letting me know he'd approached while I surveyed the security measures around the building.

I didn't let him shake me, though. It would take a lot more than Deacon to worry me. "This is all pretty easy exercise. I don't need to focus much on it." I offered him a dismissive look. "Not all of us get winded when running."

He narrowed his eyes but didn't rise to the jab. Then again, it was yet another thing that annoyed me about Deacon. He controlled his temper better than I ever could. Then again, he was a meta and not a shade. He didn't have another thing inside him, driving him, altering his normal reactions. He was some twisted mix of human and shade, but he differed greatly from me.

"You know, if you get Hera killed…"

That brought me to a stop and made me rise to my feet and face him. "Aren't you a little too worried about some female shade? Doesn't seem appropriate given your job, does it?"

"I just don't want to see her suffer because you want to use her."

"That it? Because I don't think she needs you watching over her." *She has me. She sure as fuck doesn't need you.*

The jealous, possessive thought shocked me. It came to me so fast, I hadn't even really thought about it, like it was some truth buried deep inside me.

"She doesn't see people for who they really are, and you're exactly the sort of asshole who would happily take advantage of that."

Hadn't I thought that same exact thing before? That Hera wasn't careful enough, that she didn't realize how dangerous people were? I didn't much care about it being twisted around to apply to me, though.

"Funny for you to say that, given you're at least as dangerous to her as I am."

Deacon snorted. "Hardly. *I'm* not helping her try to escape."

That made me go completely still. While I knew Deacon suspected something, him coming right out and saying it showed his confidence in his guess.

"No idea what you mean," I said, though I doubted it was all that convincing.

"Right. Look, I know she's got some naïve, romantic idea that she's going to find a life outside of Larkwood, but you've been here long enough to know better. I have no idea what you, Wade, Brax and she have cooked up, but whatever it is, let it go. Tell her to accept her place here, to make the best of it."

"Easy for you to say. It's always people who are free telling those who aren't to learn to accept what is. It's like people with homes telling those without to learn to be happy with wherever they are." I spat the words as I approached him, my temper slipping.

Deacon didn't pull away, didn't show any signs of fear. Then again, he wasn't exactly human or some weakling. "I've seen shades get dragged off to the North Tower. I've *been* in the North Tower. I know better than you do what happens when shades step outside the line, when they pay the price for it. I don't want to see Hera end up there for some pipe dream that will never happen. If you help her with this fool's errand, then you're on the hook for what happens to her."

Wasn't that similar to what I'd told Kit days earlier?

I ended up standing right in front of him, so close that if someone didn't know us, we could have almost seemed like lovers. Funny how similar love and hate could look. "Hera is going to do what she wants. Sometimes a life trapped somewhere isn't a life worth living, and risking it is worth anything."

The purple of his eyes shone bright, almost as if glowing. "It isn't just about dying. It's easy to say you'd rather die than live imprisoned, because if you die, that's it. It's all over. Shades don't get to just die here, though. Don't you get that? Larkwood doesn't let anyone go, not if they can use them. So if Hera gets caught, if she lands herself in serious trouble, she isn't going to just die. She doesn't get to close her eyes and head off to some magical afterlife where everything is perfect. She'll get taken to the North Tower, she'll be experimented on, tortured, forced to do things you can't even imagine, and destroyed until there is nothing but a husk left."

I swallowed hard because I knew he wasn't lying. Larkwood didn't remove its claws from anyone. Still... "If you have something to say to her, say it to her. You might see her as a thing you can control, but I don't. She's not property, and she can make her own choices."

Deacon pulled his shoulders back, the level of aggression rolling off him making me wish we could go a few rounds. I wanted to beat on one another until we were both too bloody and tired to think about any of this anymore. It wouldn't solve anything, wouldn't fix the problems, but fuck, I'd feel better.

It wasn't possible, though. If I laid a finger on him, it would just come down on me, would ruin the plans I had that were far more important than rearranging this asshole's face.

"Let me make myself clear," Deacon said. "If Hera pays the price for whatever bullshit you, Knox and Wade are helping her with, I'm not going to let it go. Whatever she suffers, I'll make fucking sure you suffer tenfold."

As I stared at him, I didn't bother to respond, because what was the point? The reality was that he was right. Even without him intervening, if Hera got caught, if things didn't go right, I knew I'd suffer more than I'd ever experienced before.

That girl was important to me, no matter how much I'd tried to keep it from happening, and losing her would be a wound I didn't think I could come back from.

* * * *

Hera

I didn't bother to knock on the door to Knox's room. Knocking on front doors like that didn't happen in Larkwood. Privacy wasn't a thing people expected here, so I'd gotten used to just walking in.

Not that it hadn't bit me in the ass before.

I recalled walking in on Knox and that demon before, and the uncomfortable moment that had happened afterward.

However, that had stopped happening. I didn't doubt that Knox still fed on his own, but he didn't bring them back to his room at least. I had mixed feelings about it.

I didn't like him hiding things from me, but I didn't want to walk in on it again, either.

I knocked on the counter as I set down the book Knox had wanted. The knocking was less of a request to enter and more of just letting him know I'd arrived. It was my version of, *"Hey, I'm here!"*

A moment later, Knox walked in from his bedroom. He was barefoot and wore only his sweats low on his hips. It put his chest on display, and worse? He must have gotten out of a shower recently because droplets of water glistened on his chest. A towel hung around his shoulders, and when he spotted me, he gave me an absolutely mind-blowing smile.

Again I wondered how one person could tempt me this much.

Still, I shook my head, waking myself up so I didn't ogle as I dropped my gaze to the floor. I knew damn well how he felt about that, understood the reasons why, so I tried hard not to put him in that position, not to make him feel pressured or stared at.

"You never look at me," he said softly as he approached.

I shrugged, pretending it wasn't a big deal.

He set his fingers beneath my chin but didn't force my gaze up. It was a request, not a demand.

I sighed and gave in, looking up and into his green eyes

"You always glance away, like you can't stand to look at me. I can understand that, now that you know more about me, now that you know what I really am."

I frowned at his words, at how wrong he'd guessed. I didn't want to admit the truth, but I couldn't have him blaming himself or thinking he disgusted me. I pulled back enough so he could see my hands as I responded. *"I know you don't like to be stared at."*

He tilted his head as if he didn't understand. "So?"

"So I don't want to make you uncomfortable."

His eyes were hard as he watched me, as if trying to work out my point. After a moment, he spoke softly. "So you look away from me because you don't want to upset me?" At my nod, he let out an empty laugh. "I'd thought maybe you hated me, that maybe the more I pushed you away, the more you saw what I really was, that you couldn't stand the sight of me."

I shook my head, wanting him to understand that it wasn't him at all. *"I don't want you to think I'm like other people, just trying to use you, or have you think that's all I see in you."*

He pressed his lips together, the action tempting me like everything else he did. It made me remember the softness of those lips when pressed against mine, the rare times he'd touched me instead of the other way around. Finally, he let out a long breath. "You're the only person who gives a damn about what makes me uncomfortable. The funny thing is, I think you're also the only person who I *want* to look at me, who I want to want me."

That made me draw my eyebrows toward each other in confusion. *"But you always stop us – "*

"Because I'm not in the right headspace for more, because I don't want you to interact with that side of me. It's not because I don't want you to want me. You're the only person who wants *me* and not my incubus, who sees me at all. Please, don't hide that from me, don't look away anymore." His words were such a soft plea, as if he were begging me.

It struck me as strange, made me wonder if something had happened. The distance I'd kept between us crumbled, as if he didn't want that anymore.

And I didn't want it – I never had.

I let my gaze move over him at his request, allowing myself to fully take in the sight of him. He was beyond stunning. His body was flawless, lean and strong with very little body fat to hide his muscles. It wasn't just the obvious, either. Sure, his abs and his chest and his shoulders might as well have been made of marble, but it went deeper. It was his long fingers that teased me and his collarbones and the points of his hips. Every inch of him was an invitation that I desperately wanted to take him up on.

His groan came out heavy, as if he could feel the way I looked at him. "I never liked when people stared at me, but I like it when you do. I can smell how much you want me, and for the first time that scent doesn't make me sick. It doesn't make me want to run away."

I wanted to reach out, but when my hand started to lift as if on its own, I pulled back.

"It's okay," he assured me. "I want you to touch me. I want to feel someone touch me who sees *me*."

At his permission, I gave in. The touch was so soft, it had to tickle, but doing more terrified me. I brushed my fingertips against his chest, the heat of his skin searing. I traced his collarbone, then moved down into the valley between his pecs. The hard ridges of his abs tensed beneath my fingers, but he didn't stop me or pull away. He trusted me to feel the firmness of his muscles and the rapid beating of his heart.

Yet, each brush of my skin to his made me crave more, made me desperate to have more, to taste him, to lose myself with him.

And it wasn't because of what he was. Even if he doubted it, even if he thought it was because of his being an incubus, I knew it wasn't. I felt hunger like this with Brax as well, with Wade, with Deacon. While it was different with each, while we all had our own relationships, it wasn't as if what I felt for Knox was wildly different, as if it were something magical or driven by his powers.

It was just him and me. It was my own desire. It was his past and his pain and the man he was.

I wanted to go farther, to strip him down, to take off my own clothes, to enjoy the feeling of nothing between us. I'd had no idea that I'd had this sort of hunger inside me before I came to Larkwood. It was as if when I'd changed, when I'd become a shade, my libido had amped up as well. It turned me shameless against it.

I moved my lips to his neck, and that shook him free of the moment. He jerked backward as if I'd done something so much worse, like I'd just groped him without warning rather than just kissing his throat. He set his hand over the spot on his neck.

His eyes were wide, but his expression held no fear. Instead, shame hung in the depths there. He dropped his gaze from mine, his hand still covering his neck.

I wanted to ask what it was, but I had no idea how to do that, how to broach the topic when he clearly didn't want me to.

He sighed softly. "Looks like I didn't scrub enough."

I frowned, not understanding his words.

Instead of explaining, he took another step backward. "Why don't we do this another day?"

I nodded, a heavy numbness on me, the way I hated when I didn't understand what he meant, when I felt on the outside, forced to just watch him struggle. I wanted to help him, to have him rely on me. It was nearly impossible for someone to untangle their head on their own, so I wanted him to let me in.

However, he'd set his boundary, and if there was one thing that mattered with Knox, it was respecting that. No one else ever respected his wishes, so I'd already sworn to never ignore them. I didn't bother to try to say goodnight, to ask him anything else.

An uneasy quiet stretched between us before I turned and walked out, leaving Knox to himself and his pain.

Chapter Ten

Hera

Lying in Deacon's bed felt strange. I hadn't seen him beyond a quick moment since our last fight, and as it turned out, that was far too long.

And...I couldn't deny that I needed information from him.

Still, even if I didn't, I'd realized that this tension I felt from our last fight wore on me and I'd wanted to let it go.

I'd asked him earlier if I could see him, but he'd said he had to work. I had no idea if he'd told me the truth or if he'd just blown me off, but sometimes the only way to get through to stubborn people like Deacon was with a surprise attack.

In this case, that meant breaking into his room and crawling into his bed to wait for him, since he'd eventually have to return.

Of course, what had struck me as a great idea didn't seem so wonderful as the hours dragged on. Before I knew it, my eyes had fluttered closed. He hadn't been kidding about working late when the clock struck midnight.

I lost the fight eventually, and dozed off, surrounded by Deacon's scent.

* * * *

Deacon

I hurt. *Everywhere.* Going one-on-one with an enraged werewolf had proven one hell of a challenge, even for me. Even muzzled and with gloves on t0 keep fangs and claws in check, they weren't pushovers.

I rarely had to deal with that—werewolves weren't level 1 shades—but occasionally they got an especially troublesome shades in intake and would ask for help from us in level 1.

I didn't mind chipping in—I never had to see the shade again, which made things simpler. Things got messy when guards got too close to the residents, and I had enough complications in my life without adding anything to them.

I walked into my bedroom as I pulled my shirt over my head, ready to crawl into bed and close my eyes. A hot shower would have soothed my sore muscles, but my exhaustion won out. I'd managed not to get any blood on me, so I'd take that as a win.

Except, when I tossed my shirt into the laundry hamper in my open closet, I stopped dead in my tracks.

Speaking of complications…

Hera slept in my bed, her eyes closed, her breathing easy and regular. She looked so peaceful when she slept, more like the girl I'd met in that parking lot, the one I'd saved.

It was strange how much had changed over the past months. She'd arrived at Larkwood so afraid, so unsure, but she'd grown into herself. She'd started trusting herself and standing on her own two feet. The other side of that was that she'd turned more jaded, more suspicious of those around her.

That all drifted away when she slept, though. It made me wonder if she'd ever be so open with me when awake and aware, or if, the moment she woke, she'd distance herself from me.

It wasn't just her that had changed, either. Somehow, she'd altered all of Larkwood. Each person she interacted with shifted, as if the very academy had changed with her presence. Wade had seemed less distant, Brax a little softer, Knox more determined and even Kit had seemed a little more...human. Hell, even I felt different.

I wasn't sure I liked it, to be honest.

Change wasn't often a good thing, because it was unpredictable.

Hera shifted as if she sensed me, rolling toward me, her arms wrapping around my pillow and clutching it to her chest. It also twisted the blanket, which exposed her thigh.

And made it clear she'd crawled into my bed naked.

Any exhaustion I'd felt fled at the sight of the pale skin she flashed me from her toes to her hip. I rubbed my hand over my face, trying to control myself.

Talk about a losing battle. How could I expect myself to stay in control when I had Hera naked and vulnerable in my bed? When she'd come here on her own? I wanted to wake her up with me against her, wanted to claim her lips in a kiss to say what I didn't have a clue how to say, to feel her melt against me as I slid into the heat and tightness of her body. I wanted to feel close to her again, to feel that sense of home she gave me.

It was so much easier to physically communicate with her. When we tried to talk, when we tried to spend any time actually conversing, Hera and I only ended up fighting. We misunderstood each other, took everything we said and did as some sort of challenge.

I didn't enjoy fighting, but we struggled to do much else.

After another moment, I finished stripping down. If she'd come here naked, I'd return the favor. I crawled into the bed carefully, not wanting to startle her. It didn't seem I needed to worry about that since as soon as I got into the bed, she shifted toward me.

She released the pillow and curled around me instead, nuzzling against my chest, her eyes still closed.

I gave in and stroked my fingers through her hair, savoring the softness of the long strands and the warm puffs of air against my skin.

I wanted to let her sleep, but no doubt she'd come for a reason. I whispered her name softly, wanting to rouse her gently.

After a moment and a few attempts at her name, her lashes fluttered, and she stared up at me. A slight crease appeared between her eyebrows before she glanced around the room.

She was probably figuring out where she was and why. She didn't strike me as the sort of girl who normally woke up naked in random places.

Redness sprang up on her cheeks, no doubt the moment she realized where she was and how she'd gotten there. She didn't need to move her hands for me to read the apology in her expression.

"Don't apologize," I said, keeping my voice barely above a whisper. "I don't know why you're here, but I'm not mad."

She offered a hesitant smile, one that gave me a pretty good idea why she'd come. We hadn't made up since the last fight, the one about Kit, so I'd bet she'd wanted to resolve things between us.

I slid my hand behind her neck to pull her closer until I could kiss her. I couldn't resist, especially when she returned the touch. Her lips were coaxing, teasing, and I lost myself in them.

I rolled over her, yanking the bedding out of the way so nothing rested between us. Her skin was hot and soft, and all of it pressed against me. She spread her thighs around me and used a grip on my shoulders to pull me tighter to her.

Her tongue teased my lips, drawing a groan from me. How could she undo me so easily? After our last fight, I'd again thought I should end this, that I should walk away, that it was only headed for heartbreak for me. I'd told myself to cut ties, but all it took was one kiss and I was back here, trapped.

No, not even a kiss.

It had only taken a glimpse of her — hell, even just a memory — and I went tumbling back down into a sinkhole with her.

We were normally rough and rushed, but not tonight.

I wanted to take my time, to savor her, to spoil her for once. We normally couldn't do that, but tonight seemed perfect for it.

I broke the kiss and shifted down her body, pressing my lips against all the best places as I went.

The scar at her throat.

The full curve of her breast.

Her bellybutton, where her stomach dipped in.

The points of her hips.

When I reached her pussy, however, I knew I'd reached the best of them all. I slid my hands up her thighs, grateful that she didn't close her legs or hide anything from me. She really had changed, hadn't she?

I forced myself to stare up her body, to meet her gaze. "I don't know why you came, not exactly, but I just want to feel you tonight. No fighting, no arguments, no guard and resident or anything else. Just us."

It wasn't a question, but she nodded. In fact, tension left her at that, as if she needed it as much as I did.

I leaned in and kissed her inner thigh, then dragged my tongue up to the crease of her leg. She shivered, and it drew a smile from me.

She was so responsive, and she hid nothing from me.

As a reward, I moved my tongue up her wet slit.

She made no noise — she couldn't — but I'd gotten to where I could read her body without that. The way her muscles tensed, the way she bit her bottom lip, the way she arched her back, it all told me how she felt about each touch.

I delved into her cunt with my tongue, wanting to drown in her sweetness, to have every part of her. Normally I pinned her down, but this time, I chased her when she squirmed, as if to prove that I wasn't going anywhere.

It didn't matter how much we fought, how much she struggled with herself and the world and me, I'd chase her forever to stay with her.

After a moment, I focused on her clit. Maybe I should have teased her more, but I didn't have it in me. I wanted to watch her fall over that edge over and over again.

I sank two fingers into her pussy, knowing she could take it. That pushed her into her own release, because her thighs closed around my ears and her fingers gripped the back of my head, holding me against her.

The aggression in that move made me groan and keep going, sucking on her hard clit, driven by the tight grasp of her hands. Why was it that everything she did turned me on? When she was shy or unsure, I wanted her. When she was aggressive and needy, I wanted her just the same. It was like everything she did drew me in and made me desperate.

When her legs loosened, when her pussy stopped gripping my fingers, I pulled back and crawled up her body. Just like before, she kissed me. She didn't seem to care that her juices covered my lips, didn't care if she tasted herself, and that made my cock ache.

She wrapped a leg around me, her heel tugging me closer, begging me with her body.

And I was only too willing to give her what we both wanted. I pulled away just enough to grasp my cock, to press the head against her drenched cunt. I paused and savored the heat for a breath before sliding into the welcoming tightness of her body.

I went slow, wanting to take my time, to not let this be like the quickies we usually had. Instead, I tried to somehow explain what she meant to me with this.

She pressed her forehead against my chest, a reminder that she was smaller than I was. Her nails dug into me as she held on to my waist, as she urged me further.

Words of praise rested on my lips about how much I enjoyed the snugness of her cunt, the taste of her, the warmth of her, but I didn't dare loose them. When we spoke, we muddied everything, made it so much more complicated, so I kept my mouth shut and did the only thing I could.

I filled her completely, giving her everything I could in that moment, trying to use this to create something between us that couldn't be broken—not even by Larkwood.

Tomorrow we could deal with the rest—no doubt we'd have to—but for tonight?

Tonight, I would love Hera so much that she could never doubt how I felt about her again.

* * * *

Hera

I woke warm. I didn't normally wake up cold by any means, but it wasn't like *this*. I felt as though I had a heated weighted blanket over me, and it was damn near enough for me to consider going back to sleep.

"You awake yet?"

The whispered voice made me jump with the surprise at hearing it so close to my ear. In fact, the shock took over so fast, I didn't identify the voice at first while my heart raced.

I twisted, rolling over to find Deacon behind me. Along with him, the events of the night before came back to me.

And everything else we'd done when he'd gotten home…

We'd spent hours together without a word, and each time we'd finish, a kiss or a stroke from one of us would reignite that passion.

It made it hard to look him in the eyes, so I dropped my gaze.

Not that looking at his chest instead of his face made it any better. Hell, if anything, seeing a hickey over his collarbone made me even more embarrassed.

He let out a rare laugh, soft and like a secret between just the two of us. "So your confidence only lasts until the sun rises, huh?"

I lifted my hands and covered my face to hide the red that no doubt colored my cheeks.

"Come on, now. You were tough enough to sneak into my bed naked last night — you're tough enough to deal with me the next morning."

I moved my hands, not because I wanted to stop hiding but because I needed to sign. *"I'm sorry. I shouldn't have just broken in."*

He made a sound that said he found my statement stupid. "I don't care. Hell, if I could get away with it, I'd have you sleeping every damned night in my bed."

That statement took me by surprise and pushed back the shame. It was surprisingly open from Deacon, who normally kept his feelings to himself.

Instead of addressing it, though, he went on. "I know you didn't come last night just for that, though. You wanted to talk to me, right?"

I nodded, because it was true. I'd wanted to fix things between us, but I also wanted to ask him…

"Do you know where the communications center is in the North Tower?"

He sighed, his eyes clouding over. I didn't think he'd answer at first, but after a moment, he did. "You're impossible, you know that? No matter how much I tell you something is a bad idea, you just don't listen. I used to think that keeping you in the dark was protecting you, but I think now you'll just do as you damn well please either way. I've been here a long time and no one else gets the better of me, but you just bowl me over every damned time."

I wondered for a moment if I was supposed to feel bad about that, but I really didn't. I wasn't using him, wasn't doing anything that could hurt him. He just didn't agree with my plans.

"Are you going to tell me?"

"I shouldn't. What I should do is lock your ass up. I should see if I can get you assigned to me somehow and make you stay right here in my bed. Maybe if you have me on your ass every day and night, you'll stay safe." Frustration colored his words, but even with them, I wasn't afraid. He let out a bitter laugh. "But I know not even that would work. You'd still find a way to do what you wanted, and the only thing me being stubborn does is risk you."

His words tempted me to respond, but I didn't. I gave him the room to think about it, to consider my words and his response. He had to work through it himself. He wasn't an enemy, wasn't someone I was trying to trick. He deserved the ability to make his own choice.

"The communications center is on the fourth floor of the North Tower," he said softly. "But the North Tower doesn't allow any free movement. It isn't like here, where you all get a lot of room to roam. The North Tower is set up like a traditional prison, where shades stay in their cells all the time unless being experimented on or otherwise used. They house shades in cells close to the project they're involved in."

So I just had to get out of my cell, then head to the fourth floor.

He shook his head. "I see you thinking, but you don't get it. The shades that go there don't leave their cells. They can't just wander around. Even if you're sent there, you won't be able to get out of your cell, let alone get to the communications area. Even if you did all that, even if you managed to get there, get out of your cell and somehow disrupt communications for some escape attempt, you'd be stuck in the North Tower."

He thought that because he didn't know everything, because he thought it was just me.

I wasn't alone anymore, though. I had help and together, we had a good plan.

"I can take care of myself."

"It isn't that I don't believe you — it's that you don't know enough to be able to say it. I spent my whole childhood in the North Tower, subjected to experimentation and training. I don't want you to suffer that. The things they do there…"

"You mentioned Corrander and Lazarus before. What are those?"

"I don't know exactly. There are whispers, where staff from the North Tower talk about them. I know Lazarus has something to do with bringing shades back to life. I have no idea what that means, but if it is related to the North Tower, you want nothing to do with it. Trust me, you need to stay as far away from that place as you can."

"The Warden is watching me," I explained.

"Yeah, I know. She's been interested in you since you arrived. It's yet another reason to forget about whatever you're planning. She's dangerous, and she won't hesitate to remove you if she thinks you're a threat."

"Isn't that a better reason to think ahead?"

"You can't think ahead of the Warden. She's been in charge of Larkwood for thirty years and she's had all that time to rig the game in her favor. She's the type of enemy who is steps ahead, who has plans for everything an opponent could do. I've heard she even has some special escape in the event of a riot or attack. You can't win against someone as deeply entrenched as the Warden is."

"It's only a matter of time before she doesn't think I'm worth keeping around."

"Maybe, but that matter of time might be decades, and damn it, Hera, I *want* that time with you. I don't want to lose it because you're chasing a pipedream."

I looked him in the eyes before responding as truthfully as I could. *"I can't live as a prisoner. You said you wished I could spend every night here, but I can't. I can't love you when I don't have any choices, when I don't have my own life or my own future."*

"But whatever you're doing will kill you, and I'll be left here alone again and guilty because I let it happen."

I leaned in and set my forehead against his, rewarded by him wrapping a strong arm around me and pulling me closer.

"At least stay with me a little longer," he whispered in a soft, pleading voice. "Don't leave yet. Let me hold you just like this a little longer."

The way he asked sounded like a goodbye, like he knew I barreled toward a tragedy he couldn't stop.

Either I'd escape, and he'd be left here, or I'd die trying, and he'd still be alone. I understood his feelings, but they couldn't change what I had to do.

So I nodded and cuddled against him, giving him a bit more time because that was all I had to offer.

Chapter Eleven

Hera

I frowned as I walked down the unfamiliar hallway.

Usually, my work consisted of manual labor, but on my schedule for the day had been a large block of time with a room on the second floor listed.

I never went to the second floor. It housed the administrative level, and after arriving, it was off limits.

At least, until now…

I still had no answers when I'd arrived at the specified place to find Kit standing beside the door.

A moment of surprise showed on his features, but as quickly as it happened, it disappeared. He really was hard to read, wasn't he?

"I hadn't realized they'd called you here," Kit said.

"I don't know why I'm here," I admitted.

He pulled out his phone from his pocket, then scrolled across the screen as he stared. He let out a soft sound before putting his phone away. "It seems you've been assigned to the interrogations team, at least temporarily."

"Why?"

"Sirens can see glimpses of people when hearing them and can determine truth from lie. That would prove useful for interrogations. It seems they feel that is a better use of your time than pulling weeds." Kit's voice said he didn't care for the change.

Him not knowing about it made me uneasy. Kit seemed to know everything, yet they'd kept this information from him?

Why?

"I don't know what to do."

"Don't worry. I've reviewed the file already. Just follow my lead."

"You'll be with me the whole time, right?"

His eyes widened for a moment, as if the question had surprised him. Still, he nodded. "Yes. I run many of the interrogations here, so I've done this many times. You will enter the room, then take a seat at the table. I will question the suspect, so you can focus only on listening. If you need a question to be asked, write it down and show it to me in case the suspect knows ASL."

I nodded, grateful to Kit for being there. At least I wasn't alone.

Kit stared down at me for a long moment. "You will be fine, Hera." Somehow, him saying it made me think it might be true. With that, he used his wristband to open the door, and I followed him in.

The room reminded me of any interrogation room on police shows. It had a large mirror on one side, a metal table bolted to the floor and four chairs set around it. The man already at the table had handcuffs on his wrists hooked to a metal ring welded to the table.

He was in his late twenties and surprisingly well dressed. It was a stupid thought, but I'd always assumed criminals would look messy, dirty, that sort of thing. Again, it probably came from my complete lack of knowledge about the real world. Just like I'd painted all shades as evil and dangerous, I'd considered all those accused of crimes already guilty.

Knowing that didn't change my surprise that the man looked as if he could have been someone I'd met in my old life, with his suit and clean-cut look.

"Sorry to keep you waiting, Mr. Hemslock," Kit said as he walked into the room with all the confidence in the world, as if it were no big deal.

The man looked over, his eyes narrowed. "This is highly unusual, you know? I've asked repeatedly for my lawyer, and I haven't been given a chance to talk to them. I'm not sure where I've been brought or why, but rest assured, you *will* have a lawsuit on your hands." The man spoke as if assured of his own importance.

The name struck me as familiar, but it took a moment for me to realize why.

I knew him.

Or it would be better to say I had met him previously and that I knew who he was.

Charles Hemslock, the youngest son of Harold Hemslock, worked as the CEO of a research agency, but his father worked for the government agency that oversaw approving scientific advances that came from shades.

Medications developed based on shade anatomy and power had agencies such as the one Charles' father worked for to oversee and regulate them. I'd met them both when they'd come to parties my parents had thrown.

That connection to my old life put me on edge as I took a seat in the chair Kit gestured toward. I took the regular pad of paper and pen that Kit handed to me to take notes or write questions.

"This is a rather unique situation," Kit said. "And places such as this have more leeway with rules."

"Rights have no leeway," Charles responded.

"Of course they do. There are always time, place and manner restrictions. You've been brought here to answer questions because you could call us experts on the issue."

"Experts on what, exactly? I had armed people show up at my home without notice so they could drag me off without explanation. No one has told me what I'm doing here or what you want from me. I have no idea what I'm doing here."

Lie. The words scraped against me, the immediate knowledge that he was lying. It wasn't the slight unease when a person was unsure, when confused, but rather Charles was purposely lying, likely with something he'd thought of beforehand.

I wrote that down on the pad as Kit took a seat beside me, his gaze darting to the paper to read it without acknowledging the statement.

Instead, he focused on Charles. "I'm going to warn you that this will go much more smoothly if you are honest."

"I am being honest."

Kit smiled, but the edges held a dangerous threat as he opened the file he'd had with him. "You work for one of the companies that your father deals with, don't you?"

"So? Last I checked, that was hardly illegal."

"Collusion is illegal. Working at a company isn't a problem, so long as you and your father do not use your positions for personal gain. It does seem that your company has had a far higher number of approvals compared to other companies. That doesn't strike you as odd?" Kit asked.

"Not at all. My company is just better at producing advancements and running the necessary tests to ensure their safety. If other companies dislike our numbers, they should do better to improve themselves instead of focusing on us."

I closed my eyes as I listened, to try to hear deeper. It was strange, because it had been so hard to learn to control that overwhelming skill, but now it was almost harder to lower those defenses, to hear it.

The lies were easy to hear—he hadn't said much that was true thus far. Instead, I listened deeper, tried to allow myself to focus on what else I could pick up.

Flashes of him came to me, old ones where Charles appeared younger, all mixing together and flying past so quickly it was hard to pick one from another. I saw him having dinner with his father, another of him in bed with a woman I didn't recognize, another with him working at a desk, poring over paperwork. The things went by so quick I shuddered, overwhelmed.

Something touched my leg, pulling me from the spiral. I glanced over to find Kit's hand on my leg, though he didn't turn to look at me, pretending as if it hadn't happened.

Right. We were doing a job right now. His reminder helped me focus.

"What do you care anyway?" Charles said. "Even if what you're saying is true, even if there was something going on, all of our medications have been beneficial. None of them have been proven unsafe."

"That is true. The issue is that some of the medications have caused certain questions to arise. For example, the new diabetes medication your company just released officially lists the source as a level 3 werewolf."

I tried to ignore the response I got from Kit, the way his voice also sparked images. I saw him in his room alone, then another of him in his other form, his real form, in the darkness. I saw him with a woman I didn't recognize at all, one with long dark hair and light blue eyes. He kissed her, the action far sweeter than anything I had witnessed from him before.

I recalled the story he'd told me before about the woman he'd loved. Was this her? Seeing him act like that felt strange, like something I struggled to connect with the reserved man I knew.

Still, I shook that away, tried not to get overwhelmed by it.

"That's right. What's your point?" Charles' voice drew me back to the room.

"That when we had the chance to look closely at the actual medication, it could not have come from a werewolf. Rather, it uses the blood and source from a banshee as the base."

"If you had evidence about that, you wouldn't be talking to me here. You'd already have me before a court," Charles said as he leaned back in his chair, assured of his own innocence.

Or, rather, assured that he wouldn't get into trouble. Then again, I'd grown up around people like him. They thought they were untouchable, that they had enough power and connections to never get caught for anything they did. They saw themselves as innocent because they thought they were above the law.

And I was just like that until I wasn't…

I rubbed at the center of my chest because of an ache there, because of having to admit that I had been as bad as them. If I'd gotten pulled over before coming here, I hadn't been above batting my lashes and flashing my license so they could see my last name. It always worked, too.

But this place wasn't the world Charles knew the rules to. It didn't operate the way he'd grown accustomed to.

Kit didn't take the bait, remaining as calm as ever. "Again, we enjoy significantly more leeway than elsewhere. You said you didn't know where you were brought, so let me tell you. You're at Larkwood Academy."

That got through to Charles. He gulped hard, a break in his calm and cool exterior. "Why am I here?"

"Because you're right. Out there, in the world that you're used to, you can get away with a lot. Things like, for example, getting your father's influence to gain access to level-1 shades, something clearly forbidden by law."

Charles shook his head. "I would never do that. Every shade in our programs is properly documented and none above a level 2."

Lie.

Kit didn't even look over to check—he probably know damn well Charles was lying. "We keep better track than you think, and we know more than you expect. You bribed another academy to classify level 1 shades as level two or lower, so you could take them rather than having them sent to proper facilities. Let us not forget that, due to your inexperience in dealing with such shades, there have been no less than six deaths directly caused by shades you have no business housing."

"You've got it all wrong. Besides, even if a few shades were classified wrong, that fault lies with the academy who classified them, not me or my company. Whatever you think you have, you don't." Charles turned his gaze toward me, as if looking for an ally. "I don't know who this guy thinks he is but messing with me is going to bite you in the ass. You need to…"

His words trailed off, and he narrowed his eyes. His expression held confusion, as if he wasn't sure what he was looking at. After a few slow blinks, Charles asked in a small voice, "Hera?"

My stomach sank. I hadn't expected him to recognize me at all. For one, it had been years since we'd last seen each other, and even then we hadn't been close. On top of that, the perfectly dressed and primped girl I'd been was a far cry from me now, where I sat there with my natural hair in a ponytail, no makeup, and wearing sweatpants and a T-shirt.

It was the first time coming face-to-face with my past in such a way. I'd had the calls with my parents, with Aaron and Moa, but those hadn't been in person. This was the first time someone from my old life had actually laid eyes on me, and his reaction was the thing I'd been worried about.

I didn't confirm or deny his guess as he stared at me.

"It is you, isn't it? What are you doing here? I heard you were overseas, taking a year off."

So, that was the story my parents told everyone? Of course, that wasn't a shock. They didn't want the knowledge of what I'd become out in the world. It might harm their precious reputation, so they'd probably kept it to those who needed to know and crushed any rumors that went against their lie. Hell, I wondered if they wouldn't fake my death to make it all go away.

He dropped his gaze to the band on my wrist and his expression hardened. He showed no pity, as if everything suddenly made sense, as if he realized I wasn't the person he'd known before, that I wasn't worthy of his time anymore. "I see," he said. "I guess that explains it, doesn't it?"

I couldn't look him in the eyes anymore, couldn't see the revulsion there. Being seen as who I used to be was hard enough, but that instant disappointment when he realized what I'd become?

It hurt too much.

I had no idea if Kit moved on because he needed to focus or out of concern from me. Either way, he drew Charles' attention back to him. "You see my eyes, don't you? You shouldn't concern herself with her, because I am the problem here for you."

"What are you, a telepath? Because nothing you discover would be usable anyway."

Kat glanced around the room as if confused. "Do you truly not understand where you are? The rules outside of these walls don't apply here. You were brought here without anyone knowing where or why. If you never show up again, it will be treated as a missing person. Or perhaps we will simply make your death look like anything we want."

Charles narrowed his eyes, not appearing properly frightened. Then again, until I'd gotten locked up in Larkwood, I'd had no idea what a place like this was actually capable of. I'd felt so secure in my own position, in my safety, that I'd thought nothing could touch me. I'd thought everyone had to play by the rules as I understood them.

That wasn't this world, though, and I had a feeling Charles would figure that out the hard way…

"You think your life is bad here? Just *wait* until I get out of here. You have so few rights already, so just imagine how much worse I can make your life. *Both* of you." Charles looked toward me. "I'm going to guess your daddy kept your name under wraps. I can't blame him. I doubt he wanted everyone knowing he had a shade in the family." Charles let out a cruel chuckle. "In fact, knowing this, I'd bet I could gain quite a few favors from him and your mother to keep the secret."

I shouldn't give a damn about my parents. They'd both tossed me away and hadn't bothered to contact me since our first disastrous video call. Maybe it was my upbringing, the way they'd raised me to believe that the wellbeing of the family was more important than any one family member that made guilt tug at me. I didn't want to be used as a weapon against them even if they had wronged me.

It seemed I was still a Weston no matter what they did.

Or maybe I just held out some hope that I'd get the chance to return to my old life after my escape, and if everyone knew about me, that wouldn't be possible.

"Actually…" Charles' smile spread in a way that turned my stomach. "I bet Larkwood will be quick to want to smooth this over. What if I ask them for you to make amends? How would you like to become my pet? You were always so untouchable before, but now? I doubt you'd be so high and mighty if you were mine to play with."

Kit held his hand out, a flower in his palm he'd pulled out from his jacket pocket. "I find it funny how often humans fail to realize how fragile life really is. They move around in their daily routines thinking today won't be the day, never noticing just how easy it is to pluck their lives away." He took a petal between his fingers and pulled it free.

Charles didn't budge. "I've faced people a lot tougher than you. You can't intimidate me."

Kit's smile lacked any warmth. "You speak like an adult, but you're a child to me, just someone so sure the world is what you think it is, but lacking the ability to open your eyes and truly see what surrounds you. You asked if I was a telepath, and no. I'm an Elder, something beyond anything you've tried to house in your little lab. What I need is the location of your housing unit where you keep the shades you have illegal possession of."

"Such a place doesn't exist, and even if it did, I wouldn't tell you a word."

Kit held his hand out flat over the center of the table so Charles could easily see it. Kit's hand shifted, changing into his wendigo form. The flower in his palm wilted, just as the apple had done before, as if time shifted around it and it rotted before our eyes. It crumbled, then turned to dust. Kit blew the dust toward Charles, as if making the point of what he was capable of.

Charles finally looked nervous. He swallowed hard, as if he'd never realized something like Kit could exist. It was the difference between looking at a tiger through a fence and suddenly being in the same room as one. Still, he didn't seem ready to quite give in. "You wouldn't dare. We donate a lot of money to this place, and my father is too important. The Warden wouldn't be happy if she knew what you were doing here."

The door of the interrogation room opened, drawing my attention over. A woman walked in who I didn't recognize. She was well dressed in a pantsuit, appearing to be in her late fifties, her expression serious as if she was used to taking charge. "Never make the mistake of thinking I'm unaware of anything that happens in my academy." *That voice...*

I remembered it like a person would a face, recalled hearing it when I'd been in Medical. The Warden was far scarier than I'd have expected, especially because she didn't look toward me.

Anxiety tore through me, but I tried to remain calm, to not let on how she rattled me.

Charles moved his gaze to her nametag, some of the color draining from his cheeks. "You should know better than to risk this..."

"The thing about risk is that it is always balanced against reward. In the past, your family has been quite useful, that's true, but you have started to believe you are beyond reproach. You have forgotten who helped you get where you are. The way your father and you have hidden 1 shades shows you have forgotten who you owe so much to. I would call that biting the hand that feeds you."

"Maybe there was a misunderstanding," Charles said, his tone having lost most of his attitude, as if he'd just realized how much trouble he was in. "I'm sure I can look into it and resolve this."

He was clearly trying his hardest to get around admitting any guilt. He wanted to pretend he had no idea what was going on but really wanted to help us fix it.

"Where is the housing unit?" The Warden asked without giving him any room to wiggle free.

He let out a long, slow breath before his shoulders dropped. "It's in Arizona, an hour outside of Phoenix. I'll write down the address, then contact them to release the shades in question to you."

"No need," she said. "My team will be there to transport them, and the reaction of your guards doesn't matter. If they wish to fight, that will be their mistake. We will take what we want, including any research done with those illegally procured shades."

Charles opened his mouth as if to argue, but quickly shut it. He wasn't in a position to make any demands. I doubted he gave a damn about the shades or the guards—he probably only cared about saving whatever research he could.

Kit rose as if to leave, so I followed suit. It seemed we'd finished our job.

"Wait," the Warden said.

Kit went still, tension rising. "Warden?"

"This was a very large breach of trust, and I don't think Mr. Hemslock here truly understands how serious it is."

"I do," Charles said, but he wasn't submissive. He was biding his time.

I knew men like that, had grown up around them. Charles would play a part to get back to his life, then he'd no doubt double-cross them just as soon as he thought it was safe to do so. It was how men like him thought.

"He needs a reminder of our power and why betraying us is a bad idea."

Kit closed his hands into fists, which had regained their human form. "I don't think that is necessary."

The Warden gave Kit an empty look, one that lacked sympathy or understanding. "Are you refusing a direct order?"

Kit pressed his lips together, the expression odd. It appeared helpless, something I'd never associated with him before. He turned his gaze to me, and I offered a slight shake to my head, a plea for him not to do whatever the Warden wanted him to do.

I didn't know what it was, but I knew it was bad.

"Of course not," Kit said, his voice having lost any feeling in it. He turned back toward Charles, Kit's hand shifting into the claws from before.

Charles tried to pull backward, but the cuffs kept him from doing so. "What do you think you're doing?"

"Be still." Kit dropped his tone the commanding one.

Charles did so, his fight and fear leaving until he appeared almost drugged.

"No," the Warden said. "What use is a lesson if he can't remember it?"

"He'll remember it based on what he loses. There is no good reason to make him suffer more than he needs to," Kit answered.

The Warden said nothing back, rather just stared at Kit as if waiting for him to do as he should.

Kit turned his gaze back to Charles, not moving for a moment, before nodding. When he did so, Charles woke, blinking slowly before resuming his struggles.

"What did you do to me?" he asked, panic bleeding through his voice.

Kit didn't answer as he pinned Charles' arm to the table, and it seemed as if the other man's struggle was nothing to Kit. He held him down easily, then lifted his other hand.

I took a step forward. I didn't know what I'd do, but I couldn't stop myself. I wasn't sure if it was because I knew Charles, or just that I didn't want to see anyone hurt, or the hesitation from Kit. Whatever it was, I wanted to stop this, to calm everyone down.

Kit lifted his gaze to me, and the harshness there stopped me. A warning rested in his eyes, one I read easily.

Don't get involved.

He didn't need to use his command to make me go still. It was the seriousness on his face, the fear that rushed through me that rooted my feet in place.

The hand not holding Charles shifted, the claws stretching out, and even though I knew what was coming, I couldn't prepare myself for it. I'd seen him turn things to dust, but never a person, never something alive and afraid.

He set his shifted hand on Charles's arm, and Charles let out a scream that had me lifting my hands to cover my ears. It was guttural and terrified and full of pain. Before my eyes, Charles' hand and arm twisted, collapsing in on itself, until it turned to dust just like the flower and the apple had.

I couldn't watch anymore, couldn't hear more of that horrible screaming. My stomach rolled, and even with Kit's gaze locked on me, I bolted from the room. No one got in my way, and I didn't stop until I collapsed in my room.

Even then, however, the screaming echoed in my head, like a soundtrack to Larkwood I couldn't ignore anymore.

Chapter Twelve

Hera

I stayed in my room for the rest of the day since I had nothing but the interrogation scheduled. For once, I didn't welcome the free time.

The more time I spent alone, the more I thought back on what had happened, the angrier I got.

I'd thought I understood Kit better, that he wasn't the scary thing I'd seen at first. I couldn't connect the man I'd started to trust with the creature that had just destroyed a man's arm for a lesson.

The hours passed until it hit midnight, and sleep seemed no closer than it had at the start of the night.

And maybe it was foolish, but I knew exactly where I wanted to go. I'd just watched Kit turn a man's arm to *dust* in front of me, and yet as I left my room, I headed out to question him.

Even if it was stupid, I had to know. I had to reconcile the two people — the man who had looked out for me and the creature who had destroyed Charles' arm. I wouldn't be able to breathe until I got some understanding of it.

I took the elevator, then the bridge. There weren't many around—a few of the more nocturnal creatures would spend time out and about at this hour, but there they were rare. That was fine by me—I'd rather not have to deal with anyone else while in this mood.

I took myself all the way to Kit's office, then to the door in the back—the same layout as Deacon's. I knocked on the door.

A voice came through. "Go back to your room, Hera."

I turned the handle of the door as my response, but found it locked.

"This is not the time for us to talk," Kit went on. "Go to sleep. There's nothing for either of us to say."

Once again, if my brain had been working right, I'd have known what a monumentally bad idea this was. I was bothering someone who could and was probably willing to turn me to dust. That didn't matter, though.

I held my palm in front of the handle and popped the lock using my powers. As soon as the light flashed green and it clicked, I pushed the door open.

Kit stood a few feet away, as if he'd turned his back on me and had planned to leave me standing there as long as I wanted. He turned back toward me and narrowed his black eyes to slits. "Did you really just break into my place?"

I lifted my eyebrows and held out my hands as if to say, *and what are you going to do about it?*

He sighed and pinched the bridge of his nose. "I wasn't kidding. We have nothing to discuss, nothing that will do either of us any good right now."

"Why?"

He didn't bother to misunderstand the question. "I told you before—I'm as trapped as any other shade here. My cage might look a little nicer, but it is still a cage."

I clenched my jaw, wishing I could speak, that I could yell at him. Somehow raging at a person didn't feel nearly as good when done with sign language. *"He wasn't a danger. You hurt a man who wasn't a threat!"*

"Yes, I did. I've done it before, and I would be foolish to think I won't do it again. That is life here, and you would do well to understand that." Kit's voice came out flat, as if he felt nothing, as if he had no emotions at all.

But I *knew* that wasn't true. Maybe I was an idiot, maybe I put too much faith in him, but I'd seen real feelings from him. The flashes in my head, the sadness as he spoke about the woman he'd loved, it all said he wasn't this empty thing he wanted to pretend to be.

"You're a coward," I signed.

"You don't know anything. I don't see you standing up to the Warden and defying her directly."

"No, but I'm at least honest about how I feel in private. I don't hide behind some fake mask. Is it really that easy for you? To hurt others, to betray your own kind, and for what? For a nicer cage?"

The look he gave me was no longer flat, and I missed that emotionless expression for a moment. It was better than the anger he offered me now. "You think I did that because I want material possessions?"

I stared around his place, at the niceties I'd seen in no other rooms. He had a stove, a large television, leather couches. His behavior had bought him a lot of luxuries, it seemed to me.

He made a sound that reminded me of a bear before walking to shelves along one wall. He picked up a vase that seemed well-made and expensive. "You think I care about this?" He threw it, and it crashed against the far wall, shattering into pieces. He picked up another, this time a crystal bowl that held dried flowers. "This? A *gift* from the Warden after sending me on a mission that kept replaying in my head for months afterward. I spent so much time with screaming in my head that I couldn't silence. I didn't want it." He threw it, hitting the same place the vase had, the bowl ending up in just as many tiny pieces.

A sting in my arm made me flinch, but I ignored it. Whatever the cause wasn't nearly as dangerous as Kit, so I wouldn't take my attention from him.

He swiped his arm over the shelf, knocking all the rest of the fancy decor to the ground. "I didn't want any of this. I didn't ask for any of it. The Warden likes to send it to remind me of my place, like a pet she likes to spoil when it serves her well."

"So why do it all?"

"Because I don't have a choice."

"Everyone has a choice."

"You say that because you don't understand." He sighed, then picked up a photo. I expected it to join the other items, but it didn't. He stared down at the picture, his eyebrows drawn toward each other, deep lines etched into his forehead. He moved his fingers down the image.

I came closer, needing to see what could draw that expression from him.

A woman was there with short, dark hair and bright blue eyes. Was this the woman he'd loved? She looked similar, but it wasn't who I'd seen in my vision before.

Even if so, I still didn't understand. She was gone — why would that make him do anything? She couldn't be used against him if she was dead.

He shook his head. "This is my daughter."

And that was the last thing I'd ever expected to hear...

* * * *

Kit

Looking at the picture soothed me as much as it hurt. It was always like that, though. I kept it, along with the others, on a shelf to look at each day. When I walked around my place, I'd stop just so I could stare at that face, at the daughter I did everything for, the one I didn't know at all. Perhaps it was dangerous sentimentality, but it almost made me feel as if she were a part of my life.

Hera didn't respond, but she'd gone still.

Not that it surprised me. Something like me wasn't associated with paternal feelings and offspring, after all.

Did I even have those feelings? It was difficult to know, to identify them after so many years.

"She's twenty now, attending college in Florida," I explained. "Human. She looks like her mother."

Hera leaned closer to stare down at the picture, then turned to look at me. *"This is what they use?"*

I nodded. "Her name is Lilianna. Her mother picked it out. I didn't love it at the time, but even I couldn't win arguments against her."

"How did you two..." She struggled at the end, as if not sure how to phrase it.

But her question was obvious. "Unnecessary pregnancy is frowned upon, but if Larkwood believes they might benefit from it, they have no problem allowing it. When they saw me with Jasmine, they removed the pregnancy blocks that prevented conception. I think they hoped to see what might happen if we had a child, if the child could inherit my skills."

"I thought children of shades are born human."

"They are, but there is some research to show that certain types of shades may follow family lines, especially Elder types. They'd hoped that she might change into an Elder when she came of age. The only blessing of the entire thing—she never changed into a shade. They give me monthly letters about her with pictures and updates, but she knows nothing about me or her mother. I wish she knew how much her mother loved her, but at least she's been given a normal life. That is something I am grateful for."

"And you do as the Warden says because if you don't, they'll threaten Lilianna?"

I sighed, hating having it spelled out like that. It made me feel weak.

I'd always viewed my sacrifices to protect my daughter as noble, as necessary. Now, however, as Hera stared at me, I didn't feel that way. There was no nobility in this at all. I felt helpless.

"Yes," I answered. "I lost her mother because I refused to obey an order. I thought I could do that, that I was strong enough to have my own morals, my own rules, to live my own life even in this place, but Larkwood taught me such things can't exist here. Before the death of Jasmine, I had worked for the Warden, though I stopped short of anything I found too distasteful. It seems the Warden had grown tired of my rebellion, and she finally had leverage to use against me. It was all my fault, because I had too much pride, thought I could handle anything. I've worked with wardens since Larkwood first opened, since they first sent me here. I thought too much of myself and my powers. Lilianna was only six months old when the Warden had her mother murdered and took her away from me. They placed Lilianna with a loving adoptive family, and they bribe me with these updates to keep me under their thumbs, to remind me I still have things to lose."

Hera looked at me in a way that made me want to hide. I'd never felt like that before, always more than willing to face any problem head-on. There was no way to face this, though. I had no way to fix it. Larkwood had me trapped for however long my daughter lived, could force me to become a tool for the sake of a girl who would never know what I sacrificed for her, never know me, who would hate and fear me if she ever met me.

I expected Hera to look at me with anger, to storm out of my place and never speak to me again. She'd seen me disfigure a man who couldn't fight back, had watched me snap the neck of a terrified shade, all things I desperately didn't want to do but had still done.

Instead, she met my gaze head-on. *"She's very beautiful."*

I blinked slowly, unable to make sense of the statement. It made me recognize that Hera truly was kind. She had a sweetness to her, a purity that Larkwood would crush with time.

But I didn't want it to. I wanted her to keep that, which was perhaps why I'd spent so much time and effort trying to help her, at least in my own way.

A scent struck my nose, making me frown. A spot of red sat on the carpet, and another joined the first.

"You're bleeding?" I said, reaching for her arm where it seemed to stem from.

Hera yanked backward, as if the idea of my touching her was too much.

I can't blame her for that.

I tried to pretend her reaction didn't hurt, that I didn't care if she feared me. I shifted slightly to see her arm without touching her, finding a cut there and a line of blood down the back. It seemed she hadn't even noticed the injury.

I frowned as I tried to figure out what had happened, but the shimmer of glass shards on the floor made it clear.

I'd done this. I'd lost my temper, thrown the items and she'd ended up harmed by it.

Guilt tugged at me as I moved past her, careful not to get too close. I took a first-aid kit from the hallway closet, then opened it on the coffee table. I hadn't used the items there since I'd never needed to. I healed quickly enough that using bandages would have been a waste.

I nodded toward the couch. "Please, sit. Walking around with blood on you in Larkwood is a bad idea. The scent of blood makes tempers run high in many shades."

She followed the order, though she seemed uneasy, still. How couldn't she, though? After seeing what I'd done, after hearing my story, after I'd lost control and hurt her?

I really am worthless.

"I will clean your arm, then apply the bandage. It would be too difficult for you to do it yourself." I didn't want to apologize. I wanted to not mention all those things, but as I took out an alcohol wipe to clean the blood away, words fell from my lips. "I'm sorry. For what you had to see me do, for burdening you with this all, and for my behavior here. I never wished for you to be afraid of me, but I understand if you are."

She didn't respond at first, but when I went to open a second wipe, her hands moved. *"I'm not afraid of you."*

"I don't need your skills to spot that lie. It would be a normal reaction to fear me. Don't worry—I'm used to it." I wiped the rest of the blood from her upper arm, then moved down to her wrist, to where the red had dried even at her fingers. Her hand was so small compared to mine.

It made her seem fragile, made me almost afraid to touch her. "Lilianna's mother was a level-1 shade—a banshee. She was tough, the absolute embodiment of a mama bear. I remember being astounded when I met her. I found her protecting a new shade, one who was only ten at the most, when other shades had cornered them. She sent eight other level 1 shades running. I was in love at first sight."

Hera listened quietly as I cleaned the blood from her hand, moving between each finger, careful to get it all.

Or perhaps I just enjoyed touching her enough that I took my time so the moment lasted…

"I thought that because of what she was, because of how tough she was, that she would be safe. I thought between her and I, between the power we held, nothing could hurt us." I let out a cold laugh. "That didn't happen, clearly. I have so much power, and for what? I couldn't protect the only things that ever mattered to me. Lilianna's mother died and Lilianna was taken from me, and all I can do is act like a puppet for the Warden. I feel like one of those trained tigers, forced to follow the orders of things less than, forced to ignore my nature."

I balled up the last alcohol wipe and tossed it to the table in frustration before taking out a bandage. I opened it and pulled the back off so I could apply it to the small cut that had already stopped bleeding.

"This isn't who I wanted to be," I admitted, hating myself for burdening her further. Why did I want to tell her that? I'd cared little when people thought badly of me, when they had no idea why I did the things I did. It was my place in life and thinking too much about it only caused pain.

So why did I care when Hera did? Why did I want her to know that I wasn't heartless, that I did what I did for something bigger than me? It didn't change anything, wouldn't help anyone. It was selfish, and yet I went on.

"I remember before I was sent to Larkwood, my pride at how strong I was. I remember thinking I could do anything, that I would use this strength for good. When I came to Larkwood, I still believed I could be something good. I walked that line, refusing to do anything that would cause harm, holding true to my own rules even as I tried to follow the old wardens' orders. I told you before that walking that line was impossible, and I said it because I know. I tried. As soon as they had something to hold over me, all those morals meant nothing. That is why I've warned you not to have anything that can be used against you, because Larkwood will destroy you with it. I don't want to see that happen to you." I placed the bandage, then sat back to give her space.

She stared at me, silent. The weight of her gaze made me fidget, as if she could see through me. Was this what people felt like when they looked into my eyes?

Finally, she lifted her hands to respond, signing slowly as if she had to consider her words closely. *"I'm sorry."*

"Why are you apologizing? Last I checked, this is all my fault, not yours."

She reached out slowly and set her hand on mine. It shook, betraying that she still feared me.

And wasn't I pathetic for allowing it? Even knowing she feared me, even knowing she pushed herself to touch me, I accepted it, craved it. It was as if she warmed those deep, dark areas inside me, that empty void of hunger that created what I was. Even Jasmine hadn't truly warmed it. I'd never shown it to her, too afraid to let her see all of me.

Hera had seen it, knew how deep it went, but faced it head-on. Maybe she was afraid, but she wasn't running.

Which was far more than I deserved.

"I can't say I approve of what you've done, but I understand it, at least. I don't know if I'd do anything different if I was in your place, either."

"You don't need to defend me," I answered honestly. "I know what I am, and I know that my behavior is selfish. I failed Lilianna, failed Jasmine and now I hurt others to ease my own guilt. Knowing that won't change it, though. You should stay away from me, Hera, because I will follow the orders I receive in order to protect Lilianna. You should go and not come back here, because whatever you think I am, whatever you think I can be, you're wrong. I've accepted who and what I am."

She pressed her lips together and lifted her chin. It nearly made me smile at the stubbornness in her, at the way she didn't wilt even if she should have. She squeezed her hand on mine once more without moving. My gaze moved over her to the scar at her throat.

She'd suffered too, hadn't she? She'd witnessed the darkness of the world, of Larkwood, and she hadn't crumbled beneath that weight. She kept that light inside her, that purity, that strength.

If she could survive the darkness of Larkwood, maybe she could survive the darkness inside of me. Maybe it wouldn't swallow her whole and destroy her as it had so many others?

I turned my hand to interlace my fingers with hers, unable to help myself. It was dangerous, and it might end up biting us both in the ass, but I was far too weak to let her go.

Chapter Thirteen

Wade

Talk about an uncomfortable conversation…

Knox crossed his arms as he stared at me. "You going to tell me why you're here?"

"Aren't we friends?" I offered a wide smile.

"Not even close. Also, having a void in my room makes me uneasy."

I snorted. "Your little tricks don't work on me. Don't worry, I'm not interested in jumping you."

"What a pity." Knox's words were full of sarcasm. He wasn't interested in men and certainly not me, but at least the little jokes helped me feel a bit more at ease.

I walked further into his room, glancing around. I'd never been there because I'd never had a reason. We always met at Hera's place on neutral ground.

Of course, I'd never had the good sense to feel like people had the home field advantage, so Knox's place or anywhere else didn't change how I felt.

"What's that?" Knox nodded at the bag in my hand.

"Oh, right! I brought you a bribe." I reached in and pulled out a package of crackers, the ones that Hera kept that I knew Knox liked, then tossed them over.

"What are you bribing me for?" Knox didn't smile, though he caught the crackers.

"I need your help."

"This conversation is starting to bore me," Knox muttered and set the crackers down. "Can you please get to the point?"

I sighed and took a seat on his couch. It turned out it was easy to make a plan in my own room but following through now was a different case. Seeing Knox's perfect face, watching the easy sensuality he carried, it all said he was the right person to ask even if I really didn't want to.

He copied my sigh then sat in the chair beside the couch. "If you're quiet, it must be serious. Just out with it already."

Like a bandage – just rip it off.

"I wanted to ask you about sex."

And there went his eyes, widening so there was white all around the green irises. "What?" He almost sputtered.

"Didn't think that would shock an incubus so much. It's like a vampire getting weird about blood…"

He opened his mouth a few times before finally getting anything out. "I'm not here for a birds and the bees talk. I'm sure there are books in the library for that."

I rolled my eyes. "I don't need to understand the mechanics," I specified. "I'm not stupid, you know?"

"So what are you asking for?"

I gave up trying to make this less awkward than it was. It was painful and embarrassing but drawing it out wouldn't make it better. "I don't have any experience, okay? I'm sure you've guessed that much already. I was hoping you could give me some tips, so I'd feel a little more confident. It's not like I've got a dad to go to for advice, so all I've got is an incubus."

Knox sat back, tapping his fingers on the armrest of the chair. "For Hera?"

Would he refuse me because it was her?

Even if a few of us had managed to subtly ignore the way we were all connected to Hera, perhaps this was too much.

I nodded. "She says she doesn't care that I've got no idea what I'm doing, but how can she not? I just want to make sure I'm good to her, that I don't screw it up, you know?" I tried to ignore how pathetic that sounded.

"I doubt she gives a damn about your experience," Knox said, his voice soft. At my look, he went on. "Hera's sweet, and she actually cares about people. That means she's going to be interested not just in sex, but in being *with you*."

"But she's with Brax and with Deacon and with you—confident men who know what they're doing. How am I supposed to compare?"

Knox blew out a slow breath, then shook his head. "You don't understand anything, do you? Hell, most people don't understand, not really. I know exactly how meaningless and transactional sex can be. I could tutor you until you can get her off in a few seconds, but that's not what either of you wants—trust me. You don't want sex to just be mechanical. You want it to be more."

"Can't you teach me both?"

He shook his head. "I don't know anything about the sex she wants either. She and I haven't…"

That was a surprise. Knox was an incubus, so I'd assumed they'd had sex from the drop. The two clearly liked one another, so why hadn't they?

I didn't need to ask, though, because Knox laughed then went on. "I don't want to expose her to my incubus, don't want sex to be that mechanical thing I mentioned, not with her. It seems we're more alike than we realized, huh? Both of us wanting more but too damned cowardly to give in."

I went still as I considered something.

It was a horrible idea, wasn't it? Completely twisted and wrong and Hera would *never* agree…

Still…

"What if we worked together?" I asked.

He tilted his head. "What?"

"Well, it seems to me, we're both holding back, right? Me because I don't know what the hell I'm doing and you because you're afraid of your other side. What if we tried together?"

"Together?" The one word sat there between us. "You're saying…"

I finished the thought for him, forcing myself to do so even if I thought he might just punch me in the face for it. "I'm saying that I can remove a shade's power by physical contact, right? So if I were there, touching you, you'd be only you. Your incubus side would sleep. You'd be essentially human."

"I've seen people you've used your power on."

"You've seen people I'd incapacitated on purpose with my powers. It doesn't have to be like that, though. I can touch Hera and it quiets her mind, just takes her powers while she's in contact, but she doesn't get harmed. You could have her the way you want, without worrying about your powers."

He continued to tap as he stared at me. "And in exchange, you'd have some help during, so you wouldn't feel so much pressure?"

"Hey, even if I can't figure out where her clit is, you can, right? Between the two of us, maybe we could make one decent partner." My words were self-deprecating, but it helped with my nerves.

"And you think she'd agree to that? She hardly seems like that sort of woman."

"I think that she wants to be closer to both of us, and if this is what we can offer, I think she'll take what she can get."

"It sounds horrible when you put it that way."

I nodded. "Yeah, probably, but it's still true. She's sweet, and she's honest, and she shows exactly how she feels in her face. I think she'll take us up on it if we explain."

Knox pressed his lips together and stared off to the side, no doubt thinking. Maybe it wasn't as good a deal for him. Maybe he didn't care for being used in that way, for me leaning on him like that.

Or maybe the idea of having Hera with him was too far.

Still, I said nothing else, just let him have the time to figure out how he felt about it. It might not be what he wanted, but if he was serious about craving Hera but not touching her like that due to his incubus, then it might be his only option.

And I had to admit, Knox's self-restraint impressed me. Given his hunger, and how he'd resisted Hera and his own desires forced me to admit I respected him. It took some massive self-control to resist something so instinctual.

Plus, Hera was damn hard to resist on her own.

"Okay," Knox said.

"Wait, really?" I cursed myself when I said that. I was getting what I wanted—arguing was stupid.

"Yes. As long as Hera agrees, maybe it's for the best…" Even as he spoke, he seemed unsure.

I didn't think it was that he didn't want to, so much as him having to come to terms with a situation that wasn't ideal. No doubt he'd have preferred to have her to herself, but if it was between not having her or having to share, it seemed he'd rather share.

And boy did I understand that.

"Does this make us, like, brothers of some sort?"

"What?" He furrowed his eyebrows.

"I feel like sleeping with the same woman together creates some sort of bond. Spelunking buddies? Cave-diving cousins?"

Knox just stared at me as if he couldn't quite get a grip of the stupidity I was saying, but I couldn't help it. The more nervous I was, the worse my jokes got.

"Vagina twinsies?"

Knox rubbed his hand over his face as if this entire thing had been a bad idea and he'd only just realized it. "You're right. You do need my help—badly. Let me start your first lesson by telling you to remove all of what you just said from your vocabulary. If you say that to Hera, she'll kick us both out, and I don't want my chances harmed because of you."

I grinned at his annoyed response, because it meant he'd fully accepted my plan.

It meant I'd finally get to be with Hera, to taste her, to feel her, to have what I'd imagined since meeting her.

And, if nothing else, I knew she'd enjoy it because Knox would be there. I didn't have to worry about not pleasing her, at least at first.

I'd not only get to have her but I'd also get to learn from Knox, and I was a hell of a good student when I wanted to be.

I might skip out on the politics classes, but this was one subject I planned to give my full attention to.

Hera was worth it.

* * * *

Hera

Sitting in the Warden's office made me uneasy. No, not just uneasy but downright terrified. The meeting hadn't been added to my schedule—instead, a guard had shown up to escort me without notice.

In my months at Larkwood, the Warden had never summoned me before. I hadn't spoken directly to her, even. I'd heard her voice in Medical, and she'd come to the interrogation, but I'd yet to meet her directly.

And as I took a seat across from her, I really wished I still hadn't. She was beyond intimidating. It wasn't just her attitude but how she could follow through on it.

It was the difference between a puppy snarling and a wolf doing it. The Warden was the wolf—not only would she bite me, but she had the power to make it hurt if she did.

She pushed a writing pad across the desk toward me, which meant she expected a back and forth. "Thank you for your help with the interrogation."

That wasn't what I'd expected, and I had no idea what response she wanted, so I only nodded as if to tell her it was fine.

It wasn't fine, but I couldn't say that.

"Since you arrived, I'd been wondering what use you might have. As the only 1A shade we have, I expected great things from you." Her gaze moved to my throat. "At least, I did before we found out you'd been maimed. Even still, it seems your talent at reading people could serve us well."

I pulled the writing pad over, but still didn't write anything. Thanking her seemed wrong, because I didn't want her praise. It felt dirty, especially with Kit's story still fresh in my mind.

"I'm going to take you off manual labor. That should have been done before, but it seems Kit let it slide. He should have realized you'd have the skills for information extraction and assigned you there, but he didn't. I wonder why?" Even though the Warden said that like a question, her tone implied she had an idea of why.

I didn't want Kit to get in trouble for me, so I scribbled down a response. *"He's been trying to help me hone and control it. He probably didn't want to say anything until I was better at using it."*

She read the words, a cold smile spreading over her red lips as if she heard the lie. Talking to her felt like a game of chess when I didn't know the rules. She stayed steps ahead of me and each word I spoke seemed like another win for her. Worse, her voice grated on me, made me want to open myself up to what it could show me. Why did that feel so much stronger than usual? Maybe because of all the secrets she held…

"He isn't normally so careful. Interesting." She tapped her nail against her chin as she stared at me. "It doesn't really matter, though. You are a very useful individual, both due to your skills and your bloodline. I'm happy to see that you'll be moved to doing more beneficial and lucrative work than just pulling weeds. It can afford you a life more in line with what you were used to before coming here."

I wanted to tell her I enjoyed doing manual labor, but I had a feeling she didn't give a damn what I wanted or what I'd prefer, so I kept quiet.

"Now, you did help us with Mr. Hemslock, and I am a woman who likes to reward good work. Do you have any specific requests?"

Kit's warnings went through my head, the fact that this was how the Warden got people to do as she wanted. She got her claws into them like this, just a little. She pretended to offer a tiny gift that seemed harmless, but before long, she'd gain complete control.

I shook my head, not wanting to risk it. The only things I could want from her would be for the escape, and she was the last person I needed to get near that. She was too smart, too powerful. I couldn't risk asking her for anything related to our plans.

Her smile widened, as if my refusal didn't surprise her at all. "I thought you might be rather humble. It's a strange thing from someone like you, with your background. You grew up getting whatever you wanted, showered in praise and luxuries. I'd thought when you came here you'd use that same arrogance to get what you want here."

"*I don't need anything.*" I held out the writing board for her to read.

"Perhaps, or maybe you're smarter than I'd thought at first. You sure have gathered quite a collection of pawns around you. Gathering goods can only take a person so far, but people? They are a far more useful resource. Few understand that, but given what I'd heard about you, it seems you do. It makes me feel as if you and I might be somewhat similar."

I drew my hand into a fist. I didn't care for her words, for her trying to reduce my relationships and real feelings into nothing more than a plot. It uglied something precious to me, dirtied the only good things I had in my life anymore. Worse, she then acted as if the two of us were similar at all.

"Of course," she added on, "I think the most surprising is Deacon. He has been here for a long while, and after the fling with that shade years ago, he's shown no signs of repeating that mistake. For you to sway him, I must have underestimated what you can do."

I swallowed but didn't respond. Even she'd noticed that? We'd worked so hard to keep it hidden, but it seemed we'd failed.

Her smile widened, though it struck me as far more of a threat. "If you truly take to the work, if you give it your all and prove yourself indispensable, I wouldn't mind giving you time with him. In fact, there is the chance that I would offer him to you, should you be useful enough. Though, the opposite also holds true."

The way she could say that without the slightest hesitation reminded me just how dangerous she was. She'd just told me she'd give me a person as a reward if I wanted, while in the same breath, she threatened him if I didn't do as she wanted.

I spent so much time worrying about myself, I forgot at times that others could end up on the chopping block because of what I did.

The fear she spawned inside me made it harder to block her voice, and a string of images hit me. I saw the Warden in a large, empty house, eating dinner alone. Next, a young girl surrounded by blood and bodies, tears streaming down her face as she screamed for help. Then perfectly manicured fingers punching a code into a panel. The memories hit me in a torrent, one I couldn't slow down or stop or control. A first kiss. A dark tunnel. A shady conversation where money was exchanged. They came faster and faster until I closed my hands into fists and let my nails dig into my palms so the pain could focus me. It was all too much information to take in at once, and while I had no doubt I'd try to sort through it later, I needed to pay attention for now. The Warden was too big a threat to let myself fall to distraction.

Which meant I had only one answer for her. *"What kind of work do you want me to do?"*

"I want you to help with intel gathering. There are people like Mr. Hemslock who are brought here. We have interrogators, people like Kit who can convince people quite well, but you can hear the truth in their words."

"What about telepaths?"

"Telepaths can only access what a person is currently thinking. My understanding is that you can see what is beneath that, get glimpses of their past. That can all prove extremely useful. Imagine, if you will, we have someone who has important information. A telepath is easily foiled if a person has any training about keeping their thoughts focused. You, however, may see where their lover lives. You may see that they have embezzled money from the wrong person. You can find information that we can then use to convince them to work with us."

"I don't understand what that has to do with Larkwood."

"Larkwood exists because people allow it to. The public wants to lock shades away so they don't have to see them, so humans can live their little lives without worrying that a vampire or other monster will jump out at them. Larkwood is expensive, however, and it needs both financial support and the general support of the public. It means we have to take matters into our own hands to ensure we get the resources we need. Sometimes that means doing jobs that engender goodwill, but sometimes it means removing risks before they become problems." She tilted her head. "I'd think as the daughter of a politician, you would understand how this works. Your mother has both received and given plenty of favors to keep Larkwood moving, and since you arrived here, she's felt even more willing to help."

That made me frown. *"She's doing more to help me?"*

The Warden let out a chilling laugh. "No, dear. She's being extremely generous and accommodating to ensure we keep you here, out of sight and out of the media."

Oh. Just when I thought I was as hurt as I could be, somehow the world found another way to kick me. My mother was helping Larkwood not to give me a better life, but to ensure her life wasn't affected by my existence.

It reminded me of Charles, of the way he'd looked at me. No doubt that would be the reaction if the world knew that the precious Weston heir had turned into a shade. She'd lose support, possibly her place in the government. If nothing else, it would at least bring her choices into question, make people wonder if she was acting out of self-interest because of her daughter. My father, as the CEO of a pharmaceutical company who used research on shades to develop products, would be likewise at risk of bad publicity.

I sighed, the writing pad falling to my lap.

"Don't worry yourself about it," the Warden said as if she gave a damn about me or my feelings. "Your old life may be over, but you have a very bright future here in Larkwood."

And never had words that seemed kind on the surface struck me as such a threat before.

Chapter Fourteen

Hera

I couldn't help but smile as Wade and Knox bickered. None of it was serious, not like when Brax argued, when I was afraid things would end up turning bloody. Instead, it reminded me of siblings fighting over stupid things neither actually cared about.

"You always have some smart-ass remark," Knox complained. "It's impossible to get one over on you."

"It's not my fault you're not used to verbal sparring. You're used to Brax solving things with his fists."

Knox snorted, the sound the closest to agreement he'd get, no doubt.

I still had no idea why they'd both shown up. They'd arrived at the same time, which was strange, but I'd figured they wanted to talk about the plan.

Not that they'd gotten that far. They'd just come on in like they lived here and started to pick at each other as if I weren't even there. Wade sat beside me, Knox across from us, and I'd given up trying to get information from either of them.

I rather liked the noise in my place, the busyness, so I sat back and enjoyed the show.

The two were the most likely to be friends, all things considered. Then again, Wade could get along with anyone, and Knox wasn't as prickly as Deacon or Brax.

It made me happy to see them talking. There was this part of me that worried about them both, about the loneliness that all shades in Larkwood suffered from. I didn't want either to be lonely, and I wasn't selfish enough to think I could solve that for all of them.

So seeing them get along outside of me warmed me.

"What are you smiling at?" Knox asked as he tilted his head.

"You two are cute."

"Cute?" Knox huffed a laugh. "You're lucky you said that to us and not Brax or Deacon. I don't think either of them would take kindly to being called cute."

"To be fair, Brax *is* cute," Wade said. "He sulks like a toddler when he doesn't get his way."

"I'm going to pretend I didn't hear that. Hera might not find you so cute if Brax knocks out all your teeth. Besides," Knox added on, "We have other more pressing issues than whether or not my brother is cute, don't we?"

The meaning in his voice made me sit up straight. Pressing issues sounded bad, as if they had a problem they needed to address but didn't want to bring up.

Was it that bad? Fear gripped me as I went over the options. Had our plan already failed? Had they figured out some huge problem I hadn't considered? Was Brax hurt? Was it something outside of Larkwood that I wasn't aware of?

A sting in my ear made me turn to find that Wade had flicked me. "Stop spiraling. It's nothing bad."

I narrowed my eyes but let it go. His little trick had worked to stop the worry that had consumed me, like an annoying reset button.

"So what is it about?" I asked.

Instead of answering, Wade leaned in and kissed me. His lips were warm and soft, teasing as he often was, and I gave in.

It was impossible to fight it, really. His palm went to the side of my neck, his hand larger than I'd expected. He wasn't dominant or rough, which was why the size of his hands always threw me for a loop. It also helped because his kiss dimmed the world around me, quieting it, like shutting off the radio when overwhelmed and basking in the silence.

It only took a moment for me to lose my mind, for his kiss to throw me off so much that I gave in, kissing him back.

At least, until my sanity returned, and I recalled that Knox was sitting *right there.*

I pulled away and wiped my lips, as if that made it better. While it wasn't a secret that I was involved with a few different men, seeing it was far different from just being aware of it.

Especially because Knox couldn't touch me. It felt cruel to do this in front of him.

"What are you doing?" I asked.

"I thought it was a kiss. I know I'm still new to this, but I'm pretty sure I did it right…" Wade behaved as if unsure, but I knew damned well he was just making a joke.

Talk about a smart-ass.

"You know exactly what I mean. We aren't alone."

"I don't mind," Knox said from his spot.

It forced my gaze to him, and I sucked in a breath at the heated look in his green eyes. I'd seen glimpses of his incubus, of the thing that prowled inside of him, the thing he hated. The flashes where his gaze turned predatory, where he seemed ravenous when he looked at me, they were nothing compared to this.

Which made me think he wasn't being entirely honest, because that didn't look at all like the expression of a man who was comfortable.

Knox must have guessed my thoughts because he offered me a smile that was anything but gentle and sweet. "It really is fine. I can't help my reaction when a sight like this rouses my darker side. It's wanted you since it first saw you, after all. Still, I'm not asking you to stop."

"It's not right," I argued and shook my head.

"Because it makes you uncomfortable?" Knox asked.

"No, because it makes you uncomfortable."

Knox's smile softened the smallest amount, as if my response charmed him despite the obvious tension still inside him. "It is unfair how sweet you can be, you know that? Maybe that's why I struggle to win against you, because I'm never prepared for what you're about to say." He came over and took a seat on my other side, closing me in between the two men. "I said I didn't mind because I really don't. In fact, Wade and I have already discussed this. If you don't want to because *you* don't want to, that's fine. We'll both back off and not press the issue. If you want to stop only because you're worried about Wade or me, well, neither of us want that."

I frowned as I tried to make sense of his words. I turned my head in question toward Wade, who hadn't said anything else.

Despite his usual smile, his eyes held a hardness that said he hid a lot. Still, he answered my unasked question. "I'll take the blame here. I've been dragging my feet with us because I'm nervous. I know you want more, and hell, I do also, but I've been so afraid I'd screw it all up, that I'd make a fool of myself, that we'd go further and I'd end up disappointing you."

I grasped his hand and shook my head, trying to reassure him. Wade was a virgin. I didn't expect some marathon of perfectly choreographed sex that would last all night. I didn't *want* that. I just wanted him, to feel him, to have that moment where we showed each other just how much we cared for the other.

He smiled and patted my hand. "I know that's me thinking that and not you, don't worry. Still, I went and talked to Knox for some advice, and I realized we might actually help one another." He paused, then glanced at Knox as if to give him the chance to speak for himself.

"You know how much I want you, but the idea of letting my incubus anywhere near you makes me ill. I don't want you to be food, to be taken in by that power instead of me. It seems mutually beneficial to be here with Wade, then." Knox stopped speaking, staring at me.

Which let me put the rest together. Then again, Knox had pride, so I doubted he wanted to say everything clearly, to have to admit it all, especially in front of Wade.

That was when it all sank in. If Wade and Knox were touching, Wade could temporarily steal Knox's power. That would silence his incubus, render it helpless, allow him to be with me without worry about his other side. And with him there, Wade would feel more comfortable despite his lack of experience.

Maybe the fact that they'd not only come up with this idea but also discussed having sex with me behind my back should have annoyed me.

But, even if a flash of irritation or embarrassment hit me, it couldn't stand against the overpowering desire that combusted inside me. I had a picture of Wade over me, against me, inside me, with Knox taking my lips in a deep kiss, his hand cupping my breast, teasing me.

"I don't think she needs to really answer," Wade said with a laugh, "given that blush."

"That's *nothing* compared to her scent. Trust me, she's on board with the plan."

I swallowed hard, trying not to let myself get carried away. *Are you sure? I don't want you to change yourself for me. I don't need that,* I directed at Knox.

He came over to sit beside me and brushed his lips to mine in the same featherlight kiss he tended to give me, the type he felt like he could pull away from afterward, that wouldn't make him lose control. As always, he broke it almost immediately. "I want to change me. It isn't about you, not exactly. I didn't agree because I was afraid of how you'd react—I did it because I wanted to, for me. I want to have you and not worry, not have to keep myself in control, to hold back. With Wade here, I won't need to. It'll just be you and me."

"And me," Wade chimed in as if we'd forgotten him. "I know I'm not a stud muffin or anything, but I have feelings."

The words drew a look from Knox and me, and after a moment, we both laughed. That was part of what I adored about Wade, the way he could change the entire vibe of a room, the way he could wipe out the stress, how he could make me smile no matter what.

And that was what sealed the choice for me.

Was I nervous? Sure. Sleeping with one man could be overwhelming enough, but it was nothing compared with two men…

Still, that wouldn't stop me. After everything I'd been through, everything I'd survived and worked toward, I couldn't let this scare me off.

So I nodded as I set a hand on each of their thighs.

I was more than willing to have sex with Wade and Knox, even if it killed me.

Knox

I didn't think I'd ever had a moment of *now what* like this during sex. Given I hadn't had sex until I'd become an incubus, I'd never gone through the worry, the questioning about what to do and how.

Instead, my incubus had guided me, an innate instinct for how to please a partner, for what they craved, for how to chase all their little reactions.

Hell, I hadn't even had to do much given how my pheromones and draw worked. Beyond that, thanks to my incubus, I changed based on my partner, became whatever they wanted.

Which made me unusually uncertain as I sat beside Hera, her hand on my leg, her having agreed to Wade's and my plan.

"First things first…" I muttered and looked toward Wade. I didn't want to get started until we'd done the most important thing, until we'd put my other side to sleep.

I didn't trust myself to even try before that, because I had no idea how my instincts might react. I desired Hera with a strength I'd never experienced before.

Wade nodded and pulled off his gloves. It made me realize how rarely I saw any of the other man. He was careful to remain covered, to prevent even the accidental brush of his skin against another. The clothing was so much a part of him I didn't even notice it anymore.

That couldn't have been easy. I recalled how I hid away when hungry and tried to picture keeping that sort of distance up all the time. It had to be even harder because of Wade's personality, the fact that he seemed like a puppy who would have been happy to curl up on someone's lap in bliss if he could. Instead of that, however, he'd been forced to cut himself off from everyone around him.

"Don't be so nervous," he said, the barb no doubt meant to distract me.

"Yeah, well, I've seen what this can do to others. Sorry if I'm not all that thrilled about the idea of ending up the same way."

"If I knocked you out, that would defeat my purpose, wouldn't it? You wouldn't be that useful in that condition."

I narrowed my eyes but held my hand out in offering. We needed to get it over with so I didn't have to worry anymore.

Wade wrapped his hand around my wrist. The sensation hit me immediately, like being dunked under cold water. I tried to yank back, but he kept his hold. It felt like someone had pulled a plug inside me, as if a part of me swirled down a drain and poured out of me and into Wade.

He shuddered, as if the transfer did something to him as well. Then again, I'd seen him use the powers of others after he stole them. It wasn't complete, it wasn't like he became an incubus, but he no doubt could feel that hunger, that desire.

And staring at him, I *saw* the draw. I hadn't spent time around others of my type, so I'd never experienced the pull of an incubus. I got a small taste at that moment, though. Even though I'd never felt attracted to a man before—at least not real attraction that came from me—I felt it then. I wanted to touch him, to feel him.

I shook my head to clear that away. If anyone understood how that power could twist a person, could make them think they wanted things they didn't, it was me.

Instead, I used the change to turn toward Hera and take her lips in a deep kiss. It was what I'd wanted but had denied myself, the ability to feel her lips against mine, to slip my tongue into her, to taste her very breath without worrying I'd lose control.

She gasped in surprise, but just as quickly, she returned the kiss and even took more. Was she really this ravenous for me? This desperate for me? Not just my incubus, but *me?*

As much as I craved drowning in her, I broke the kiss. We had too many things I wanted to do to her, too many things I'd looked forward to, that I'd imagined.

"How long will this work?" I asked Wade, the question so obvious it surprised me that I hadn't asked before. Maybe a part of me had doubted it would work, hadn't been willing to really trust it.

"Since I didn't pull the power away roughly, it won't last long. Maybe a few minutes? It means we'll have to continue to touch during to make sure it keeps going."

"You can't make it last longer?"

"The more I yank, the worse the reaction is. That's how I end up making others pass out, when it takes days to recover. It's the difference between poking a tiny hole in a bucket or just turning it over. Stealing power on purpose will last longer, but it would hurt, and you wouldn't be all that useful in the state you'd end up in."

I pressed my lips together, not caring for the answer. Honestly, there had been a part of me that had wondered if Wade would have been able to silence my incubus longer, if, in the future, he could have given me peace so I could be with Hera alone, just her and I without my darker urges.

I pushed away the disappointment and questions. Thinking about that would only hurt me now, only cause me to ruin the time I was lucky enough to have. Worse, I didn't want Hera to notice my upset, to risk her feeling guilty.

Besides, it wasn't as if I hadn't had sex with men plenty of times, so one being involved while I had Hera, touching one during, was hardly some new thing. Having that with Wade made it even less bothersome.

I pulled away from Hera so I could remove her shirt. I wanted to see all of her, to enjoy the sight of her naked body, to savor it. Wade took that moment to remove his own shirt, then took off his other glove. Hera reached for my shirt, looking as greedy as I felt.

It seemed she wanted this as much as I did. The fact that she even looked at me when Wade seemed to have a draw made me worry I'd blush.

Which was odd.

I wasn't some virgin who would react just to the sight of someone else. How many perverted things had I done? As an incubus, I changed into what my partner wanted, into their dream object. That meant sometimes I was the sweet boyfriend and other times I was a twisted, dominant being who humiliated the person I was with.

So how could she make me feel so…inexperienced?

And excited?

It was an odd feeling, one I wasn't sure what to do with beyond leaning in and pressing a kiss to Hera's collarbone.

I acted on my own instinct and desires rather than those of my other side. I didn't use my abilities to figure out what she wanted, to do as she pleased, to become what she wanted. It was the first time I got to enjoy, to do as I wanted as my own person.

Hell, I wasn't sure what I even liked.

I like this… The thought floated into my head as I moved my lips to her left breast, as I traced my tongue along the edge of her nipple, tattooing the sight and feeling to my heart. I never wanted to forget a moment of this.

Not just the look or feeling, but the chance to feel like a man with a woman he loved rather than the monster with a meal I normally felt like.

Wade set his hand on my shoulder, the touch making me jump. How I could so quickly forget about him was almost embarrassing, how Hera distracted me.

He let out an amused chuckle.

But it reminded me that this wasn't just about me. I pulled back and turned my gaze to Wade. "Why don't you kneel here?" I gestured at the floor in front of Hera.

Redness covered Wade's cheeks. I didn't need my powers to tell that he was just as aroused as he was embarrassed by the idea. Still, he lowered himself to his knees right where I'd instructed.

"She's still overdressed, and it's keeping you from your goal, isn't it?"

Wade nodded, his eyes clouded over. I hated to admit it, but I was pretty sure I enjoyed this. I enjoyed telling him what to do, seeing the flush on his cheeks, the slight tremble to his hands as he reached for the waist of her sweats.

I didn't bother to wonder why — I just accepted it.

Hera lifted her hips to let Wade drag her sweats down her legs, taking her underwear with them. He worked them off her, freeing them from each of her feet, then tossed the clothing away.

His gaze locked onto her knees, since she'd pinned her thighs together. The moment of shyness charmed me, reminded me that Hera was sexy and sensual, but she wasn't fake. She wasn't someone who played this like some game. Instead, she was just a real person who wanted to be closer to those who mattered to her. That did more to me than any seductive ploy would have.

"Set your hands on her knees and press them open slowly."

Wade did so, curling his thumbs into the insides of her knees. He wasn't Brax, didn't have incredible strength, couldn't just yank her thighs open. It was better this way, though. His touch was a request, and Hera only shivered for a moment before obeying.

The sight of her spreading her legs wide made my cock ache desperately.

Wade ran his palms up her thighs, the touch something he wanted as opposed to me telling him what to do. His gaze locked on her pussy, which told me they'd never gotten this far before.

Perfect. I wanted to experience this all with them. The mechanics of sex were no mystery to me, so getting to feel this uncertainty with them felt like getting to feel it myself for the first time when I never had.

"Brush your fingers up her cunt," I said, my voice dropping an octave, not bothering to soften the terms.

Wade's hand trembled as he obeyed, his touch so light, I wondered if she felt it. At least, I did until he reached the top and stroked over her clit. *That* got a reaction from her.

Hera jerked at the touch, and Wade yanked backward. "I'm sorry," he rushed out. "Did that hurt?"

She shook her head, but I'd bet she was so distracted she couldn't make her hands work for a response.

Which meant we were at the teaching point, and that made me smile. "Women are especially sensitive here." I reached in and brushed against her hard little clit. She reacted the same, gasping in a breath. I rubbed her gently, then shifted my fingers to a *V* so I could spread her open and pull the hood out of the way. "So you have to be gentle, especially at first. See, it swells and gets hard as she gets turned on, like it's begging for the attention."

Hera set her hand on my forearm, digging her nails into me. Seeing her so undone already pleased me. We'd hardly touched her, really, and she already teetered on the edge.

Which meant there was no doubt this would be fun…

"Now, taste her," I said, my voice low and commanding.

And Wade obeyed as if he couldn't help it. He leaned in, and the sight of his pink tongue stroking up Hera's slit made me groan. He dragged it up her entire pussy in a slow, tortuous stroke. At the top, he touched her clit along with my fingers.

Wade reached out and set a hand on my leg, the action almost mindless, as if drawn to do so despite how he focused on his task.

"That's good," I praised him. "Now, keep going. Go ahead and point your tongue so you can dip in deeper. It's like you're reminding her of what's to come, of how good your fingers and your cock will feel."

Each thing that I told Wade to do, he did. My words mingled with Wade's tongue until Hera panted as if struggling to draw breath.

"Deeper," I ordered him. "I want you to *drown* in her, to have her wetness all over your face. You're going to make her come just like this, feel her break apart on your tongue. If you want to know how to please a woman, how to bring her to her knees, this is it." I shifted to use the fingers still exposing her clit to rub the firm nub.

Hera shivered, so close to release that I knew I'd been right. She'd come soon, unable to help it between my words and Wade's tongue.

"See how her hips move? How the muscles in her thighs twitch? Those are all signs that she's close. You can go harder, now. Focus on her clit, rubbing it more firmly. You can press your lips around it and suck as well. Listen to the sounds she makes to see how much she wants."

Wade followed the order so fast it was as if he didn't have to even consider it. He danced his tongue up to her clit, to where I spread my fingers more to expose her fully. Wade flicked his tongue against her once more, then narrowed his focus to just that tiny spot, as if the world outside of her clit had disappeared.

He ground the flat top of his tongue against her clit, then swirled around it. Wade worked her without mercy. How long had he imagined this? How long had he wanted this? A long damned time if his hunger meant anything.

Then she tipped over that edge, her head falling back, her mouth open on a wordless cry as she came.

Wade

Hera's muscles tensing as she came felt like a baptism. I usually made a joke of everything, made light of the world around me. It had been an easy way to feel in control.

No matter how terrible life was, how tragic, how overwhelming, I could make it manageable by turning it into a joke. It was like seeing a terrifying wolf and calling it a puppy just to make it into something I could comprehend and handle.

However, I couldn't make a joke right then. Nothing came to mind, nothing to make this all a little easier to deal with.

And for once, that was okay with me. I didn't *want* to make this smaller. I wanted to feel Hera, to have this moment of bliss, to watch her come undone because of *me*. I wanted to be that important to her right then.

She had others in her life, had things larger than me going on, but I'd been the one to turn her mindless in this way for a moment.

She tensed as she came without a sound, then went limp, her legs falling further apart as if all the energy she'd possessed had left her. I licked her again, and she jerked as if startled.

Knox laughed softly. "After a woman comes, she's extremely sensitive." He pulled Hera toward him, and she didn't fight him at all. She didn't seem entirely with it, at least not enough to argue with Knox.

He tugged her into his lap after removing his sweats. It left me still there on my knees, now before them both.

And I couldn't look away from the compelling sight.

Knox's shaft was hard, and it rested up along Hera's bare, wet pussy. The sight burned into me. I wanted more.

I had no idea what more meant, exactly, but it consumed me. I wanted more of this feeling, more of her, more of him, more of all of it. None of us were shades or trapped right then—we were just people driven to satisfy this hunger inside us.

Knox kissed Hera's ear, and she shivered in response. "I like this," he said. I got the feeling the words were more for Hera, but still, I listened intently as he went on. "Normally, even if I like someone, I'm not *me* during. I'm whoever they want me to be. I don't even know what I like, because it's never mattered. This is the first time I've gotten to be myself, that I've gotten to do what I want, feel what I want, to chase my desires."

Hera reached behind her, setting her hand on the back of Knox's neck. The action stretched her out, made me notice just how beautiful she was. Her body was amazingly soft, which had drawn me in at first.

I'd touched nothing so soft, so tempting. From the fullness of her breasts to the gentle curve of her hips, every part of her was giving.

"I'm going to take you now," Knox said, almost whispering to her ear. "I'm going to slide deep into you finally. I've thought about this from the moment I saw you that first day, but I never thought I'd get it." He turned his gaze down, toward me. There was an honesty in his gaze, as if he wanted me to understand something.

He got this with her because of me. I knew what he tried to say without him having to utter the words. I gave him a half-smile, my attempt to assure him I was getting as much out of it as he was.

that the sweat on Hera's brow, the lust that clouded her pretty eyes, it all showed that I'd gotten more than my fair share out of this.

Hera arched her back, the action moving her hips so Knox's dick rubbed against her.

Knox chuckled, then cupped her breast, teasing her nipple with his fingers. "I knew you would be like this — insatiable. Then again, that's how you make me feel, so I can hardly blame you for it. Now, I'm going to have you ride me, and you'll do that for me, won't you?"

She nodded as if we'd broken her resolve, as if she would have agreed to anything if he just kept touching her.

"Good girl," Knox said before he released her breast and grasped her hips. He urged her up slightly, his smile spreading more when Hera twitched as his cock rubbed against her sensitive pussy.

Except, he didn't quite hit the right spot. He seemed reluctant to release her, to guide himself to where he needed to be, and Hera was too lost to the want and sensation to do so herself.

I didn't need anyone to tell me to do anything—I knew exactly what I wanted.

I reached out and wrapped my hand around his cock. It was solid and incredibly hot in my palm, something I'd never expected to feel. Sure, I'd touched myself plenty of times—being a virgin at my age wound a man up—but touching someone else was different.

Knox groaned but didn't tell me to stop, didn't set a limit there.

I stroked him once, allowing myself to savor the heat of him, the desire I'd never experienced before. I knew it wasn't his incubus side, since he was without any of those powers.

Maybe it was a moment when I discovered something about myself I hadn't known before?

I didn't think I cared enough to figure it out right then. Instead, I stroked him once more, then positioned the head of his cock against the entrance of Hera's pussy.

She closed her eyes, giving herself over to us, to it all.

That trust humbled me.

Knox used his grip on her waist to pull her down, to slide into her. As close as I was, I got to watch closely, see how Knox's thick cock spread her pussy, to see the way her wetness clung to his shaft and made him glisten as he sank inch after inch into her.

"You are *so* tight," Knox said, his voice strained. "Do you like this? Do you like to feel me spreading you open like this?"

She nodded, the motion quick as if afraid he'd stop if she didn't answer.

Not that Knox appeared anywhere near ready to stop. He kept up the pressure until her body met his, until he filled her, giving me a good look at where they were joined, where the lips of her cunt hugged his thick shaft.

Knox released her waist and set a hand on her lower stomach. "You're so full, aren't you?" He nipped her ear, then used the hand still on her waist to guide her motions.

Hera rose and fell again, though not far, as if she couldn't stand the idea of losing that feeling of connection. Watching her move hypnotized me, the roll of her hips, the way she hid nothing. I hid everything, kept it all to myself, so honesty terrified me.

Still, I refused to hide from it, either. Not here.

Knox reached down farther with the hand on her stomach until his fingers reached her clit. He rubbed softly before locking his gaze on me and lifted his eyebrow. "Why don't you push her right over that edge again?"

And I was only too happy to do that. I scooted until I knelt close enough, then leaned in to drag my tongue along her clit. Hera jerked against my touch, but I did it again. I chased her as she moved, the strokes of my tongue less direct, but that didn't seem to matter.

I lost myself to the feeling, to the moment. I licked her sweetness while she rode Knox, the room filled with heavy breathing, with the sounds of pleasure from Knox and me.

Hera shook, and I knew damn well it meant she was close. After just the one time I'd watched her come, I could spot the signs now. I almost felt bad, almost pulled back when I suspected the sensation overwhelmed her.

I didn't, though. I wanted to be her everything, to push her beyond her limits, so I wrapped my hands around her hips to hold her still before locking my lips on her clit. I sucked hard, as Knox had told me to earlier. I might not have been strong like Brax, like Knox, but I was strong enough to keep her imprisoned for my touch.

It didn't take more than a few moments to force her body into that abyss.

Knox took the moment to lift his hips since she'd stopped moving, probably chasing his own release, his own desire.

Hera came harder this time than the last. I couldn't help the sadness at not hearing her cry out, not getting to savor the sound of her voice as the pleasure washed through her.

Knox released a sound darker than I'd heard before. His hand on her hip tightened, and they came at the same time, both drowning in their own feelings.

I let go of Hera's clit, though I didn't pull away. Instead, I softened the touch until I hardly brushed against her. Even when that wonderful limpness took over, when she leaned back against Knox fully exhausted, I didn't stop.

I dragged my tongue along her wet folds and around where her pussy wrapped around Knox's dick. I tasted both the softness of her body and the hardness of his, savoring that place where they met.

After a moment, Knox shifted enough so his softening cock slid free, giving me a view of where his cum leaked from her.

"Once more?" Knox whispered against Hera's ear, drawing my gaze up.

Hera opened her eyes and stared down at me, locking me in place with her honest eyes. She reached for me despite the tiredness that hung on her, the welcome enough for a stinging in my eyes.

I didn't deserve her—I didn't deserve any of this. I'd spent so much of my life without acceptance, being hated and feared, and here she was, accepting all of me without reservation.

And I couldn't turn that down.

I rose off my knees, swallowing hard as I slid down my sweats, ready to feel nothing but her and him against me. I leaned in over her, crowding her small, soft body as I placed my foot beside them on the couch for balance.

Knox grasped her hips, scooting her down a bit to make for a better angle. It was funny how nervous I'd been before, when I'd considered this moment, when I'd lain in bed at night and fantasized. Terror had mixed with desire as I'd worried about what to do, how to touch her, how to know if she enjoyed it, how not to hurt her.

Perhaps it was like skydiving. While it was terrifying to think about it, when actually there, when a person jumped, the fear ended. Likewise, now that I'd gotten here, instinct took over.

I grasped my cock and rubbed myself along her slit. She was drenched from her own pleasure, but also from Knox's cum.

And why didn't that bother me at all?

When the head of my cock brushed her clit, she yanked backward.

Knox's laugh came out breathless. "After coming twice, she's going to be *very* sensitive. It's why I thought it was good for you to go last, to enjoy the way she's going to squeeze down around you, the way she'll struggle."

I swallowed hard at his words, at how right he was even if I didn't want to admit it. It also took the stress off me about performance.

She shut down my brain, my questions, my worries. I pressed forward, letting out what was probably a pathetic groan as I sank into the snug grip of her pussy. She took me easily, almost feeling as if she pulled me in.

At least, that was how her cunt felt. Just as Knox had said, the rest of her went wild. She shifted, her breath sawing in and out of her chest in rough and rapid panting. Even so, she didn't reject me, didn't push me away. She wrapped the arm not behind Knox's neck around me, pulling me closer, letting me rest against her and trap her between Knox and myself.

It was perfect.

The heat and tightness of her pussy drove me mad, especially because each time I moved at all, she squeezed around me in a snug grip that made the sensations all the better.

I didn't worry about skill or finesse, not then. I refused to let myself get lost in the worry about pleasing her and gave myself over to instinct. It seemed even I had it, as I set a hard pace, plunging as deep as I could, getting as close as possible.

"I had no idea," I muttered, mostly to myself.

A grasp to my chin tilted my head up. Something warm and wet touched my lips. *A tongue?* It teased around my mouth, and it took a moment to realize it was licking the wetness from my face.

I opened my eyes, ready to kiss Hera back, except that wasn't who I found.

Instead, it was Knox. He had a hold of my chin and ran his tongue along the seam of my lips. I groaned at the feeling, at the way I opened for him, letting him lick into my mouth.

I brushed my tongue to his, unable to help it, especially as Hera's arm around me held closer, her nails digging into me. The pain of that along with the way she struggled as she came yet again and the impossibly hot grip of her cunt overwhelmed me.

I'd come plenty of times by my own hand, but those felt like a joke compared to this. The orgasm rushed through me, a tensing in my back, in my thighs, shutting off every thought in my brain other than the places I touched these two people.

I spilled into her, adding my own cum to Knox's, marking her in a way that felt like a claim I'd needed. I groaned, breaking the pseudo-kiss with Knox to rest my forehead on Hera's shoulder, giving myself entirely to the feeling.

I'd always assumed I'd die alone in Larkwood, had accepted it as the only future available to me. I didn't have to like it, but fighting against the inevitable had never seemed worth it. Even helping Hera, even thinking about an escape had been nothing more than a way to pass the time, a way to fill the endless days.

Now, however?

Now I felt like I finally had something that might just be worth hoping for.

Chapter Fifteen

Hera

Seeing the three men in one place made me even more nervous.

Then again, flashes from a few days before, when I'd slept with Knox and Wade, kept playing in my head like a dirty movie I couldn't find the pause button for.

It had ended too soon, really. After Wade had finished, we'd washed up, the quiet awkward as if no one knew how to break the silence. I'd have happily let them stay, to not let the night end yet, but Knox had pressed a sweet kiss to my forehead and reminded me that he didn't want me too sore afterward.

Which was probably fair.

It wasn't like threesomes and marathons were something I was all that used to.

Still, it meant that seeing them both together now, especially with Brax there too, made me uneasy.

Could Brax tell? Or had Knox told him? My cheeks heated as I sat there, on the stools of the kitchen island as if the distance made it easier.

It didn't.

"Why are you all the way over there?" Brax asked, his usual annoyance in his tone.

At least that never changes.

"I'm just comfortable here."

"Well, it's stupid to need to yell. Get over here if we're going to talk."

I shifted on the stool, wanting nothing more than to keep that distance. I was easy to read, and I didn't need *anyone* to figure out what swirled in my head.

Knox sighed softly, his gaze at least kind. "Come on, songbird. We don't bite."

Bite. How was it that he knew exactly what to say to drive me mad? Was it because he was back to normal after Wade's trick? Because his incubus liked to toy with me?

Wade said nothing, but a smirk on his lips said he knew why I struggled, and, worse, that it amused him.

Still, I came no closer.

Brax let out the longest sigh ever, as if entirely exasperated by the conversation and my stubbornness. He nailed me with a hard look. "You fucked these two. Is that really any reason to act like we're all suddenly strangers? For fuck's sake, Hera, get your ass over here so we can discuss the plan already."

His words were so blunt that they hit me like a kick to the stomach. At the very least, he shook loose my spiraling thought process. That answered whether or not Brax knew, didn't it?

Knox reached out and smacked Brax in the back of his head, the action making them look like brothers again. Despite appearing nearly identical, it was times like this, when they behaved like fighting siblings, that I really saw it. "You are the worst, you know that?"

"What? She's over there because she's worrying about it, worrying about if I know, what I think about it, how to act. Now there's nothing for her to stress about. I know, I don't care, we're good. Let's move on."

I tilted my head at that, unsure if I was more relieved or disappointed by his words. Sure, I didn't want Brax angry, didn't want a fight, but him not caring at all? Did I really mean so little to him?

He stared at me, then pressed his lips together and shook his head. "You don't get it. You're still pretty slow, you know that?" His tight expression said he planned to say something else, but instead, he turned his gaze toward the poster on the table. "Let's just focus on the plan, okay? For my part, I've checked out the generators. It'll be easy to take them down. I'll wait until the security gets shut down, that way it'll lock everything open." He turned his gaze to Wade. "How about you?"

Wade nodded, still sitting back in his chair as if relaxing instead of planning an extremely dangerous escape. "We're good. I was able to get a simple virus from a tech mage. Since it's just a framework, he has no idea what it's for, so we don't have to worry about being found out. It'll also throw a false alarm to draw guards to the front entrance. I'll plug it into the main computer in the server room and it'll unlock all security measures. The thing is, that means *all* security measures. There isn't any way to target only certain areas. Every door in every area of Larkwood will go green. It'll be chaos. Think full-blown riot."

Brax smiled for a moment before it faded away, his gaze shifting to me, then to Knox, then to Wade. I read him easily. He might enjoy a good fight, but it was a different matter when he had others around who might not be as safe. He cursed softly. "I have to get rid of the generators, but as soon as they're down, when we rally, I can handle anything that gets thrown at us. You all just have to get to the meetup place safely."

Wade grinned. "Are you worried about me? That's cute."

Brax did not return the smile. "I'm not worried about you. I just want to make sure you reach that point because your worthless ass would make good fodder."

The joking helped to ease my worries, so I slid from the stool and made my way into the living room. I knelt down beside the table, bringing me close enough to read and write.

Next, I glanced at Knox, who hadn't mentioned his progress yet.

"I'm meeting with someone later today who is going to give me a key for the roof exit." He left it at that, and it would have been impossible to not hear the stress in his voice. Even without my skills, I would have caught it.

A flash in my head showed Knox and that woman whose shoe I'd broken, his body near hers, her lips at his throat.

I jerked my gaze away from him, hoping he didn't see my expression, that he didn't notice. The last thing he needed was my jealousy or censure over anything he did. He needed to feed, and using his skills was how he got what we needed.

I avoided looking at him again, unwilling to see whatever rested there. No matter how much I told myself to ignore it, I couldn't. It wasn't just jealousy, either, but pity. I hated that he had to do what he didn't want to.

It only reinforced *why* we were doing this, why we were escaping. I wanted him free, to have the freedom to do as he wanted, to not have anyone take advantage of him anymore.

Of course, if he heard that, no doubt it would just piss him off.

"And you?" Brax said, breaking the tension with his no-nonsense voice.

I let myself look at him. *"I found where the communications center is and the layout of the North Tower."*

Brax tipped his lips down. "I thought we decided that you getting sent to the North Tower was a bad idea…"

"No. You just decided you didn't like it," I signed. *"I'll be fine. The security measures will be for there too, so it'll pop all the locks for me. Even if it didn't, I can open each door on my own. I'm pretty good at it now."*

As I gave my part of the plan, none of the men looked pleased. Had I ever had *all* of them glaring at me at once? It almost felt like some achievement.

"Hera…" Wade said.

I lifted my hand to silence him before responding. *"Wade, you're sneaking into the main server room to plant a virus. Knox, you've been manipulating someone who could have you thrown to the North Tower in a heartbeat, all for roof access. Brax, you're going to destroy the generators which will clearly draw some attention. Then you all have to make it through a riot to reach the rally point. We are all doing dangerous things to make this work. I'm not special."*

At least all three looked slightly shamed by my scolding, by the reminder that they were putting themselves at risk as well. I might be a woman, but that didn't mean I needed their protection while they took all the danger on themselves.

I wasn't useless. I finally understood and accepted it. I was tough. I had skills.

"You're a little special," Wade said. The words seemed sweet until I saw the smirk on his lips. "I mean, if something happens to you, I'm left with these two. I have a feeling that orgies will be a lot less fun without you."

The words drew heat to my cheeks as they brought back the memory of what had happened, but at least it broke the tension from before. Wade really did know how to calm things down, didn't he?

He made it almost impossible to keep fighting or stay angry when he did that, when he disarmed us with a well-timed and perfectly inappropriate joke.

"We all have to risk things," I signed, wanting them to understand. *"And getting out of here is worth any risk. I can do this — trust me."*

All three sighed and exchanged loaded looks. Finally, they nodded, one at a time.

"So, if we have the plan set, when do we do this?" Brax asked.

"I'll need tonight to get the key," Knox answered. "But after that, I'm good."

"I'm ready whenever," Wade answered.

"Tomorrow during the day, I'll make my move. The transfer to the North Tower should happen right away, but I don't know how long it'll take me to get to communications after that." It wasn't as if I had a guidebook of how much time it took to get a shade into the North Tower, before

I could slip my cell and get to communications. A few hours? A day or two?

"So how do we coordinate it? It isn't like Brax can just wait at the generator for days until it's time," Knox said.

"*I have an idea about that...*" I admitted with a sigh.

Talk about a horrible idea...

* * * *

Knox

I peered around the roof as I frowned. I couldn't recall the last time I'd been outside without a guard.

Sure, I sometimes had jobs that Larkwood sent me on, or otherwise was allowed in the yard area, but never without some musclehead watching me and waiting for a chance to pull his weapon.

Instead of that, I only had one human woman.

Yet I suspected I might have preferred the weapon over the scent of want that clung to Nisha, the Warden's assistant.

A small hand slid over the expanse of my back, through the shirt that covered me. "You look good out here, under the stars."

Her praise did nothing for me. I didn't want to hear how good she thought I looked, how much she wanted me. The only reason I'd come here with her was for that key, so all her empty words and sickening touches did nothing for me.

Worse, where I'd hated this before, it had never felt quite as wrong as it did now. Was that because of Hera? Because after being with her and Wade, I'd finally tasted true passion? Now I fully understood how empty this all felt.

Still, I couldn't let that get in the way of my plan. If I failed, if we had no way to escape Larkwood, then I had no future. No matter how much I hated this, I had to play along.

I tilted my face up to look at the expansive sky, the bright stars that dotted the darkness. "It's been a long time since I've gotten to see the sky like this."

She stroked over my back, then brought her other hand up as well. She moved those hands to my sides of my waist, her breath warming a spot between my shoulder blades. "I was surprised when you contacted me. I thought you'd turned me down."

I had, but telling her I just needed to use her wouldn't get me what I needed. Instead, I forced myself to play my part. "I guess I was nervous."

"Nervous? Why?"

"I get hit on a lot by other shades, by guards, but never someone like you."

"Like me?" The way she asked screamed 'praise me.'

So I gave her what she wanted. "You're a good woman — too good for me. I was surprised, and I kept thinking that it was a mistake, that it wasn't a good idea. I just thought there was no way you really wanted me."

She pressed her lips to my back in a soft kiss, then whispered against me. "You worry too much. I'm not that good of a woman, either. I'm married, you know?"

That surprised me. Few people who worked at Larkwood had families, given how far Larkwood sat from anything else. Most staff spent six weeks or so at Larkwood, took two weeks off, then repeated that process. Not many marriages survived hours like that.

She laughed softly, though it held pain. "He's always worked a lot, which is why I took this job. It's hard to be apart so much. I guess I got tired of sitting in an empty house waiting for a man who wasn't coming home."

"Do you love him?" The question surprised me as it left my lips. It was the last thing I should have said to her, but I couldn't help it. The longer I spent with Hera, the more I found myself thinking about love, about how relationships worked.

That made her pause and pull back a bit. "Of course I do."

I turned to face her, staring down into her eyes. My incubus snarled in my head with want, demanding I kiss her, that I take her in my arms and gorge myself on her. "How can you be here then?"

"Have you ever fallen in love?"

I swallowed hard and nodded. Admitting the truth might have been stupid but denying Hera in any way felt wrong. I wouldn't tell Nisha the name, but I wouldn't hide my feelings, either. "Yeah. Just once."

"It's deeper than anything else, right? Even if things change, even if you're apart, it's more than that. It's a commitment to stay together, to build a life together, to honor that no matter what."

I frowned as I considered her words. I understood it in a weird way. I thought about Hera, about how she had slept with Brax and Deacon, that she loved both of them. Yet, I didn't feel she loved me less because of that. It was more than something so trivial. My feelings for her, our relationship, were big enough for things like that not to matter. "I guess so," I admitted.

"Then you should understand. What happens between us doesn't change what I have with my husband. They don't have anything to do with one another. I just don't want to feel so lonely anymore."

But was that true? I accepted Hera having other loves in her life because she loved them, because they mattered to her. I doubted I'd feel the same way if she simply indulged in her desires without thought, with anyone she wanted.

The difference struck me then.

"Sex without love is empty," I said.

She frowned, a deep crease appearing between her eyebrows. "What?"

"Love can overcome distance, it might be more important than any little problems, but that doesn't change that sex without it is like a candy cane made of ice—it might resemble something more but lacks substance. As someone who understands sex well, I can say that with absolute certainty." I cursed myself as I spoke, frustrated with my own lack of focus.

I was here to get the key, to ensure us an escape route, to follow a plan, and yet instead I risked it all by opening my mouth.

Shut up. Take off your pants and do what you're good for.

Nisha blinked slowly, some of the lust that had swum in those eyes of hers cooling. "I never thought I'd hear something like that from you."

"No one is more surprised than I am, trust me." I let out a harsh laugh, frustrated with myself, with the way my brain warred with my incubus, the way I felt out of control and unable to bring either to heel. I turned my face toward the sky once again, trying to imagine a future where I could feel this all the time. If we succeeded, I could have this, I could live my life the way I wanted and never get pushed into something I didn't want to do again.

"You don't want me, do you?" Nisha asked, her voice tinged with sadness that made me suspect the words were about so much more than this moment.

I shook my head. "It's not you, though. I don't want anyone, I think, not unless I love them. After years doing things I hated, of submitting when I wanted to fight, of smiling when I wanted to yell, I'm tired of it."

After I spoke, I held my breath, waiting. Had I ruined everything? Would she get angry? Would she storm in and call a guard to have me hauled to solitary? If it went that way, I could still give in to my incubus, could allow it free rein. No matter how angry she was, it wouldn't take much to convince her to forgive me, to make her believe anything I told her.

Something pressed into my palm, making me drop my gaze to my hand. "Why?" I asked her as I stared at the key to the roof she'd placed there.

She took a step backward, putting distance between us. "I wasn't kidding—you do look good under the stars. I think it's because the freedom agrees with you. I can't do much about you being here, but maybe the roof can be your own little getaway."

I furrowed my eyebrows, unable to understand, to accept it. In all my years at Larkwood, no one had done anything for me unless they got something out of. They certainly didn't give up what they wanted for my own benefit. Was it a trick?

Nisha sighed and offered me a lopsided smile, looking less like the seductive woman she'd seemed before and more like a young lady embarrassed by her own behavior. "Maybe it's because we're out here with the breeze, but I feel like I can think a little more clearly. So, I'm going to go and give my husband a call. I've got a lot of vacation time saved up, so maybe I'll take a trip home. This place…"

She peered around the roof as if she could see the entire filthy history of Larkwood just like that. "It does bad things to every person who comes here. Whether shade or staff, it twists us all like a poison. I don't think I like the person I've become here. Take as much time as you want up here."

When she went to pass me, to go back to the staircase that led to the door, I caught her wrist to stop her. She jerked her gaze to mine, a moment of fear there that mixed with the lust that still simmered. It reminded me that even if she fought that desire, it didn't completely rid her of it. "Thank you," I said, trying to make sure she understood that I meant it.

She nodded, then pulled away and left me there alone.

I took the chance to stare out at the empty desert outside of Larkwood's walls, enjoy the way the breeze cooled my cheeks, to feel the weight of the key in my palm.

I'd hidden how I really felt for so long, had refused to admit it because the truth had terrified me. I'd worried that if I ever uttered how I really felt, if I had to give in to things I hated after that, the pain would overwhelm me.

Yet, now, on the eve of everything changing, as I prepared to take on the biggest challenge of my life, the truth had saved me. I'd trusted another person and rather than using it against me, they'd helped me.

Hera had given me the strength to do this, to look at those parts of myself I didn't like and accept them. She'd taught me to rely on others, to let them in, to stop hiding so much of myself.

I closed my hand around the key in a tight fist as I swore to do whatever it took to repay her. No matter what happened, I'd make sure she got to taste the freedom she craved.

* * * *

Kit

I swirled the whiskey in my glass as I sat in the dimly lit room. Why was it that drinking alone in a room was so depressing?

The dichotomy of alcohol always struck me as odd. If drinking with friends, it was seen as social, as a happy thing. When done alone, however, it transformed into something incredibly sad.

Though, it wasn't as though drinking with others was an option for me. Who exactly was I to have a drink with?

The guards who hated me? The shades who hated me? The Warden who was far too fond of me?

Hera?

That name made me sigh as I took another sip of the surprisingly smooth liquor. I still couldn't break that connection with her, the leash she seemed to hold on my thoughts.

Even after she'd seen what I was, what I'd done, she hadn't cast me away. She hadn't reached out to me since, but that was fine. It wasn't as if I needed to see her every day.

Though I would like to...

I growled at my own wayward thought. It was dangerous and pointless. Wanting things was a quick trip to sorrow—nothing more.

I wished alcohol worked on me, that it numbed my thoughts the way it would for most humans and shades. I would have welcomed that blurring of my far too lucid memories. Instead, my only relief came from the burn as I swallowed the strong liquor.

"Kit?" Hera's voice stopped me. When I lifted my gaze, I found a shimmering vision of her in front of me.

Ah, that's right, our connection. Hearing her voice should have clued me in on that.

"I didn't expect you to reach out to me like this again," I admitted.

She'd slept many times after that first night when she'd been in Medical, but she hadn't tried to speak to me in this way again. The first time was no doubt an accident, caused by her stress and the newly formed bond. After that, the bond functioned more like a doorway that a person had to choose to walk through.

"I need your help," she said.

That made me go still, a feeling so close to fear in my chest. "What do you need?" I asked, ready to do whatever she requested.

Which I refused to think about too much.

"Can I talk to you like this even when I'm awake?"

I nodded. "It isn't as clear as this, but yes. It is more like an ability to send single thoughts, like a message rather than a conversation."

"How?"

"Just as you do when asleep. You need only to reach out through that bond between us, to feel those threads, then push the thought to me. Why do you need to do that?"

She tore her gaze away, as if she couldn't bear to look me in the eye while she spoke. It made me dread whatever horrible idea she'd come up with…

"I need you to pass a message to someone."

"Again, I ask why."

She blew out a breath and started to pace. Her feet made no sound against the floor, of course, since she wasn't physically there. "I can't tell you that. I need you to give a message to Wade, tomorrow. It'll be an easy message, but it needs to happen as soon as I send it."

I struggled with my response. I wanted to say yes immediately, to be her rock, to help her. She relied on herself too much, too unwilling to lean on others. The other part of me wanted to tell her hell no, since I had no doubt that I'd dislike what she wanted. What if the message endangered her? What if it was part of a plan that would end up getting her killed?

"You expect me to do this without knowing why? Without understanding what it is a part of?" I asked.

She nodded, then stared back at me. "Yes. I'm sorry to ask you this, because you've already done so much for me, but I can't tell you why."

"Because you don't trust me?" The words hurt even as I forced myself to ask.

She didn't answer right away, as if trying to decide. Finally, she sat down on the couch beside me, an odd thing since without a true physical form she didn't move the cushions at all. "That's not it. I trust that you wouldn't hurt me or betray me, but you also have other priorities, other things to think about. I don't want you to risk yourself, so I don't want you involved."

Her words caught me off guard. I'd expected her to lie and tell me she trusted me, to make up a story about why she needed my help, or to admit that she didn't trust me. Instead, she'd said she did, but she worried about me?

She wasn't the type to lie, and especially not to lie well, so I suspected she answered truthfully.

"You have Lilianna to think about," she added on. "I can't put you in a position that could endanger her. If anything happened to her because of me? I don't think I could live with that. So, please, just agree to this and don't ask anymore."

I stared at her, at an absolute loss for words.

Had anyone *ever* really worried about me? Had they prioritized me above what they could use me for? No doubt, whatever nonsense she had in her head, it would have been easier if I'd been part of it. I didn't say that out of arrogance, it was simply a fact.

Yet, she hadn't. She hadn't tried to trick me, to manipulate me, to use me at all. She asked for help, but only seemed to want to involve me in a way that wouldn't lead back to me.

If she'd have tried those other options, I'd have said no. Somehow, she made it far more difficult to turn her down when she treated me like this.

"I don't know what you're planning," I said as I set my hand on her knee. Since she wasn't physical, it differed from touching a person. Because of our bond, it was more like touching energy, something solid only to me. "But if you want my help, you need to promise me that you will be careful. You need to promise me that if you get in over your head, you will reach out to me to ask for help."

"But Lilianna—"

I silenced her by leaning in and brushing my lips to hers. It wasn't a real kiss, not the one I wanted that I'd told myself to stop thinking about. It lacked her warmth, her scent, her taste. Still, it was more than I'd thought I'd ever get. "You matter to me as well, Hera. I don't think I could look at myself anymore if I turned my back on you, if I allowed you to get hurt out of my own cowardice. I won't press about what you're doing, so long as you can make that promise to me."

Her eyes went wide, as if the kiss were the last thing she'd ever expected. Was that because she'd never seen me that way or because I'd done a good enough job hiding my feelings that it had taken her by surprise?

Would she slap me for the kiss? Yell at me? Reject me?

I waited, ready for it.

Instead, she leaned in and returned the kiss, though it remained chaste. She let her forehead rest against mine, the touch strange, almost sad.

It made that spark of fear inside me grow. Just what was she planning? What was she after? Why did she look so sad all of a sudden?

"I promise," she said in a whisper.

And no matter how difficult…I'd have to trust her.

Chapter Sixteen

Hera

I stared at Deacon from across the large cafeteria. Just how much I enjoyed watching him work surprised me. He was tough, no doubt about that. He didn't take shit from anyone, but he was fair, too.

Even if others never understood it, never saw it, he worked hard to protect the shades he could.

The thought of never seeing him again made my chest hurt. How could I live without his smile, that rare one he showed only to me? How could I not hear his voice anymore, never glare as he lectured me again?

A selfish part of me wanted to ask him to come with me, but I knew better. Deacon didn't believe there was a life outside of Larkwood for him — for any of us. He'd grown up within the walls of the North Tower, and while he could leave, he didn't truly know about the outside world.

He would never come, and he'd probably work to keep me from doing it as well. I'd thought at first it was because he was an asshole, because he wanted me locked up. Now, I understood him better.

Deacon had learned that no life existed outside these walls. He would stop me not out of hate but out of fear. He didn't want me to die trying to escape, especially because he didn't believe a person could ever actually escape.

The Warden's words came back to me, though. She knew about the connection between Deacon and I, and I couldn't leave him with that mess. I didn't want him to pay the price for what I would do, which meant making it clear to everyone that we were not together.

The aching in my chest didn't stop as I rose and walked toward where Deacon stood. He spoke with a few other guards, their voices low but conversation seeming friendly enough.

At least, on the surface. A tension there still remained, a clear sign that the other guards didn't consider Deacon one of them. It wasn't like that would change after I left, but I didn't want him to suffer anymore because of me.

"You can't just target the female residents for searches," Deacon said, in a low voice to a guard I'd seen around but never dealt with personally.

"I don't," the other guard argued.

"Really? Because even the official searches you report are ninety-two percent female despite the population being nearly fifty-fifty." Deacon crossed his arms over his chest.

"Come on," the guard complained. "You know how boring this job gets. You've got to let people blow off a little steam or we'll go crazy."

The argument didn't seem to affect Deacon. "Doing that is not only inappropriate but it also means the male residents are left alone, that they can have more contraband because they aren't getting searched. Let me make myself perfectly clear—fix this problem. If I see another report that skews the numbers that way, you won't need to worry about boredom because you'll be busy searching for a new job."

The other guard rolled his eyes, the action disrespectful, but Deacon said nothing about it. He was probably used to others treating him like that. If he lost his temper at every eye roll or glare, he'd get nothing else done.

Still, I struggled with the desire to turn my focus on that guard instead of Deacon.

Except…that wouldn't help him in the long run.

I approached, the noise of the cafeteria almost overwhelming. I'd picked this time because of the audience, because forcing people's hands often meant doing things as publicly as possible.

I walked up to Deacon and shoved him as hard as I could.

Not that he even stepped backward, as if it meant nothing to him.

It probably doesn't.

He narrowed his eyes. "What the hell?"

The guards reached for the weapons on their belts, but Deacon snapped out a quick, "No!"

At their looks, he shook his head. "She's just a silenced siren. There's no reason to escalate things." He shifted his gaze back to mine, the look full of meaning.

No doubt he was trying to tell me to knock it off, to watch myself, to not push this any further. He could only protect me from so much, and if I went too far, he'd be helpless.

Which was exactly how far I needed to push it.

"Now, what is the meaning of this?"

"I hate you," I signed, feeling sick at the lie. *"I slept with you thinking you'd help me, but you just used me!"*

His eyes widened, then he glanced around as if to see if anyone else understood. The other guards' smirks said they could read ASL.

Which was exactly what I'd hoped for.

"I don't know what you're talking about," Deacon muttered. "But this isn't a conversation to have in the middle of a crowd. Let's go." He wrapped a hand around my arm, no doubt ready to drag me off to some corner where he could question me, where he could try to figure out just what I was doing.

But I needed an audience for my plan.

I snapped and twisted the sound, then used it to shove Deacon backward. This time it worked, the pressure far more than what I'd managed with my hands. He stumbled away but caught himself before getting knocked down.

If I didn't trust Deacon so much, I might have given up right there. The expression he gave me was full of anger, a look that said if he got me alone, I was in *deep* trouble.

And for a moment I wanted that time to feel that anger of his. I knew it was just a reaction to the truth, to how I wouldn't be able to touch him anymore, that I wanted some sort of goodbye.

But that wasn't possible.

The other guards took the batons from their waists, snapping them to full length, the electrical prod on the end sparking to life as they hit the button. They were used to dealing with dangerous shades, and I doubted they thought much of me.

At least, not yet. They'd see how wrong they were soon.

Deacon held his hand out. "Everyone calm down for a minute." His tone came out desperate. "The Warden doesn't want this one hurt."

"Yeah, well, she isn't supposed to be able to do *that*," one of the guards said, his gaze hard and locked on me. "Things change."

"Maybe the Warden already knew she could, which is why she's taking such an interest in her. Did you ever think of that? Do you want to piss off the Warden by hurting her favorite pet project?"

"So we just let her walk out after attacking a guard?" The guard dropped his voice so it didn't carry far. "All these other shades saw it. We're going to have a riot on our hands if they think they can get away with that shit."

Deacon clenched his jaw, as if trapped between two bad choices. I hated the pain on his face, the uncertainty. I'd put that there. Even if I'd done it for him, I'd never wanted to hurt him. "Okay, we take her into custody, but be careful."

"*I'm sorry,*" I signed, looking right at Deacon. The others no doubt saw it as an attempt to get out of trouble, but I could only hope Deacon truly understood it.

Or rather, that he would in time. I wanted him to know I was sorry for what I was about to do, for leaving, for everything.

He rushed forward, as if to tackle me, to stop me, which meant I'd run out of time.

I clapped my hands hard, then shoved those sound waves outwards. I did it in all directions, which threw not only Deacon back but all the guards as well. It was the most powerful time I'd done this, though I was careful to hold back some. I didn't want to risk walls or the building, but I needed to make one hell of a mess.

Those waves crashed out beyond our little group as well. The scraping of the tables against the floor as they moved, the slam of bodies against the ground, it all said it had gone far.

I turned to find nothing standing in the huge room. Every person had gotten thrown to the floor and the furniture all pushed out toward the walls. I was entirely alone on my feet in the center, staring at the chaos I'd caused so easily.

It was the first time I really wondered if I was the monster others saw me was.

I swallowed hard, meeting Deacon's gaze as he forced himself off the hard ground, blood leaking from his lip. He must have struck it when he fell.

He took a step toward me, but a sharp pain in my shoulder blade caught my attention. Before I could even turn, another hit me.

I spun to find two guards at the doorway, rifles in their hands, pointed at me. A look over my shoulder showed two darts sticking out of me, and the wave of dizziness told me what was obvious.

The drugs from the tranquilizers swam through me so fast I couldn't prepare myself before my knees gave out. The world lost its sharpness, everything blurring around me, the sounds all mixing together until they were slush in my mind.

"Well, well," came a voice I recognized. *The Warden.* "As much as I wanted to keep you here, it seems you're too dangerous. I did warn you, didn't I? If you thought it was bad here, just wait until you experience the hospitality of the North Tower."

Those were the last words I heard before the darkness dragged me under. I gave in to it, a smile on my lips.

Finally, I was going to get out of here.

* * * *

Brax

Seeing Hera hauled out of the cafeteria was more than I thought I could take. Everything inside me had wanted to rush in, to stop what was happening in front of me.

In fact, I had no idea if she knew I'd been there. I'd followed her, unable to help it, unable to stay away. I knew she'd make her move, even if I didn't know what that move was, but I hadn't expected *that*.

It reminded me that Hera was more powerful than I'd ever realized. It was easy to not notice it. She seemed small and sweet. She couldn't yell, didn't show aggression the way I did, the way most shades did. Believing her weak was an easy trap to fall into, but judging from what she'd done, it was a clear mistake.

She had brought an entire room full of dangerous, powerful shades and guards to their knees without breaking a sweat. Even I had fallen to my knees, unable to stand against the blast of her power.

Had she ever looked as beautiful and terrifying as she did standing there in the center, her hair twisting around her, her chin held high?

But I'd done nothing when the guards had shot her with a tranquilizer. I'd forced myself to remain still even as my teeth changed, as blood filled my mouth from the fangs catching my tongue, as my entire body hummed with a desire to rip apart anyone who dared touch her.

The desire overwhelmed me, and I wondered if I could resist it at all. I'd never felt that before, even when Knox had been in danger. That instinct inside me that roared in my ears terrified me.

Even now, an hour later, sitting on the top floor near the bridge to the North Tower, I couldn't calm myself. Where was she? Was she okay?

What would I do if our plan worked, but she didn't make it? Was there a fucking point of getting out if I ended up alone?

I leaned forward, my elbows on my knees, and tried to slow my breathing, to soothe the rage inside me. Maybe seeing Hera, even a glimpse, would calm it.

She'd done it before, eased my berserker, made it quiet with her touch. If I couldn't get it back under control, I'd do something to risk everything we'd planned.

A door opened, but it wasn't the person I wanted to see. Instead, Knox came up to me and took a seat to my left.

"You don't look so good," he said.

"You didn't see her go down," I muttered. "I doubt you'd be so calm if you had."

"Which was why we weren't supposed to be there," Knox pointed out.

"Fuck off. Like I was going to let her risk herself and not be there to help. What if the guards had gotten too rough? What if they'd tried to kill her?" I shook my head. "I wasn't going to just let that happen."

"You have it bad, don't you?"

I snorted. "No idea what you mean."

"Do you think if you keep saying that, it'll suddenly make it true?"

"It is true."

A tap on my hand made me drop my gaze to where Knox poked at me. "Your nails are shifted into claws. That only happens when you're on the edge."

"I'm a berserker—I'm always on edge."

"Yeah, but not like this. I have to wonder if you just don't recognize the feeling or if you're lying to yourself."

I wanted to tell him it wasn't true, but I couldn't. Maybe it was because of what I'd watched with Hera, but completely dismissing how I felt about her struck me as wrong. What if something happened? What if I never saw her again? Did I really want to pretend she meant nothing to me now?

"I should have done this part," I whispered. "I should have never let her take this risk."

"She isn't helpless. Despite how she looks sometimes, Hera is tough. She can do this."

I blew out a slow breath but nodded. I didn't know if I agreed or not, but I had no choice. We'd set the plan in motion, and we couldn't change it now. Hera would go to the North Tower. She'd have to take out the communications area there, then Wade would take care of the security system, I'd destroy the generators, and finally Knox would secure our exit.

I couldn't second guess anything because the plan required us all to do our parts. If we didn't, it would fail, and we'd all pay the price.

"You succeed last night?" I asked to try to distract myself.

He nodded. I'd expected a grimace, some sign of unhappiness as he recalled what he'd had to do to get the key. I'd known he had planned to meet Nisha, to go to the roof with her. I doubted she'd hand the key over out of the goodness of her own heart, after all.

However, none of that came. An almost serene smile crossed his lips.

Just before I could ask, the doors opened again, but this time it was what I'd hoped for. Or rather, what I'd waited for...

Hera lay on a gurney, her wrists bound together in mitts that covered her hands. Her head tilted listlessly to the side, her eyes closed, the drugs no doubt still keeping her knocked out.

I tightened my hands into fists, trying to ignore the roar of anger in my head, the desire to run over there. I could take out the guards who had her, steal her away, not let her go on with this insanity.

Then what?

I released my hands, ignoring the warm wetness from my nails digging into my own palms.

I had to let her go, had to trust her. All our lives depended on it.

So I watched as they took her through the doorway, across the bridge and to a place I couldn't follow.

I'd never prayed before, never saw a reason to, never expected, if there was some god out there, that he gave a damn about me. Still, I closed my eyes right then and begged whatever deity might be listening to watch over her. The most precious thing to me to me in this whole fucked-up world had just gone somewhere dangerous, somewhere I couldn't follow.

Don't let this be the end...

Chapter Seventeen

Hera

I woke with a gasp, bolting upright. I didn't know what had happened, where I was, but something inside me screamed *danger*.

My bare feet hit the hard floor, my body unsteady, my hands bound together. I glanced down to find them in cuffs with gloves that covered my hands. A fogginess in my head was far too familiar, and it took me a moment to realize the reason.

Right, I got shot with tranquilizers.

It meant that Kit's toxin no longer worked in my system, though that was probably for the best. No doubt the guards had taken me in without much damage because they'd knocked me out.

I peered around the unfamiliar room, frowning. Rather than a bed, only a thin pad that could barely pass as a mattress sat on the floor. No windows, no chairs, no other furniture filled the room. The door wasn't solid metal, though. Instead, it appeared to be glass, though I'd bet it was actually some sort of specialized plastic.

No way would they trust some basic glass to keep in shades.

I went to the door and peered out at a long hallway and another matching door across the way. More doors lined the hallway as far as I could see. How many there were, and how many had shades trapped inside, I couldn't guess.

I closed my eyes to listen.

Rustling came back, muffled steps farther down, but no speaking, no conversations, just movement. Then again, if each cell only held a single person in it, it made sense they wouldn't speak.

A face appeared before me, on the other side of the door, and I couldn't stop myself from stumbling backward. The man there grinned, his expression not in the least bit reassuring. He moved his lips, but a distorted sound came out.

It told me that the room must have some serious sound proofing. That was probably to prevent me from using my skills, to dampen sound waves and weaken me.

Still, I could catch the words. "Well, aren't you a lovely little bird? We don't normally get ones as pretty as you. By the time they get here, they're all pretty used up."

His words made me sick, but I refused to cower or look away.

His gaze moved to my throat, his smile widening. "They even took care of silencing you, huh? How kind. Makes our job a lot easier, though it makes you less useful. In fact, if I hadn't seen the videos of what you pulled in the cafeteria with my own two eyes, I would never have believed it."

"Quiet." A different voice had the man pulling to the side as if put in his place by that one word.

And here I thought I was done with the Warden…

She shooed the man away with a hard look—a warning no doubt—before she turned back to me. "I find that I have mixed feelings about you being here. On one hand, I had hoped to keep you in the main population. More freedom there could offer more opportunities for us both. See, keeping you here will force us to change you, to make you a part of our special programs. That necessitates we remove you from most of our official files and limits how much I can use you as a card against your parents. However, after what I saw you do, I'm rather excited to see how useful a tool you can be."

"What programs?" I signed in response.

"Don't bother." She waved me off. "I've never learned sign language. Honestly, I don't much care what you have to say. I've been Warden here for thirty years, and I've found that unless a shade is reporting to me about a mission, what they say rarely matters. However, I can guess what you're asking. You see, the North Tower is basically an entire lab. We take the worst of the worst here, and we make them useful."

She turned her head to the side and signaled to a guard. The door slid open.

"Before you get your hopes up," she said, "I'll warn you that while security was good in Larkwood, it is nothing compared to here. You will not leave your cell unless tests or jobs require it. When you do leave, should you cause additional trouble, we will have tranquilizers trained on you. In addition, we have speakers." She pointed inside the room, then also at small boxes on the walls of the hallway. "They have a sound ready to go. Should you do anything we don't like, they'll incapacitate you."

I narrowed my eyes, not trusting her a bit. While I'd heard of such a thing in the book Deacon had given me, I hadn't witnessed it. Besides, I'd proven myself stronger than normal sirens, able to do things others couldn't, so perhaps it wouldn't work on me anyway.

The Warden smiled as though she'd read my mind. "You don't believe it will work on you? Well, what better time than now to check?" She nodded down the hallway, toward a window that had a guard stationed behind more of that plastic.

A moment later, the world turned to static around me. I didn't even *hear* the sound that came from the speakers, but it hit me like a wave, shoving me under. It scratched over every one of my nerves like sandpaper, and I couldn't even string thoughts together.

As quickly as it happened, it went away. Or maybe it had taken minutes, and I just didn't realize it. I really had no idea. I found myself panting hard on the floor with no memory of when I'd fallen, of how I'd gotten there.

Above me the Warden stood, her expression just as pleased as I'd ever seen her. "It does work. Wonderful to know. Take that tiny taste as an example of what will happen should you ignore my rules, if you act up, if you consider using those powers of yours for anything other than what I allow. Do we understand one another?"

I wanted to argue, to tell her where she could shove it. However, a memory of the agony the sound had put me through made me nod slowly before forcing my body from the floor, the action harder with my hands bound and my head still foggy.

"I'm glad we understand one another. Follow me, please." She turned and walked without waiting to see if I'd follow.

The guards watched from the small room, but I saw no cameras. It was strange given how many were in the other areas of Larkwood. Then again, they probably didn't want any hard evidence on the sort of things that happened here.

That fact made me gulp as I followed the Warden.

We passed cell after cell, and whereas I'd thought before they might be empty, I was shocked to find the majority full.

"We take shades from the main buildings of Larkwood but also from elsewhere. While we house the most dangerous at Larkwood, other academies occasionally end up with shades they can't handle, or ones that might further our research, so they send them here," the Warden explained. "We have the expertise and facilities to take in and deal with the most difficult cases."

Inside one cell, I spotted a vampire, his eyes a bright red, a sure sign of bloodlust. He sat on a chair and rocked back and forth, his eyes locked on a spot on the wall. He didn't seem even close to sane.

As I passed the cells, I found more of the same. Person after person filled them, all with a crazed, frantic silence about them. They didn't pace like trapped animals attempting to escape. They had a violence about them, a tension that screamed dangerous, but they also seemed content with where they were.

Which made no sense. Could Larkwood have drugged them? Somehow broken their spirits?

I didn't know, but each step I took made me more and more uneasy.

"This floor houses the members of our Corrander Project. Consider these shades your new partners. You'll grow quite close over time as you work together."

Corrander? So it seemed they'd sent me to that project. As long as it was in the North Tower, that was all I really cared about.

"I know this might seem upsetting right now." The Warden paused at the far end of the hallway, at a closed door that had no window like the cells did. She turned to face me. "It may not be much of a consolation, but I can promise you won't be upset soon."

With those ominous words, the Warden ran her wrist past the sensor to open the door, then waited. Her meaning was clear enough. She wanted me to enter, and whatever had happened to those shades, whatever she wanted from me, rested in that room.

A desire to pull back overcame me, the same sort of fear a person would experience when they peered into a deep, dark cave, but I refused to give in. I had a plan to stick to, and whatever sat inside that room couldn't have been worse that what I'd already faced.

I forced myself forward, one slow step after another, into the dark room. The door shut behind me, leaving the Warden outside. I squinted, trying to peer into the dark room.

"A new toy," said a voice that struck me as soft yet hard. It threw me as I couldn't place it. It was a girl, but the high tone told me she was still rather young. Still, it lacked the uncertainty I would have expected from a girl of that age. It sounded grizzled, as if the girl had lived through hell and come out on top of it.

Light bathed the room, so bright I squinted against it as my eyes adjusted. When they did, when I could take in the room, I saw the one who spoke.

The girl appeared to be a teenager at most. She had long black hair that reached the middle of her back, and she wore a simple white sundress. She sat cross-legged on a stool in the center of the room, the menace surrounding her keeping my attention on her rather than anywhere else. The rest of the room, the furniture, the bed, the desks, none of it could pull my gaze from her.

Especially because of her eyes.

Pure black eyes stared at me.

* * * *

Deacon

I couldn't stop pacing, couldn't stop thinking. I'd worked out until my muscles hadn't wanted to move at all, until a fear I'd pass out drove me back to my room, but it hadn't helped. Nothing helped.

I'd showered, tried to distract myself with books, with trash tv, even tried a few beers to take the edge off.

Nothing worked.

Each time I stopped for a moment, my brain went right back to Hera, to the strike of her powers against me, to the accusations she'd thrown.

Had I really gotten it all wrong?

I'd thought we were…

Something.

I didn't know what it was, exactly, but it wasn't whatever she'd said. Had I been confused? Had she been using me all along? Was I just as stupid as I'd been before?

Had I really learned nothing over the past years?

The anger and frustration grew inside me until I couldn't handle it, when I twisted to throw the damned beer bottle against the wall. I chucked it, wanting to hear it shatter into a million pieces.

It didn't, though.

Instead, I found Kit standing inside my place, next to the door, holding the bottle in his hand.

The asshole had caught it. It reminded me why I hated him so much. Or rather, one of many reasons.

"The fuck are you doing here?" I asked.

"I seemed as though you could use a visit."

"Fuck off. I don't need some pep talk from you." By which I meant that he was one of the last people I needed in my business. I didn't need him to see my pain, to witness the way Hera had thrown me aside — both literally and figuratively in this case.

Kit poured the last of the beer into the sink, then put the bottle into the recycling as if he gave a damn about making a mess in my place. His calmness annoyed me, as it only made my lack of control all the more obvious.

I crossed my arms before I was tempted to do anything more and stared at him. "I've been here a long fucking time and you've never felt the need to stop by for a little chat before."

"You've never been thrown across the room by the woman you love before, either."

The words pierced me, more dangerous than Kit's claws, no doubt. I dropped my gaze, unable to look at him. "Clearly it wasn't love. Let's not pretend it's something it isn't. We aren't kids."

Kit's steps filled the room, and he took a seat in one of the kitchen table chairs. While the idea of him making himself at home annoyed me, I knew that wasn't his point. No doubt he sat to prove he hadn't come for some territorial battle, that he didn't want to play some dominance game.

And as much as I hated it, it helped. I pulled in a deep breath, then let it out slowly. "Why are you really here?"

"I can imagine how I'd feel in your place, and I suppose I don't like to see people in pain."

"I doubt you give a fuck about me."

He nodded, as if that were a given. "Fair point. Perhaps it is better to say that your upset would upset Hera, and I don't wish to see her hurt any more than can be helped."

"Given what happened, I really doubt she's all that worried."

"Then you truly are as stupid as people think."

And there went that bit of calm I'd found. I nailed Kit with a hard look, wanting to wrap my hands around his throat, to mess up his perfect suit, to watch blood stain his white shirt. He'd always walked around Larkwood as if different or better than the other shades. I wanted to beat that out of him. "I'm gonna give you one warning here—I'm not in the mood for this bullshit, not today."

"Then listen carefully and you will get me out of your hair sooner. You should know Hera well enough to read between the lines."

Hearing him mention her again snapped the leash on my temper. I went after him, even knowing it was stupid. Kit was a wendigo, one of the most dangerous things Larkwood had ever housed, and I doubted any of us had a real grasp on what he was capable of.

None of that mattered. Hell, there was even a part of me that figured if he turned me to dust, who the fuck cared? At least it would stop the pain in my chest.

"Don't talk about her," I snarled as I took him to the ground, my weight knocking him from the chair.

We hit the floor, but Kit did nothing, as though he didn't even notice. "Why not? We're both bound to her in our own ways."

"I'm not bound to anyone." I threw a punch, landing it on his cheek.

His head jerked to the side from the impact, but he made no noise, didn't seem to feel any pain. "So you're foaming at the mouth now because you don't give a damn?"

"She betrayed me!" I yelled the words, the truth torn from my throat. I went to nail him in the face again, wanting to break him, to take my anger out on him.

Except just before I made contact, his form shimmered. Instead of the flesh and blood face I'd aimed for, the bone of his other form, the head of a deer skull, appeared.

I snarled at the pain in my hand when I made contact, because bone didn't give the way a human face would have.

He threw me off as if I weighed nothing, then wrapped a hand around my throat after pinning me. It was one of those lessons I hated, one that felt like an adult dog reminding a puppy why the adult was in charge.

Not that it mattered to me all that much. I hadn't gone into this thinking I was on the same level as Kit. Strength wasn't the only thing that mattered.

"She didn't betray you," Kit said, his voice having dropped to his other one, the one from his wendigo form, but it didn't do anything to me.

"What would you call it, then? She said she was using me. She *attacked* me."

"And why do you think she did that?"

"Because I never knew her in the first place. Because I was so pathetic that I believed all her pretty lies."

Kit made a low sound as if disappointed before he released my throat and stood. He went back to his human form, and only the redness from my first hit showed on his face. "You aren't stupid, Deacon. If you were, I wouldn't be here. That means you are being willfully ignorant, choosing to believe what is not true simply because it is easier. Hera would protect anyone, even those who don't deserve it."

I wanted to argue, but Kit was right. I recalled the way she looked at the world, the way she tried to save everyone else.

Even me…

As soon as I thought that, I sighed and scrubbed my hands over my scalp. Hera had always been careful of me, never wanted me to take the blame for anything. It was why I'd never told her I'd taken the punishment for when she'd broken into the filing room, because I knew she'd blame herself.

"I've had a rough day. Could you just get to the point already?" I asked.

Kit straightened his clothing, fixing his tie and brushing off his pants. "We both know Hera has been setting up her own little plan, even if I don't know the details. Clearly she wanted to go to the North Tower."

"And she didn't give a fuck who she ran over to get there?"

"That is your pride speaking, not your brain. What would happen if Hera got herself into trouble again? Who would fall under suspicion?"

"Me," I admitted. Already, I'd been watched more closely, as if the Warden knew my loyalties might have changed. "If she got herself into trouble, I would be the likely person they'd think had helped her, especially after the last time she was thrown into solitary."

"And do you think she'd allow that? That she would accept you paying the price for her choices?"

As Kit's words hit me, my knees gave out. I all but collapsed backward into one of the kitchen chairs.

He was right.

Hera wasn't the type to betray someone, to crush them for her own wants. If she did what she'd done, it had been to help someone. In this case, me.

"She attacked me in public and said those things to paint me as a victim. She wanted to take the spotlight off me." How hadn't I seen that? Why did it take Kit explaining it to me for me to see it?

Because I didn't want to see it.

If I admitted the truth, it was worse. Before, I could be heartbroken and angry, but Hera was the bad person. No matter what happened, I didn't need to care, because she'd screwed me over. She didn't give a damn about me.

Now, though? Knowing the truth? Now I knew she'd done it for me, and now a different, far worse kind of pain ran through me.

"What the fuck is she thinking?" I asked, probably to myself more than Kit.

"That I can't say. As it turns out, she didn't let me in on her plan, either. All I can say is that she wanted to get to the North Tower, and she wanted to make sure you weren't blamed when she went."

"The North Tower…" I couldn't stop the tremble in my voice as I recalled that place, as I remembered the years of pain and terror I'd spent there. It wasn't somewhere I'd ever wanted her to end up, and now that she was there?

I saw no way to help her. I couldn't fix this. I was stuck here with no path forward.

"So what now?" I asked.

Kit set a hand on my shoulder and squeezed. "Now we trust Hera. We believe she has a plan, that she will come out on top, that not even the North Tower is enough to take her out."

"And if we're wrong?"

Kit let go of me and headed for the door. I didn't think he'd answer at first, but his voice floated over his shoulder when he reached the exit. "I suspect Larkwood isn't ready for the hell that will rain down if Hera does not return safely."

And there was one thing I could agree with him on.

Chapter Eighteen

Hera

Fear froze me in place as I stared at the young girl, as I struggled not to fall into the abyss that was her eyes. It was crazy how much it reminded me of Kit, and it also reminded me how much I didn't want to meet another wendigo. Kit's power was terrifying, but I trusted him not to use it against me. Knowing someone could do those things who I didn't trust was a whole different story.

The girl had long, straight black hair that hung down around her face and made her black eyes even more intimidating. Her pale skin had a number of moles, though the sickly pallor made me suspect she never went outside. I had to guess she was in her teens somewhere, though I wasn't sure. Besides, wendigos didn't age normally, according to Kit, so I couldn't guess her actual age.

She tilted her head as she watched me. "It's gotten tiresome to make so many toys. So many voices in my head…"

I lifted my hands before realizing there was no chance that she'd understand sign language. It wasn't a language people learned without reason.

"Most people scream or beg by now, but you're still silent. Why?"

I pointed at the scar at my throat.

She got off the chair, her motions strangely fluid as she came closer. She leaned down, bringing her face close to my throat.

Which I *really* didn't like. I'd gotten a glimpse of the danger Kit could present before, but never like this. Then again, Kit was old enough to have learned to hide it, perhaps, whereas this girl was too young to have learned.

Or perhaps she didn't care to learn.

So exposing my throat to her seemed all sorts of bad, but I didn't have many choices. She didn't strike me as the type who would back off just because she made me uncomfortable.

"They stole your voice?" She frowned as she brought her fingers to the scar, touching it gently. "That is unforgivable. Someone should never declaw monsters. They must be leashed or destroyed at times, but they should not be mutilated. That is cruel."

The girl shook her head and stepped backward, as if what I'd suffered were nothing but a sad inconvenience. "I have to wonder why you're here, though. The toys I make are always strong, always useful. You must be a siren, right? But a siren without her voice would be a useless toy, like a sword with no blade." Her gaze moved to my hands. "Oh, but you're bound, aren't you? If you're bound, you must have talents beyond your voice or there would be no reason to bind your hands."

The way she spoke was odd, as if she were used to working through issues on her own, as if she didn't know how to handle conversations that went both ways. Then again, all of her struck me as strange.

Her room was clearly set up to live in, meaning she was as trapped here as the rest of us. I'd seen how Larkwood treated shades, and even those they gave more trust to were still prisoners.

There was a childishness to the room, yet at the same time, she didn't strike me as a child. Just how long had she been locked up here? Perhaps she was an unfortunate soul who changed very young, like Wade had, and found herself trapped here most of her life?

The idea of that made me want to sit her down, to reassure her. She might be a terrifying shade capable of so much damage, but she was also a child.

Still, the girl waved toward a table in the room. "Sit."

I didn't at first, and her voice shifted, dropping like I'd heard from Kit before. Except, when she tried it this time, nothing happened.

No, that wasn't quite right. I felt a pull, but it wasn't like it was from Kit. It wasn't as strong, as if I knew I was supposed to obey but didn't need to.

She took a step back, her eyes widening. She repeated the command, but when it worked no better than the first time, she moved back another step. "Why didn't that work?" Her tone came out confused and frightened. "It *always* works." She dropped her gaze, her lips moving as she spoke to herself. "It has always worked. Sirens shouldn't be special, shouldn't be able to resist. Could she be unique? I sense higher source levels than usual, but nothing beyond that. Perhaps she's had training to resist? Perhaps they sent her in to test me? To see if I can still manage? Perhaps they worry I've lost my touch? Have I? I don't think so…"

I shrugged, trying to tell her I didn't understand either, before I took a seat where she'd indicated willingly. I had a feeling annoying her wouldn't go well for me.

She narrowed her eyes, but took a seat across from me.

I lifted my hand and positioned it as if holding a pencil, then made a writing motion.

She shook her head. "That wouldn't work. I can't read."

At her age?

The theory that she'd been locked up here for a very long time hit me again, and a stinging in my chest said I didn't care for it. She might be the most dangerous thing to me at the moment, but that didn't mean I liked the idea of anyone suffering, especially a child who had no choice.

People easily twisted into whatever their environment made them into. Even the most loving, sweet person could turn into a monster if put into a situation where that was the only way to survive. It was even truer with children, who had less life experience to anchor them into whatever they wanted to be.

Just look at how much I've changed already…

"They don't like when I talk to the toys much, but I do it anyway, sometimes to pass the time."

I shrugged and lifted my hands to ask why.

"They said it is like talking to one's food. It only makes the job harder. Is it strange that the first toy I've really wanted to speak to can't speak back?" She let out a soft laugh, as if fate were cruel and laughing was the only response a person could have. "Perhaps they're right."

She leaned in, staring into my eyes, and that was when I experienced the full wash of her power. The command in her voice had been a whisper against my defenses, but her eyes pulled me into that dark void I'd seen inside Kit. It yanked me beneath it, made me unable to surface again.

I found myself in darkness, in a black, endless shadow. I spun around, finding nothing around, having no idea where I was.

"We can speak privately now." The girl's voice had me turning again to find her behind me.

But not exactly. It had the same feeling as when I saw Kit in my dreams, a knowledge that it wasn't exactly real, that we weren't there. "Where are we?" Just as before, my voice left my lips this time, telling me again this wasn't the real world.

The corner of her lips on one side tilted up. "You have a lovely voice. It is a shame it was taken from you. As for where we are, it isn't anywhere, really. We are still there, in that room, but we can communicate here. Think of it as the emptiness inside me, the endless hunger where we can talk privately."

"What do you want with me? What do you mean by toy?"

"You saw the others that you passed when you came here, didn't you? Those are the toys. They are empty vessels to be used for the betterment of the world. They are monsters on leashes."

"I don't understand."

"You don't?" She frowned, as if surprised and disappointed at having to repeat herself or explain. "I can remove what they are, their will, their memories, everything that makes them who they are. I consume it until they are docile, until they are obedient. They become toys, just shells to be moved about and played with, who follow only the order of the Warden."

"How does that better the world?" I pushed the question out past the fear that threatened to lock my throat down. Of all the things I'd suffered through in Larkwood, the idea of losing myself ranked as the most terrifying. My past slipping away, not being who I was anymore, that was a nightmare beyond anything I'd considered before.

"We are monsters," she said, though her words came out softer, as if she'd heard them so many times that she knew them by heart. "We destroy the world. We are unnatural and we do not belong here. However, we are also stronger than we should be. That means creating toys to keep the balance is necessary."

The self-hatred in her voice broke my heart. I'd heard it before, from Wade, from Knox, but never like this. I'd heard it from people who had other voices in their heads, who had a life before turning into shades. This girl spoke with the certainty of someone who had learned nothing else, as if she'd lived her entire life hearing only that she was evil.

"You're not a monster," I said.

"Of course I am. We all are. How can you see what we do and not realize that? How can you see the damage shades can inflict and not realize we don't belong here? That we are unnatural?" She paused, her gaze moving away as if she were thinking. "I can *feel* the tears through which source flows. Did you know that? You might feel them too, if you learned to, but I can feel them all the time. I've heard whispers through them, and it makes me wonder...what is on the other side? Is that where we belong? Perhaps we are creatures that are natural to the other side of the tears but somehow end up here?"

I got the sense that she didn't expect an answer, and I really didn't have one for her. I'd never heard that, never considered there might be something beyond our realm. Where source came from? How it leaked in through tears? How those tears were made? Those things were never spoken about, they were ignored and pushed aside as just facts of life.

It was like wondering if life existed on another planet. The question was beyond me and would never have any meaningful effect on me, thus I ignore it.

"I don't know," I admitted. "I came to Larkwood as soon as I changed, so I don't know anything about that."

"So you lived outside of these walls before?" She leaned forward, as if drawn by my answer.

"I was nineteen when I changed, so I lived most of my life with my parents."

A sad longing crossed her features, and it told me what she didn't need to say. She'd been raised here, without a family, without access to anything else.

It made me want to save her, made me hope she could escape as well.

After a moment, she shook her head. "I guess we're about out of time."

I stepped backward and shook my head. "You don't have to do this. I want to help, to save people."

"There are many ways to save others. One is to ensure that we can't harm others. That's why I do this. It won't hurt, and you wouldn't remember if it did, anyway. Perhaps you should be grateful, because when

I finish, you won't remember what you've lost, who you were. All the pain in your life will go away and you won't have to carry it anymore. You will be happy to follow orders, won't have to worry or be sad or lonely ever again. That is a gift that few are lucky enough to receive."

The word lonely stuck out. No doubt she best identified with that feeling. Her tone even had an odd kindness, as if erasing that loneliness mattered to her.

She moved so fast that I couldn't retreat, couldn't do anything. She wrapped her hand around my throat, the skin shifting to a familiar form. It elongated, thinned, and had long claws at the tips of each finger. It was what I'd seen so many times from Kit.

Her face changed, shimmering until a skull stared at me instead of her young face. Her voice was disembodied and darker when she spoke again. "Don't fight—there's no point to it. Just let everything you were pour out of you, become an empty shell. It'll happen either way, but it will be easier on you if you don't struggle."

A darkness slipped into me, her eyes drawing me deeper down. Except, as soon as it happened, something else slid through me.

I recognized the sensation. I even heard a dark growl, and a whispered, *mine* in my head.

The girl yanked backward, shifting back to her human form as if startled. "What was that?" She stared at me as if I'd done something, as if I had suddenly become dangerous. "You're already bound, aren't you?"

I nodded as I realized what she meant.

"So there is another like me? I'm not alone?"

"His name is Kit," I told her. "He's just like you are."

"But you aren't a toy. Why would he bind you but not make you into a toy?"

"He bound me to protect me," I explained.

"But why not consume you? Why help you but allow you to go about on your own? It makes no sense..."

I didn't know how to answer her, but I had to try. "If I were a toy, I couldn't talk to him. He'd be alone again."

She frowned, but seemed to be unwilling to break eye contact, as if afraid to look away. "I could break that bond, you know? He's powerful, much more powerful than I am, but he isn't here. I could consume everything inside you, turn you into a shell, and snap the bond you have to him, make you mine." After that, she lowered her voice, again seeming to speak to herself. "But then he might come after me. I couldn't stand against him, not from what I felt, and so if I damage his toy, he might kill me." She pressed her lips together, as if arguing with herself. "Then again, maybe he'll find me if I do... I could see another like me, and if I die? Maybe he'll make me a toy and I won't have to question or feel lonely anymore..."

I shook my head. "You don't need to do that. I'll tell him about you, then you can meet him. You don't need to bind me."

She tilted her head, looking almost like a confused dog. "I could break the bond, but that feels...wrong? Like a line I'm not supposed to cross. How strange. Is this old instinct? Something inside me that warns that I shouldn't do that?" After a moment, she shook her head. "I will leave you as you are for now..."

"Thank you," I answered, amazed I could get anything out at all given how fast my heart raced.

"It usually takes a few times before toys lose all their fight, before all parts of them are consumed, so the guards won't expect you to be like the others just yet. Still, keep this between us for now."

I nodded. "Of course. I won't say a word."

"You said his name was Kit, right?" There was a question in those words, something beneath it where she wanted to know more but perhaps didn't know what to ask.

"Yeah. He's sort of like a teacher, helping other shades, teaching them to use their skills."

"He helps people?"

"He taught me to use my powers, and he tries to protect whoever he can." Saying that lifted a weight from me, made me realize the truth of it. Even if Kit made choices I didn't agree with, even if he could be shady, even if he seemed like someone I couldn't fully understand, he also did whatever he could to help others.

"I didn't realize…" She paused, her expression tight as if she had trouble understanding something important. Then again, it seemed she thought she was alone in the world. Finding out she wasn't would be a shock.

"I know when he finds out that there is another like him, he'll be happy. No one wants to be alone, to be the only of their type, and he's never met another like him."

She gave me a slight smile, one full of hesitation. It almost made me wonder if she ever smiled, if she ever had anything to smile about. "I think I would like to meet him." The smile fell. "Not that that is likely possible, I suppose. Though, life for us is long, so who knows? Now, it is time for you to go back."

"And what happens next?"

"Shades require a few days; rest for each process to take effect. After that, you would be brought back to me for another pass. It takes anywhere from three to ten attempts to fully consume a shade's being. The more powerful the shade, the more attempts it takes."

"What will you do next time?"

"I don't know yet. Perhaps I'll let you go again, or perhaps I'll realize it's time to do as I'm commanded. I supposed we'll only know when it happens."

That response didn't reassure me, but I understood it. It was all she could offer.

"We are done. You'll return to your body, to the physical world, and they'll take you back to your cell."

"Wait. What's your name? I didn't get to ask."

She blinked slowly, as if she hadn't been asked that before. "They call me Corrander One."

"No, not what *they* call you, but what is *your* name?"

She frowned. It didn't seem she was unwilling to say, more that my question confused her, as if she thought back to find an answer.

When she spoke, her voice came out low, as if she were speaking to herself again. "I don't know, but I remember a name, one whispered to me in my dreams. I think it's mine, or it was once. Or perhaps loneliness will curse a person until they create the things they crave the most."

"What is it?"

The familiar black eyes locked with mine when she answered, my chest tightening as the truth became obvious, as it all came together.

"Lilianna."

Which meant…this girl was Kit's daughter.

* * * *

Hours later, back in my cell, I struggled to decide if I should send a message to Kit about his daughter. I wanted to, and he deserved to know, but was now really the time?

Too much depended on our plan. What if Kit did something foolish when he found out? What if he couldn't pass the message to Wade, then? What if his reaction caused a change in security that ruined the rest of our plan?

I would tell him, of course, but not until after we finished our plan. I'd make sure he knew, but with any luck, he'd be free along with her after the escape. With all the security measures down, every shade in Larkwood would have the chance to escape.

I sent up a silent apology for keeping it from him for now.

Pushing the thought aside, I focused instead on the door. They didn't have guards here the way Larkwood did, not ones who patrolled the hallways. It was more like Medical, where they only used guards when moving shades. The rest of the time, the shades were locked up, so there wasn't a point.

That gave me a good chance to move around without drawing any attention.

I took a deep breath, then held my hands out. The cuffs were annoying, but not all that troublesome. They'd put them on as if I had claws that needed to be covered. The way I used my powers, however, meant the cuffs didn't do much to stop me. The false sense of security benefited me.

When I got to communications, I could probably get them off. I didn't want to yet in case it tripped an alarm. For all I knew, they had sensors which would detect sounds large enough to cause damage.

I snapped my fingers, then twisted the sound and sent it into the door lock. It clicked and flashed green, opening for me with ease. The lights were lower, signaling nighttime. I doubted lowering the lights had anything to do with our comfort and was likely only because too much light would affect anybody and throw off hormones. I doubted they gave a damn about the wellbeing or happiness of the shades beyond their usefulness.

The darkness helped, though. It would allow me to move with less chance of getting caught.

I crept from my cell and headed in the opposite direction from Lilianna's room. They'd brought me here unconscious, which meant I didn't know the layout beyond what Deacon had told me, and his information was quite a bit out of date. Still, if I couldn't go one way, the other only made sense.

I passed cells, but the shades inside them didn't take notice of me. There were so many types, so many shades that sat there as if not aware or alive. They acted like the toys Lilianna called them.

I paused after moving past one, then went back. Inside sat a shade I recognized. It was the dragon shifter whose neck Kit had broken, Gerald. He didn't sit in the room but paced. So far, he was the only one I'd seen moving at all.

I knocked on the door to get his attention.

He turned his head toward me, but he wasn't the boy I'd seen before, the frightened one who had pled with Kit for help. I hadn't understood Kit's actions before, but now, after knowing what the North Tower really was, I struggled to condemn Kit as I once had.

If it was between dying painlessly as myself or living on as an empty shell?

I could see how death could be a kinder choice.

His eyes moved to me but held no recognition. It was as if he didn't remember me, didn't remember anything. He looked at me instead like prey, as if he considered just how to kill me.

It wasn't out of anger, but rather reminded me of a wild animal, one who killed because it was what they did rather than out of any actual malice. That frightened me even more.

I swallowed hard at the look, but he blinked right after. Some sanity returned to his eyes. It made me wonder just how many times he'd had Lilianna consume parts of him. How much of him was still left?

"I saw you before," he said, his voice muffled and rough.

I nodded and set my hand on the door. It wasn't much, but I wanted him to have some comfort, to feel as though he wasn't abandoned.

He blinked then set his hand on the door as well, on the other side as mine. "You need to get out of here. They'll turn you into something else, something evil and empty." His voice wavered, full of fear. It was so different from the way he'd acted moments before.

It seemed he still held a speck of himself.

I pointed at the door, mimed it opening, then held up a single finger. I wanted him to understand that I would let him out, but he had to wait a little longer.

He shook his head. "You can't. You can't let anyone here go, not even me. We aren't who we were. You don't know what we'll do if we get out. If you can, kill us all. Don't open the doors here, just set off the emergency overrides to flood the cells with poison." His voice trembled with terror. He meant every word — he'd rather I kill them all rather than let him out.

I couldn't do that, though. They were alive. Maybe I could find a way to help them, to get them to remember who they had once been. Even if there wasn't, I couldn't just murder unarmed and trapped people. I shook my head, trying to tell him I wouldn't do that.

He came closer and rested his forehead against the door. "You don't understand, you haven't *felt* everything you are draining out of you. The things I've already done, the blood I've already spilled for them, I don't want to carry those memories anymore. I'd rather die than let them use me anymore. If I get out, I'll kill you, too. If I'm free, I'll slaughter every shade I see without mercy just like they've trained us to." As he spoke, his voice dropped and slowed.

He curled his hand, and a high pitch screeching sound drew my attention. His hand had shifted, and he dug his claws into the door. Despite how strong it had to be, he managed to leave deep grooves in it. The fearful expression he'd had melted away until it was the blank expression he'd had when I'd first seen him returned. He no longer recognized me, no longer saw me as a person.

Just as quickly, he threw himself against the door, as if he could barrel through it and at me.

I stumbled backward just as his body shifted, changing into his other form. It was as if he were proving his point, making sure I understood that if I let them out, they'd not run. They'd kill every shade they could find because that was what they'd been programmed to do.

I rushed down the hallway, away from the horrible sounds he made, from the memory of that emptiness in his eyes, from the future I nearly shared in. At the far end, I found an elevator. I hit the button for floor three, praying that Deacon's information was still good, that the layout was still the same.

I went down the hallway after the elevator stopped, pausing at the first door to the left. After popping the lock on that door as well, I entered it to find a room full of servers and lights and cables running between it all.

Which meant that I'd found the communications room.

I took a deep breath, then sent my message to Kit, only able to hope it reached him. "*It's time.*"

Chapter Nineteen

Wade

I didn't mind Kit in general, but he made for boring company.

Well, in a way. I enjoyed harassing him, given how buttoned up he behaved, but he rarely gave me enough of a reaction to make it worth the effort. He worked better as a lightning rod, as someone I could mock with others around rather than just us. I needed an audience to really get into it.

However, given I stayed calm better than Knox or Brax, it made sense for me to wait for Hera's message. The other two might end up getting into it with Kit, whereas I could hold my tongue when needed.

Kit blinked slowly, going unnaturally still. The change in his expression told me something had happened.

"Was that her?" I asked.

Kit turned and looked toward me, as if just remembering I was there. "She said, '*It's time.*' What does that mean?"

I hopped to my feet. If she just said that, it meant we had ten minutes until showtime. Ten minutes until we reached the point of no return, when we couldn't stop what was going to happen.

I headed for the door, but Kit slid in front of me. When had the quick bastard even moved?

"What are you all up to? I knew it wasn't anything good, but that the way you're rushing out like this says whatever you're doing is serious and time-sensitive." Kit sure had the presence of someone dangerous. Even a look from him made me want to take a few big steps backward. I forced myself not to, though. He didn't need the ego boost of knowing he intimidated even me.

"Sorry, buddy, trade secrets. If you'll just excuse me…" I tried to move past him, but he again placed himself between me and the door.

"Tell me what is happening," he said, his voice low. Was he trying to command me?

It didn't seem to work. Maybe because I was a void? Sometimes powers didn't work on me, as if my skills made them useless immediately.

"Not happening," I said with a shrug. "Hera asked you for help and you agreed, remember?"

"That was before the look on your face or before I saw Brax and Knox sitting just outside the elevator, waiting for word. Please tell me you aren't all stupid enough to plan some sort of escape? I let this go because I assumed you would never come up with an actual workable plan and would realize the futility of trying, but it seems I overestimated your intelligence. This isn't a movie, where you all plan a magical heist that works and allows you to go live out your days on a beach somewhere."

I moved my gaze past him, the delay a problem. "If you give a damn about Hera, you need to let me go."

"I want to help her."

"Then let me leave. Like you guessed, we're on a timer here. If I don't do my part, Hera will be the one to suffer. Hell, she might even die." The last word stuck in my throat, but I forced myself to admit it. "She's in the North Tower, and if you don't let me go, she won't ever make it back."

This wasn't a game. If we failed, none of us would see tomorrow.

Doubt showed on Kit's face, but he didn't seem willing to give in just yet. "Then let me help."

But I couldn't trust him, and I didn't have time to argue with him anymore.

"Please, don't hate me in the morning," I muttered before yanking off one of my gloves and setting my hand on his cheek.

The feeling of his power flowing into me was easily the worst thing I'd ever experienced. Perhaps I'd gotten used to doing this with Hera, with Knox, where it didn't hurt. No, that wasn't it. This was on a level I'd never felt before. The power I stole from Kit *hurt*. It didn't burn, but rather froze, like the deepest part of the ocean had suddenly rushed through my veins.

Still, I didn't let go. He collapsed to his knees as I pulled as much of his power as I could. The last thing I wanted was to risk him recovering too fast and coming after me. I only got one shot at incapacitating a man like Kit. If I failed, he wouldn't give me a second.

"Sorry," I said. "But this is too important. You'll understand if it all goes well. And don't you dare get yourself killed—I hate to see Hera cry."

Kit collapsed to the ground, panting hard as if drawing breath had become difficult. I let him fall, trying to ignore the pain from the way his power scratched at the inside of my body. It was like it wanted to escape, to get back to Kit. How did he keep this much power inside of him? How did it not destroy him?

This forced me to respect and fear him all over again.

Still, I didn't have the time to think about it. I took off, leaving his room and running down the hallway. Outside the elevator, Knox and Brax waited. A nod from me had them heading off in opposite directions for their own tasks.

For me, I had to get to the server room and start the virus. If we didn't get this done in the right order, all was lost.

And I'd come too far, gained too much to let it all go now.

* * * *

Brax

I stood outside the line of sight of the cameras as I watched the door to the generator room. The light on the lock remained red, which forced me to wait.

I'd memorized the plan, knew the steps that should happen. Still, having to wait to see if it all worked tortured me.

I couldn't do anything until Wade started the virus, until he unlocked all the doors and threw the false alarm. If I took out the power before that, the doors would remain locked. As soon as he did that, Hera needed to take down the communications, as well.

We had it all perfectly planned, but a single fuck-up could throw it into chaos.

Trust was something I had little of, but here I was, forced to trust Wade and Hera to take care of their parts.

What would I do if that light never turned green? What if they failed, and I never saw Hera again? What if this little bit of happiness I'd somehow found ended so soon? Could I just walk away? Go back to my old life?

I shook my head.

It wasn't possible. Hera had made me want more, made me believe I could have more. This was all her fault.

I let out an angry sigh. Berserkers were the first into a fight. Waiting wasn't something we did well, yet here I stood. I doubted I'd do it for anyone else.

But Hera had shown me a taste of a future, that I could actually protect Knox, that there was more to my life than just surviving Larkwood.

I glanced toward the North Tower, wondering how she was. Hera had sent the message to Kit, which meant she lived at least, and that she'd arrived in communications. I held on to that, tried to let it calm me.

The red signal on the door flickered to green, and the lights around the camera went dark. That meant Wade had managed his job.

Now I'm up.

I went forward, opening the door to get my first look at the generators. They sat in rows, along with batteries that held the charge from the solar panels. Larkwood had prepared for blackouts, for anything other than a pissed-off berserker.

Then again, no one could really prepare for a pissed-off berserker.

I gave myself over to that side of me, to my anger, to my fear for Hera, for Knox, even for Wade. After so long holding back, fearing this part of myself, controlling it, I gave in fully.

The roar I released as my body shifted would have chilled the blood of any person, but for me? It sounded like home, like a long-lost friend.

My head clouded, my thoughts turning simple, as I held on to the only things that matter.

Destroy the generators.

Protect my mate.

* * * *

Hera

Taking out the communications servers had turned out easier than expected. The second the lock flickered to green, proving Wade had released the virus, I unleashed a blast of my powers. It only took a minute until the room filled with smoke and darkness, every bit of technology in there in pieces. Right after, I directed a smaller wave of my power at my cuffs, popping the metal around my wrists so they fell to the floor.

Just after that, the lights went out, plunging the room into darkness.

I rushed from the room and headed for the stairs. With the power out, I couldn't use the elevators. I pushed the door open for the stairway when a roar echoed through the space. It wasn't from close to me but still shook the walls.

It had to be one of the Corrander shades, and I couldn't stop the fear that swamped me at it. I recalled their vacant gazes and Gerald's warning.

I pushed myself, rushing up the stairs as fast as I could. I needed to get across the bridge and to our rally point. I needed to warn Brax and the others about what was coming, about what I'd released.

My legs burned, but I didn't let it slow me. I took the stairs two steps at a time, hauling myself up as fast as I could. When I reached the top floor, more sounds came from beneath me, as if others had entered the stairway. Voices of guards yelled in confusion, and the inhuman sounds of shades, full of violence, followed me.

I went through the stairway door at the top floor, then rushed toward the bridge. The top floor sat empty, a near copy of the ones on the other floors, with large glass windows. It even had the benches along the sides, but I had to guess it was for the scientists and staff since no shades got to walk around.

The other buildings remained dark, telling me Brax had successfully taken out all the power. Because of the isolation of Larkwood, even outside the walls sat only darkness as far as I could see. It was eerie, but I didn't have time to dwell. I pushed myself forward, toward the bridge, ignoring the burning in my legs and the way my bare feet ached from the run.

When I reached the door that usually kept the North Tower closed from the main building, the door to the stairwell slammed open.

No, it didn't slam open—It broke, shattering out. A shade I didn't recognize stood there, his eyes empty.

So this is one of Lilianna's toys?

I stepped backward, afraid to take my eyes off him. The shade was a man who appeared in his forties. He shimmered, with other forms swirling around him like ghosts.

He held his hands out, palms up, not smiling or showing even signs of anger. It was as if he were just driven forward out of a desire of someone else's.

Which did not reassure me. If someone was angry, if they wanted something, I could negotiate with them. If they acted only on the orders of someone else, if only the commands of another mattered to them, then I couldn't talk them out of it.

I backed away, then lifted my hands and shoved a wave of my power toward him. He lifted his arms and somehow blocked it, as if he'd created a knife that split the wave around him.

I swallowed hard as he advanced, those other forms around him catching my attention as much as he did. They appeared like spirits, and when he shot a hand toward me, one of them rushed forward.

I tried to jerk out of the way, but I couldn't avoid it. The place the apparition struck me, when it passed through me, felt as though something pulled all my energy from me. I gasped and stumbled against the glass wall of the bridge. The spirit retreated, returning to the man.

Did it just give him whatever it had stolen from me?

The man shuddered, and when he opened his eyes again, they shone brighter, as if a flashlight were directed through them.

Which meant that not only couldn't I hurt him but he'd grow more powerful each time I weakened.

I recalled what Gerald had told me, that they were monsters, that they had nothing left inside them.

Lilianna's words came back to me as well, how she'd turned them into toys with no will of their own beyond what the Warden wanted. They were shade killers, plain and simple.

I couldn't talk my way out of this, couldn't get him to understand. I continued to back away, holding on to the wall since my body still dragged.

I reached the end of the bridge, but the man advanced slowly, as if in no hurry. He felt like the passing of time, something steady and impossible to stop.

But if I let this go on, he'd win. I'd keep losing energy until I couldn't fight anymore, until he caught me. I'd fall here, if I was lucky, or get taken back to the North Tower if I wasn't. I pictured Wade's mischievous smirk, Brax's scowl and Knox's gentle touches. I thought about how Deacon held me so tightly when we'd fallen asleep together, and the way Kit looked at me as if I mattered.

If I let this man kill me, that all ended for me. I'd never see them again.

And that was worth fighting for, worth lashing out for.

I clapped my hands, then twisted those sound waves, turning them, forcing them to multiply.

The man lifted his arm in front of him again, no doubt expecting me to send it at him.

He was wrong, though. I made countless mistakes, but I didn't like to make the same one twice.

I released the power, using every bit of it I could, but I didn't direct it toward him. Instead, I sent it down toward the supports that held up the bridge.

The moment he realized what I'd done, he pulled backward. It was too late, though, given he stood at the center of the bridge. The glass shattered, and the metal groaned before giving way from the strength of the power I released.

I stumbled, the building shaking as the bridge collapsed before me. The debris fell, crashing down, and my feet slipped. I tried to catch the side of the building, to keep myself from following the bridge and that man down, but there was nothing to hold on to.

I had a split second of anger that after everything I'd done to get here, it would end like this. I wouldn't get that future I'd wanted, wouldn't see how much closer we could get.

Of course, at least I'd done what I needed to. I could only hope that the others escaped without me, that they didn't wait or get themselves caught. If I'd taken down Larkwood, if I freed the men I loved from this hell, then no matter what happened to me, it was all worth it.

Just as I accepted it, however, something pulled hard on the back of my shirt, yanking me away from the ledge and from certain death.

Wade

After spending most of my life in a place like Larkwood, how could I still experience new levels of fear like this? I had faced off against the worst of the worst, had put a wendigo on his back not that long ago, and none of that had scared me.

However, seeing Hera standing on that edge, the wind whipping through her hair, and watching as she started to go over had spawned a fear inside me I'd never known I was capable of.

If I'd been seconds later, I'd have missed her. If I hadn't come straight here, if anything had slowed me down, I wouldn't have been able to reach her, wouldn't have been able to wrap my fingers in her shirt and yanked her backward, to safety.

I pulled her hard enough that she tumbled against me, taking us both down. She twisted—probably just as scared about whoever had grabbed her—but she stilled when she locked eyes with me.

She put her hands on my cheeks, pulled me closer and pressed her lips to mine. The kiss was wild and deep, as if she needed to reassure herself that one or both of us were still alive. Her lips were heated and aggressive, so unlike how she normally acted. She was normally careful not to push, not to pressure me, yet she kissed me now as if she were starved for me.

And I couldn't not return the kiss.

A sound behind us made her break away to look over her shoulder. Across the wide, empty expanse between this building and the North Tower stood others, staring as if they couldn't figure out how to pass.

They weren't guards, but they were also not friendly. I could sense that even from this distance. Them being shades didn't change anything.

I didn't care what someone was, if they meant harm to Hera or me, I'd do whatever it took to protect us.

Hera got to her feet, her motions slow. I didn't see any physical injuries, but that didn't mean she wasn't suffering from whatever had happened in the North Tower.

"As much as I'd love to sit here and keep going—I mean, I obviously enjoy an audience," I said as I stood, "now might not be the time. We don't need you helpless."

She stared at me, that moment of exasperation possibly better than the kiss. After that, though, she smiled and nodded. *"Let's get out of here."*

And that sounded like a damn good plan.

* * * *

Knox

I held my hands in fists, frustration eating away at me. I hated having to stand back and wait with no information about what was happening.

Darkness covered Larkwood, with only red emergency lights to give the slightest ability to see. I stood there, at our rally point, alone. My job had been to secure an escape route, which meant I had to wait *here* until the others arrived.

Had Hera made it back? Was Wade safe? Had Brax escaped after destroying the generators? I knew they'd all completed their parts of the plan, but that didn't mean they'd survive to get to the rally point.

An entire school full of angry, free shades clashed with terrified and trigger-happy guards. It would only take one stray bullet to take out Wade or Hera.

Brax was tougher than that, but not indestructible.

A huge body appeared at the far end of the hallway, nothing more than a silhouette in the darkness. Red eyes flashed, but I knew they weren't from the lights.

I'd rarely come face-to-face with Brax's berserker like this. I'd asked him once what it felt like, and he'd admitted he didn't remember all of it. Part of his brain turned off and he operated on instinct and basic thoughts. That also made him so dangerous, because he wasn't fully himself. It was easy to go too far, to mistake friend for foe.

Not that I feared him. If he recognized one person, it would be me.

"Brax," I said, drawing his gaze to me.

He came forward, his movements not at all human-like. He slumped forward to fit in the room, having grown so much larger than usual. When he reached me, he crouched down to stare at my face.

It was like getting sniffed by a wolf and hoping they liked what they smelled.

He huffed, the hot air blowing across my face, but I recognized that as relief. It seemed he'd recognized me, that he was happy enough I was unharmed.

His skin had taken on a reddish tint, but even in the darkness, I could tell that wasn't the only red on him. Instead, slick maroon dripped from him.

I highly doubted that much of that was his blood.

I swallowed hard at the reminder of just how dangerous he was. It didn't scare me. In fact, it was one of the few times I found myself thankful for that. Given the screams and roars that echoed through the building, the chaos surrounding us, this side of him would come in handy.

He turned his gaze around as if searching.

"They aren't here yet," I told him. The plan was that if anyone didn't show up in time, anyone else would still go. We'd all gone into it knowing we might not all make it, but standing there in that moment made that promise far heavier.

Accepting something in the hypothetical was easy, but leaving without Hera and Wade in reality felt impossible.

The building shook, as if something had exploded, and it tossed me toward the wall. I kept myself upright, then stared at Brax, a question there.

Were we going to leave the others? Would we prioritize our own lives and freedom over Wade and Hera? A year ago, I would have said absolutely, but a lot had happened since then.

Brax moved his gaze behind him and huffed again, his answer clear.

"All right," I said. "Let's go gather the trouble-makers."

Chapter Twenty

Hera

I held my trembling hands out in front of me, so tired that I couldn't believe I remained on my feet. I wouldn't have if Wade hadn't stood beside me.

If I had done this alone, I probably would have given up. Each floor we went through, each hallway housed something else.

And everything wanted to kill us.

The shades, the guards, all of them attacked us on sight. I doubted it was just us, either. Larkwood had devolved into so much chaos that violence was all it knew. It wanted to tear itself apart at the seams, the anger and pain from so many years exploding out.

I'd used my powers to put down person after person, knocking them aside, trying to clear us a path. I knew it was too late, that our plan would have had Knox and Brax escaping without us already.

Still, we had to try. What other option did we have?

"I've wanted to tear you to pieces since you got here," said a shade who had backed us into a corner in a large classroom. It was a woman I didn't recognize, one I didn't know.

It meant that I had no idea why exactly she hated me, but the reason didn't matter.

"Don't you think you've got bigger problems than us?" Wade asked with his usual carefree tone. "Isn't now the time to try and get out?"

"Get out?" She laughed as though she'd never heard anything dumber. "There is no getting out. Do you really think they don't already have guards at the front doors? Guards watching the fence line? There is no escape, so I might as well use this chance to remove things I don't want to be here when they gain control again."

"And by that you mean us?" Wade let out a thin laugh full of stress. "I feel like if I wanted to get rid of someone, I wouldn't waste my time on folks like us. I'd go after the person who guards the chocolate."

The woman shook her head and came forward. A glance at her wristband told me what she was. *Dryad.* That meant little to me, but when she lifted her hands and a tree grew from the cracking tile floor, it made it clear.

Wade yanked me to the side, out of the way, when a branch swung toward us from the rapidly growing tree.

I shook, wanting nothing more than to collapse to my knees, but a glance at Wade told me I couldn't.

He could steal her power if he got close enough, but closing the distance was dangerous. One wrong hit could put him down.

It left it to me, and I couldn't let him get hurt, couldn't let him fall because of me. I forced myself to use my power, to twist the sounds of the tree and send them toward her no matter how I staggered.

It struck her, knocking her down, but we had no time to celebrate. The hit was weak, not enough to do more than slow her down, and as she got up, another few shades came into the room.

Any hope I might have felt that the new people would help us disappeared when I saw who it was. Gina, the girl Kit had used to knock me around stood there, along with a few others I didn't know. Their expressions showed they wanted nothing good with me.

I fell to my knees, unable to keep myself upright anymore. Wade crouched beside me, grabbing at me without touching my skin, trying to help me, but I shook my head. I'd never used my powers like this before, hadn't realized I had a limit, that it could tire me out. Between the fight with the shade on the bridge and our trip here, I'd run out of power.

We were so close to the rally point, so close to finding Brax and Knox, but I had nothing else to give.

I looked toward Wade, then moved my hands quickly. *"Go. Just leave me here."*

He shook his head. "Not a chance—I'm not leaving you." He rose and stood between the others and I, his expression hard.

"You think you can stop us?" Gina sneered as if amused. "As long as you can't touch us, you're useless."

"Not quite."

She lifted her eyebrow. "Oh really?"

Wade nodded, and I had to admit, his resolve surprised me. He usually looked like a kid, making jokes and taking nothing serious. Despite his power, he'd never struck me as all that scary.

That wasn't the case at the moment, and as he spoke, a shiver ran through me at his resolve. "I've been pulling power from shade after shade. You know that I don't just steal it, right? I can use it." He held his hand out and set it on the tree the dryad had created, and the entire thing turned to dust, drawing a scream from the dryad, telling me they were connected.

Kit's power…

I wanted to ask about Kit, to find out if he was okay since it appeared Wade had stolen his power, but I couldn't right now. I had to trust that Wade wouldn't seriously hurt Kit.

The shades in the room stepped backward, as if unsure. It seemed when they thought they were facing enemies they could easily kill they were all in, but the moment they realized it might be a fair fight, they hesitated.

I wanted to laugh at them, but I lacked the strength.

"Unless you want to end up the same, you're going to want to turn around and leave," Wade warned, none of that friendliness he usually had in his voice.

Gina hesitated. "You might be bluffing. If you could actually take us all on, you would have. Maybe that means you don't have as much power as you want to pretend."

Wade held his arms out. "You're welcome to test that theory."

Gina rushed forward, but before she reached us, a roar echoed from outside. It was familiar, but not because I'd heard it before. Rather than that, it felt more like something I recognized but not from where.

Even if I couldn't place it, the others seemed to at least know they didn't want to play with it. Everyone turned their gazes back to the door just as something huge came through, the skin red, the eyes flashing brightly.

I looked at its face and realized when we locked eyes who it was. *Brax.* I'd only seen him shift slightly before, but even still, I saw him in those red eyes. He was every bit the terrifying beast he'd claimed he could be.

"Fuck," Gina said. "It's Brax." She took a step backward. "We don't have a problem with you. We just want the girl."

Brax peeled his lips back to show pointed fangs that were each easily the size of my hand. It seemed he didn't care for her statement. *"Mine,"* Brax said, though his voice was guttural and so deep, it was hard to decipher.

As soon as he said it, he darted forward.

Something heavy landed on me, and I didn't know what it was at first. Wade's voice clued me in. "Just stay still. Brax isn't in his right mind when he's like this, so we don't want to become targets."

A crash to the side made me twist enough to see the open and vacant eyes of the dryad there. Screams hit my ears, and I wanted so badly to shut it all out.

So much death, so much pain—it all overwhelmed me.

A touch to my head made me jump, but I found it was just Wade stroking his fingers through my hair. "I won't let anything happen to you," he whispered, but I wondered if he'd said it to me at all or if it was just a promise to himself.

Before I knew it, everything stopped. A suffocating silence took the place of the violence before. The room was full of only the panting breaths of something large and angry—*Brax.*

"You should get off her." Knox's voice could have made me smile, just knowing he was alive, that we'd all ended up together.

Wade twisted, but I couldn't see where he was looking. "What if he—"

"He won't hurt her. You didn't hear him growl out *mine*? Trust me, she's the safest thing in the whole damned world right now, and the fact that you're still in one piece says he must recognize you on some level as well. Let's not push our luck any further."

Wade hesitated for only a moment before getting off me. He didn't move far, however. No doubt he planned that if anything happened, he could try to take Brax out if he could touch him.

Though when I sat up, when I found Brax crouching over me, I had to admit that I doubted even Wade had a chance.

Brax was terrifying up close, with blood covering him. It even stained his teeth, and I didn't want to think about what was stuck between them. While Wade had hidden me from having to witness all the carnage, that didn't mean I didn't have a pretty good idea of what had happened, especially with the maimed, lifeless bodies around.

"Mine," he repeated and came closer.

I wanted to pull away, to reject him, but something stopped me.

He'd done this for me. He'd allowed himself to become this because of his worry about me. Even if his eyes were different, they were still his, and he stared at me as if I were his whole world.

I swallowed down my fear and rose to my feet. Even with him crouching, I hardly came to eye-level with him. It made me realize just how large he'd grown, how intimidating.

I set my hand on his face, ignoring the wetness, the blood that no doubt smeared my palm now. I couldn't speak, couldn't tell him thank you, couldn't reassure him, so I did the only thing I could think of.

I leaned forward and pressed my forehead to his, then closed my eyes. It was a surrender, a submission, a way for him to know what he meant to me even in this form, even covered in blood, even as terrifying as he was.

He huffed softly, his shoulders slumping as if that had worked, as though the tension drifted away.

"I hate to break into this," Knox said, "Especially because I would like my arms to stay right where they are, but we need to get going before reinforcements get here."

I turned to find Knox there, a smile on his face. He held his hand out, and I took it. He brushed his lips to mine, just a quick kiss as if he needed it to be sure I was okay, before he nodded behind him. "Ready to go?"

I nodded.

It was time to get the hell out of Larkwood.

* * * *

Warden

I smiled as I stood there, waiting.

Maybe smiling wasn't appropriate. The bridge between the North Tower and the main building had been destroyed, and while I had no hard numbers, I knew we had lost many guards. In addition, countless shades were dead.

This was a day Larkwood would never forget, one that had changed the very fabric of this place. After never having lost a shade to escape, never having anything of this type happen, it seemed we'd underestimated the problems just one siren could cause.

Being angry wouldn't change that, however. All I could do was stand there and wait, knowing that no matter how much trouble Hera and her little consorts could cause, they wouldn't escape. I'd have them soon enough, and she would discover the ruthless side of me that had managed to run Larkwood for so many years.

"You're sure they'll come here?" a guard asked.

I nodded. "They were overconfident. My assistant already told me about Knox taking the key to the roof. They set up a fake alarm for the entry to draw guards there and leave the roof undefended."

"How were they planning on getting down from here?" the guard asked.

"They likely planned to scale down the sides. A number of ropes disappeared from a storage room a few days ago. Not that it matters much, now."

Because I stopped them. Because I outsmarted them.

Hera had been my surprise attack for a while now, the one who so many of my plans hinged on. I might have underestimated how powerful she could become, but if nothing else, this showed me how right I'd been to take an interest in her. No great leaps forward occurred without sacrifice, and those who died tonight were that sacrifice.

We would capture her again, send her back to the North Tower, and allow Corrander One to tear her mind apart. When she became an obedient little toy, she would prove immeasurably useful. Between what she could do with her power and what she could buy me with her connections and name, there was no end to the ways I could use her.

The rest of them?

Perhaps I wouldn't kill them. Maybe I would have Corrander One change them as well, then offer them as presents to Hera. If she became as important as I suspected she would, giving her her own little harem would prove no hardship to me. It was a cheap payoff that might give me more power, more leverage.

I glanced at my watch. With communications still down, updates about Larkwood's state were all but nonexistent. I'd sent word for reinforcements from outside Larkwood through a special line in my office that ran off its own battery backup. They would arrive in the next hour or two to clean up the mess, to help secure the shades, to regain order.

We could sweep most of this under the rug and keep the truth of it from the public.

Not all of it, though. I would never let a good crisis go to waste. I could use the story of a small riot to garner an increase in security funds. People wanted to feel safe, and they'd happily pay anyone willing to give them that illusion.

I shook my head, because that was a concern for tomorrow. For tonight, the number one task was to regain custody of Hera. Little else mattered. I'd happily burn half of Larkwood down—guards and shades included—just to get her back.

Still, I would have expected them to appear by now. The guards stood on the roof, off to the side enough that Hera and the others appeared, they wouldn't see any of us. Countless rifles were trained on the entry, tranqs at the ready.

This was it.

I'd get her back, and she'd realize she had no chance, that she couldn't hope to stand against Larkwood or me.

My phone made a noise, making me pull it out and frown. With the communications down, I hadn't expected to receive anything to my cell.

I froze when I read the notification.

Access to Warden panic room.

Which meant…

They'd just tricked us all.

Chapter Twenty-One

Hera

I held my breath as the door to the panic room in the Warden's office slid open after I entered the code I'd seen in her memories. I'd wanted so badly to feel confident in our plan, but I hadn't truly believed this room existed until I saw it with my own eyes.

So many things had gone wrong already, that I hadn't accepted this could have been true. I'd expected to get all the way here only to find I'd been as foolish as Deacon and Kit liked to say I was. Instead, the door sat open like a sign from the heavens to keep going.

With the Warden's forces no doubt split between the entrance and the roof, we'd gotten a clear shot into the staff floor and her office. It seemed letting myself examine all those memories I'd seen from her had paid off.

"Let's go," Knox said and tugged me forward, his arm around me to help me. I'd tried to walk on my own, but I'd stumbled time and time again before Knox had stepped in to help.

Brax went in first, his body still in its berserker form. He peered around, as if checking for danger, then huffed softly. It was funny that I already felt as though I understood him better and could read him in this form.

Maybe that skill came from my inability to speak, allowing me to read body language instead.

Wade entered next, and his voice from inside made me smile. "This is nice, I've gotta say. Seems like being the evil overlord has some benefits. Maybe we are all turned around on this thing. Let's become evil overlords, too!" After a moment, he made an excited sound from farther in. "She has chocolate chip cookies! Honest to god real ones."

Knox shook his head before helping me to follow, walking us through the doorway behind her desk, the one that had hidden behind a camouflaged piece of the wall.

Wade wasn't wrong—the room was nice. They'd placed it here so in the event of a riot, the Warden would have a safe escape. Just past the panic room, which held food, medical supplies and weapons, was a secondary door. As long as I'd read the memories right, it would lead down to a tunnel that would take us outside the walls.

In other words?

It led to freedom.

"Hera…"

I turned to find Deacon standing in the doorway to the office across the room, his purple eyes wide. So many things played across his features.

Relief, surprise, fear. He hid none of them as he stared at me.

I swallowed hard, angry at myself for having to face him. I'd wanted to leave without having to face him, without having to witness the look of anguish on his face. I didn't want to see that, and I sure didn't want it to be the memory that stuck with me, the one I'd have to see when I thought back after this. I should have known better, though. If anyone could have predicted my plan, if anyone could have guessed where I'd go, it would have been Deacon.

"Don't go," he said. "You don't understand what they'll do to find you, to drag you back here." His voice dropped as he took a step closer, moving into the office but still across the room. "Don't leave me, Hera, don't leave me alone again."

Pain in my chest made me want to give in, to beg him to come with us, to return to him. I thought about the child he'd been for so long, when he'd suffered on his own. I thought about how he had looked those first days after I'd arrived, and how much he had changed over the months.

I didn't want him to go back to that isolation, to that despair.

Then I felt Knox's fingers on my side, and I had to remember, I had more to think about than just myself. I had others relying on me, others who would pay the price if I gave in, and I couldn't do that to them.

I moved my lips, mouthing the word "*sorry*" to Deacon.

He sucked in a breath and charged forward, as if he'd realized what it meant, but it was too late. I hit the button inside the panic room, the one that slammed down a heavy door and latched it closed between us.

He pounded against the door, making me stumble backward. Pain gripped me, and the sight of his betrayed face haunted me. I didn't want to leave Deacon, but he had to make his own choices. I couldn't force him to crave freedom the way I did.

Knox tugged me toward the secondary door. "You can cry later, songbird. For now, we need to go."

I didn't argue or resist as he pulled me, as we followed Brax and Wade into the tunnel. Maybe it was almost being out, or maybe I'd just gone numb, but the exhaustion didn't drag me down as much. I trailed behind Knox, moving through the poorly lit tunnel, having no idea how long it took.

At the end, Brax shoved open a heavy metal hatch, then hopped up and out of the tunnel. He reached in, helping to pull Wade up, then Knox. Finally, he lowered his large hand, and I grasped it.

He lifted me from the tunnel without trouble, and the light from the sun that peeked over the mountains lit the world around us.

I turned to stare back at Larkwood, at the place that had trapped me for nearly a year, the place that had stolen everything from me, that had nearly killed me more than once.

Fires raged, and even from this distance, the screaming reached me. It was in chaos, and I couldn't even guess at the death toll.

I could only hope that the shades there took advantage of the chance, that they made their way out, that Larkwood fell.

That Kit escaped. That Lilianna escaped. That Deacon escaped. I wanted them all to live happy lives, even if I wasn't a part of it.

The sight of Larkwood in flames and chaos soothed some part of me. My problems weren't close to over yet, but at the very least, I was alive, and I was free.

Larkwood had wanted to destroy me, but only one of us was in ruins right now.

It might be a monster, one that wanted my blood, but I'd bare my own teeth. I glanced beside me, at the men who had risked everything to stand here beside me.

I had things bigger than myself to protect now, and if Larkwood wanted to come after us, I'd teach it just how dangerous I could be.

Want to see more from this author?
Here's a taster for you to enjoy!

Larkwood Academy: Screaming
Jayce Carter

Coming November 2022

Excerpt

I might have escaped Larkwood, but I couldn't shake the feeling they were right behind me, that if I let my guard down for even a moment, they'd grab me again and drag me back to hell. Every sound, every person that passed, it all put me on edge.

"Here." Knox made me jump when he caught my hand from behind and pressed something into my palm.

I glanced down to find a couple of folded twenties there. I frowned, then offered him a questioning glance.

"Don't worry—I didn't do anything weird to get it. I just used my powers to convince someone to hand over his wallet. Given the very nice sports car he was driving, I doubt he'll miss it all that much."

I let out a relieved breath. If it were Brax, I'd have worried he might have left a body behind. With Knox, a fear that he'd done something he hadn't wanted to get the money had hit me. Hearing he hadn't soothed my fears.

It had been nearly a week since we'd gotten out of Larkwood. The first trek through the open desert had been the worst, and we'd moved fast, pushing ourselves to our limits. Thankfully, with my hearing, I'd been able to identify helicopters and patrols before they got close. This was the second town we'd stopped at, since we hadn't wanted to stay long in the first. We'd only remained in the first long enough to get a change of clothing.

We'd picked up some items from a thrift store, paying for it all with money Brax had — I sure didn't ask him how he'd gotten it. It had left me in a baggy knit-cable sweater, and jeans with large rips in them — far more casual than I'd been used to in my old life and yet not the clothing I'd had in my life at Larkwood.

Wade had found a pair of slacks and a long-sleeve shirt, Brax a large hoodie and jeans, and Knox wore a rather loud Hawaiian button-up short-sleeve shirt, a windbreaker and a pair of shorts that made him look like a surfer. It made the four of us look like hopeless fashion rejects, but at least we didn't look like escaped prisoners. The long sleeves allowed us to hide our Larkwood bands as well.

I tossed food into my basket as Knox walked beside me, picking things with a good shelf life and plenty of calories. I had no idea what the future held, where we'd go, what we'd find there, which meant we needed to make the best out of what we could find when we got the chance.

I peered behind me, wondering where Brax and Wade had run off to. It was best for us not to be too close in public, since a group of four brought more attention than a pair did, but I struggled not to worry when I couldn't see them.

"They're picking up some goods at the general store down the street," Knox said. "I gave them some of the cash I'd gotten."

I nodded to acknowledge the information, then reached for a pack of cookies from the shelf. They made me pause as I looked at them, the same brand that Brax and Wade had fought over in my room before.

"You sure we need those?"

I thought back to Larkwood, to the chaos we'd left behind. I remembered the way Wade had stood between me and the shades who had wanted to kill me. Next, I recalled Brax fully changed into his berserker form, blood dripping from his huge body, the way he'd taken out everything that risked me before he'd rumbled out *'mine.'*

We'd gone through so much, suffered so much pain to get us here. Cookies seemed a small price to pay.

Knox set his palm over mine, which made me realize my hand still hung mid-air. He guided me back to drop the cookies into the basket while offering a kind smile. "Comfort food is important, right? In fact…" Knox pulled away and walked toward the end of the aisle for a moment. He plucked something from a shelf, then jogged back and tossed it into the basket.

I peered down to find a king-sized chocolate bar.

"You complained about the lack of chocolate before. I figured you deserved something nice, too."

I couldn't stop my smile, not just at the thought of tasting the candy but also at Knox's sweetness.

Now is not the time to act all smitten.

We had bigger things to deal with than my feelings toward Knox.

"You haven't been sleeping well," Knox said, the words so unexpected I frowned at the change in topic.

I tucked the basket into the crook of my elbow so I could sign. *"What?"*

"You've been waking up from nightmares. Are you reliving what happened?"

I gulped but shook my head. *"I'm tumbling into this endless void of darkness. It feels like I'm drowning, and no matter how I kick, I can't reach the surface."* Even admitting the dreams that had plagued me every night made me shudder.

"Kit."

That took me by surprise, and I jerked to a stop.

Knox, however, kept speaking as if the topic weren't awkward at all. "Your bond with Kit. I'm going to guess he's trying to reach you through it, and when you resist, that's why you get that sinking feeling."

"He wouldn't hurt me like that." I might not be certain of many things, but that I knew for sure.

"No, he wouldn't on purpose. However, he may not realize it's causing you any distress. It might be like…being blindfolded and screaming for someone, not realizing they're right next to you. He might be reaching for you but have no idea you can feel it."

Now *that* sounded like the man I know. *"What should I do?"*

"Talk to him." At my look, he laughed softly. "If Kit wants to find you, he can. You need your sleep, though, and you won't get any if this keeps up. So talk to him." After a moment, he added quietly, "You'll probably feel better after checking in with him anyway."

Which was true… Leaving the way I had without a real goodbye to either Kit or Deacon hurt. The memory of Deacon's face, the way he'd stared at me as if I'd broken his heart, was almost as bad as the nightmares.

So I told myself I'd brave it, that when I fell asleep that night, I'd force myself to confront that darkness and Kit.

I owed him that much, didn't I?

"Shit." Knox's curse took me off guard, pulling me from my little pep talk. He wasn't the sort to curse much, and I hadn't done anything to earn a reaction like that as far as I knew.

I pulled back enough to peer at his face, finding his gaze not on me but up and to the left.

I turned, my blood running cold when I realized what he stared at. On the television a breaking story ran and above the newscaster's shoulder? Knox, Wade and Brax's faces stared back at me.

The words that ran along the bottom edge of the screen talked about the escape from Larkwood, though they only mentioned the other three. Nowhere did they imply a fourth person had participated.

Why doesn't it include me?

"We should get going," Knox said, his voice low. "You check out, and I'll head next door to grab Wade and Brax. Meet us on the side of the building."

After I nodded, he headed out, his face down. Thankfully, the three looked different enough in regular clothing than the sweats the pictures showed. Besides, most people ignored news reports like those, assuming that such things would never touch their lives.

I paid quickly, a gesture toward the large scar at my throat when the cashier had tried to strike up a conversation. My fingers ached from the heavy bags, but just as Knox had said, I found all three men around the side of the building.

And boy did Brax look angry. Still, the expression fit rather well on his face. In fact, if he really wanted to hide who he was, the best way would have probably been to smile. No would recognize him like that.

Brax narrowed his eyes before swiping his hand out and taking the bags from me without asking. "No idea what you're thinking, but I don't like that smirk."

I shrugged rather than admitting or denying anything.

"Looks like this might be our last family outing," Wade said.

"Why wouldn't they include Hera, though?" Brax asked.

"It has to be a ploy." Knox pressed his lips together for a moment. "Maybe the Warden hopes that will get us stuck, that it'll force her to act alone so guards can look for Hera?"

Maybe... though the more I thought about it, the less that made sense. *"I think she doesn't want it known I'm at Larkwood at all. She's keeping it secret to leverage that information, which means she can't admit I'm not there anymore. She probably can't even tell my parents, because if she did, they'd stop helping her."* Even saying that hurt, making a deep spot inside my chest ache, the part that still craved a family.

Wade reached for me and entwined his gloved hand with mine, his tight grip reassuring.

His touch made his point loud and clear — whether or not my parents ever accepted me, I had people. No matter how hard it had been to lose my voice, it had taught me how much a person could say without ever speaking a word.

So I squeezed back as we headed off toward the empty store we'd broken into the night before to sleep at.

Things might look bad, and they might just get worse, but I wasn't alone.

* * * *

That horrible sinking sensation took over me again when I went to bed, made me cry out in fear. Even asleep, even locked in this dream, Knox's words came back to me.

This was Kit's call. Now that I knew that, I could feel it. That darkness, that cold, it was exactly like him. After almost a week outside of Larkwood, I couldn't avoid him anymore, could I?

No matter how difficult it was, how much I wanted to avoid this, I couldn't any longer.

So rather than trying to run from the connection, from the bond that tugged at me, I followed it. I walked through that door I'd discovered during my first dream, when I'd spoken to him after the forming of our bond.

And the moment I saw Kit, I nearly collapsed. He looked so much as he had before, the sight threatening to yank me backward, to Larkwood, to the hell of that place, but also to *him.*

He lifted his gaze to mine, and his black eyes widened. Any doubts I had disappeared in that moment, in the hunger there that said he wanted to consume me.

He came forward in such a rush that I backed away — not that it mattered. He slid a hand behind my neck and yanked me against him, lowering his head until he took my lips in a kiss that was nothing like the ones he'd given me before. Those had been innocent and sweet, but now I suspected he'd held himself back the other times.

He held *nothing* back this time. His mouth took mine, deep and aggressive, not letting me have an inch of space, and even though I didn't feel his touch as I did in person, even though the tingle from it wasn't quite right, it made my heart speed and my body crave so much more.

Except I couldn't lose myself in this, not when we had important things to discuss. I set my hands on his chest and pushed away.

Not that he let me go. He broke the kiss but left his large, strong hand on the back of my neck, keeping me up against him as if afraid I'd get away again.

Staring up into his fathomless black eyes managed to blank my head, to steal all my thoughts.

"You should have told me." His voice was dark and so similar to that terrifying one he used to command others.

I dragged my tongue over my bottom lip, missing the taste of him but glad I could at least speak with him here. "I'm sorry."

"Sorry?" He let out a harsh snort before yanking away from me and moving to pace. It seemed he had energy he didn't know what to do with. Perhaps he thought doing that would keep him from grabbing me again? "What does sorry matter? You could have been killed! I knew you were planning something, but never would I have suspected anything like *this*. All the years at Larkwood I've spent, and you managed what no other shade ever could." He paused to stare at me as if he couldn't understand me, as if I were something different all of a sudden.

"It wasn't me," I said.

"No? Because it sure seems like it to me, seeing as you are not here."

"It wasn't *just* me," I clarified. "The only reason we pulled it off was because I wasn't alone. The Warden could anticipate any one shade, but she couldn't keep ahead of us when we worked together. That's why

Larkwood worked so hard to pit us all against each other, but because otherwise, we are too powerful."

Kit took a deep breath, his chest rising then falling as he exhaled. Finally, he faced me again. "That's what you don't understand. Only you could have done that. Brax, Knox and Wade had been here for years, but they never managed to work together. You brought them together — you gave them reason enough to put aside their petty disagreements. I don't think you understand just how amazing that is."

His praise made my cheeks burn, so I turned my gaze from his, unable to hold that scrutiny. "You and Deacon didn't get into any trouble, right?"

"No. Your trick with Deacon worked to throw suspicion off him. Larkwood is already almost back to normal. It seems as if nothing at all happened. A new bridge was put up the next day between the North Tower and the main building, and with the reinforcements, the Warden gained control again by noon. It's strange how such a violent event can so quickly be swept away." He shook his head, then offered me a hard look. "Are you really okay?"

I nodded, struggling with how to answer. "We're all safe. I won't say the escape went without trouble, but we got out uninjured." I paused, then forced myself to go on. "You know, I would have taken you with me if I thought you'd come, right?"

He offered me a smile that lacked humor. "I wouldn't have gone. I didn't believe it possible to do what you did. You know what they say about old dogs and new tricks."

But now we were at the point I couldn't turn away from. Even if I wanted to keep things like they were, I owed him the truth. "I need to tell you something," I said.

He furrowed his eyebrows, as if the very words were unpleasant. "That doesn't sound good."

And it wasn't good. Kit believed his daughter was human, that she lived some normal, happy life somewhere, completely ignorant of the horrors of Larkwood and shades. While he missed her, no doubt, her living the happy life she wanted to no doubt eased him.

Discovering that wasn't the case would hurt him, but he still deserved to know.

"I was taken to the North Tower," I explained, unsure how to start the conversation. His expression pressed me to continue. "I saw what Project Corrander was. You probably saw it as well."

"Those shade soldiers," he responded. "A few showed up to guard the Warden until reinforcements came."

I nodded, rubbing my hands together to try to ease the anxiety inside me. "I also met the shade who created them."

He went still at that, a frown appearing on his features as he put it together. Leave it to Kit to figure things out so quickly. "A few shades can do that, but if you're talking to me, I assume it's a wendigo. To think they had one so close and I never knew..." He shook his head. "No, I suspected, I think. Sometimes, I felt a presence, but I brushed it off as nothing more than a desire to find another like myself." He went still, and when he brought his gaze to mine, anger rested there. "I remember something before the escape, this anger that struck me, and someone trying to pull you away."

"You said *mine*."

His eyes widened. "So that wasn't just a feeling?"

I shook my head. "It was real. The wendigo wanted to turn me into one of those soldiers, had expected to, but when they felt your bond with me, they decided not to."

He approached more slowly than the last time, as if once again worried about frightening me after that story. He cupped my cheek in his large hand. "I'm sorry you went through that, but I'm glad our bond saved you. I don't know what I'd do if some other wendigo broke that, if they tried to claim you, to take you from me."

I let myself melt at his words for a moment, enjoying that connection between us before forcing myself to tell him what I needed to. "That's not all."

He pulled back enough to stare down at me, waiting for me to go on.

"The wendigo they're using there is a young girl with long black hair."

He went impossibly still but didn't interrupt me.

"She's lived her entire short life in the North Tower."

"You don't mean..." He didn't finish the thought.

I nodded, swallowing hard once before speaking. "She said she remembered someone calling her a name once—Lilianna."

Kit yanked away from me, his face a mixture of pain and anger. "She was so close? All this time?"

I grabbed his arm, fear over taking me at what he might do. I didn't want him to go charging in, to try and do anything without thinking it through.

He peered down at where I touched him. I expected him to throw off the touch, to tell me it wasn't my business. Instead, he set his hand over mine. "Don't worry, I'm too old to react carelessly. She has been this close her entire life, and I never realized. A little more time to plan carefully won't change anything." He opened his mouth as if to ask something, then closed it again.

"Do you want me to tell you about her?"

He nodded, but before I could, he pulled me against his chest, wrapping his strong arms around me. "You know this isn't over, right? I don't care where you go, or how far you run, I won't just give up on you. I wasn't kidding. You are *mine*."

I let myself rest against him, nodding instead of answering.

Kit pressed a kiss to the top of my head, then released me. "Okay, tell me about my daughter."

* * * *

Brax

How was it that even now, wearing clothing that didn't quite fit her and with no makeup, Hera could still manage to tempt me so much? I'd seen women all dolled up who had barely gotten an eyebrow raise from me, yet here Hera was, checking to make sure she had everything, not trying in the least, and she had me pathetically smitten.

She turned toward me as if she'd sensed my gaze. The way she smiled warmed me, especially since there weren't many people who would smile when they saw me.

"Getting ready to go?" I asked.

She nodded, patting her hands down her sides as if to check for everything.

"I don't like you going by yourself. I'm not good for a lot of things, but bodyguard is a readymade role for me. It pisses me off that I have to stay behind."

She smiled wider, as if charmed by my pouting. *"We can't risk you or the others getting seen. I'm just going to pick up the last of the supplies for the next leg of our trip, because we can't stay here any longer. Don't worry,"* she signed.

"How can I not worry? Sure, you weren't mentioned in the news, but that doesn't mean the Warden doesn't have people looking for you."

She frowned, and it took a moment for me to realize why. The moment I did, I jerked my gaze away, ashamed that I'd been so stupid as to make that mistake.

Her hands flew a second time, signing faster than the first. *"You could understand me, couldn't you?"*

I let out a long sigh at my frustration with my own idiocy. I'd stupidly opened my mouth and admitted something I'd never planned on admitting. Still, with no good way to get out of it, I nodded and answered truthfully. "Yeah, I can."

"For how long?"

"Not long. Couple weeks before we left?"

Hera narrowed her eyes. *"Then why didn't you tell me?"*

I rubbed the back of my neck, not caring for the scrutiny. "I'm not very good at it yet. In case you haven't noticed, I'm not really a studying sort of guy — never was. Turns out that learning sign language isn't all that easy. Didn't want to say anything until I didn't embarrass myself, especially if I couldn't get the hang of it."

"So you started learning a couple weeks ago?"

And here went the part I'd not wanted to discuss. "No. I started a few months ago, after our first night together. I just couldn't get a good grip of it for a while."

I stared at the floor, now wanting to see her disappointed when she realized just how hard it was for me to grasp some more delicate information. I wasn't stupid, but unless it had to do with tactics or warfare, my brain just didn't like to convert it into long term storage. It meant that learning ASL had taken months of study at night with that damned book, sitting up late while I tried to beat the information into my thick skull.

It had burned that I'd needed Wade or Knox to translate for me for so long, when no matter how many nights I worked toward it, I just couldn't understand with how quickly her hands moved. But I'd kept going, wanting to communicate with her on my own.

A warmth on my cheek made me lift my gaze again. She said nothing — with her hand on my cheek it wasn't as though she could sign — but the smile she gave me said more than anything else could have. She came closer and leaned up, onto her tiptoes, then brushed her soft, warm lips against mine.

It reminded me of when I'd been in my berserker form, the memories fuzzy as they often were after I returned to myself, but *this* I remembered. She'd pressed her forehead to mine, the touch so unbearably gentle that it had reached past the haze of my bloodlust.

And just like the time before, it made me shudder and give in. How could do she that to me so easily?

It hit me especially hard when she crossed that line, when she reached out for me. Too often our relationship had been me crossing it. I'd gone to her room. I'd touched her. I'd craved and she'd given in. That meant when she made the first move, when she showed that she didn't fear me, that she wanted me in some way, it completely took me down. Any resistance I might have mustered went away immediately. She had a line past all those other feelings, right down to something deeper, to the real me that rested beneath my berserker.

So I kissed her back, taking her first move and running with it. I pushed her until I had her trapped between the wall and my hard body, wanting to keep her still. She felt like something that kept slipping away, like holding her was trying to grasp smoke, but for the moment I had her.

I had to let her go out alone, because my face was plastered on every TV screen around. I'd caused her far more trouble than I'd help her with, which meant no matter how much I hated it, I had to keep my ass planted right where it was.

And I *really* hated it.

I kissed her deeper, tasting her, slipping my tongue past her lips. I ran the hand not behind her neck down her, tempted by her soft and giving body. She wore another outfit from the thrift store, something that didn't quite fit but made her look better than women who wore expensive tailored gowns. It was just her, though, and she drew me as no other had. I didn't care what she wore. I didn't care how she styled her hair — I wanted her no matter what.

I reached beneath her sweater to find her warm skin, dancing my fingertips over her stomach, her ribs, the sensitive flesh beneath her the line of her bra. It all made me want to strip her bare right then, to forget others were in the shop, that we had things to do, that dangerous problems plagued us. We could toss that all aside and just lose ourselves in each other for a short while. When I did that, the rest of the world didn't seem so overwhelming or imposing.

A door opening farther back in the shop woke her up, at least. I didn't know if I cared — if Knox or Wade walked in, what did that matter? We were all adults, and we were well aware of what happened between adults.

Yet, it seemed Hera was less willing to let others walk in on us naked and tangled together, because she pressed her small hands to my chest and pushed.

I broke the kiss but rested my forehead against hers. "Saved by the incubus, huh?" I knew Knox's footsteps as if they were my own, so as soon as he got close enough for me to catch them, I easily knew who approached. "Normally incubi lead to more sex, not less. Figures my brother would end up being a cock-block."

I leaned in and pressed my lips to her throat, not willing to let her go without something. I sucked hard at a spot on the side of her neck, a place difficult to hide.

She arched against me, pulling in a harsh breath at what was no doubt a sting, but I didn't stop.

Finally, I released her, pulling back. I stroked my fingers over the red mark I'd left. "If I've got to stay put here while you go out, you damn well will wear my mark when you go." A hazy memory of myself from my other form, when I'd thought of her as my mate, hit me.

I'd never felt that way before, never wanted any one female over another, had never really cared, but clearly Hera wasn't like anyone else.

Was that why a rush took over me at the sight of the darkening hickey on her neck, the sign that she had someone? It felt like a huge warning signal to anyone who would dare even consider touching her.

And it soothed me. It let me take a step backward before Knox walked into the entryway where Hera and I stood.

"Not gone yet?" Knox asked the question with a grin, as if he knew exactly the reason and it amused him.

Then again, as an incubus, he could probably *smell* Hera's interest, could taste the lust in the room, and Knox didn't take sex seriously as a lot of others did. He didn't give a damn if I slept with Hera — he'd made that clear enough after the first time.

He wanted her, of course, but me having tasted her, me being with her, that didn't change his feelings about her.

His gaze moved to her neck, to the mark, and his smile widened. While the thought of anyone walking in on me fucking Hera didn't bother me, as it turned out, Knox seeing the mark made me shy.

Maybe because I'd never wanted to leave proof on anyone else, never wanted to claim anyone else, that it felt far more personal, more special.

I ignored the heat in my cheeks and pulled back from Hera, putting distance between us. "Be careful," I warned her again. "If you run into any problems, don't face them yourself. Just get the hell out of there and back to us."

"You worry too much," Knox told me.

"I saw her tear down the bridge to the North Tower, then take down damn near every shade between there and you. Trust me, she can manage some shopping on her own." Wade walked into the room, a cup in his hand. "In fact, next Black Friday, I'm taking her with me to score the best deals. She'll be able to clear out any competition."

I frowned and gestured at his coffee. "Where'd you get that?"

"Gas station."

"You aren't supposed to go out." I shoved the words out through gritted teeth.

"It's *fine*," he assured me before taking a drink of the coffee. "Whereas you two look like the type people notice, I am unfailingly forgettable. It is one of my few redeeming qualities. I look like any young college student, or even like a high school senior trying to look older. No one looks twice at me."

"And you didn't get me any?" Knox managed to look downright offended. "I thought we were friends."

"You share women with your friends — not coffee. Come on, now, some things are sacred!"

Knox reached out and snatched the cup from Wade, who gasped and pressed his now empty hand to his chest. "You just wait, buddy. The next time you want to quiet your incubus, I'll leave you flat on your ass!"

I turned from the two and back to Hera, trying to ignore the bickering of the children. "You should just get going. They'll keep this up for a long time."

Hera nodded, fumbling with the strap of her bag as if uncomfortable. It made me chuckle, that oddly innocent sweetness she had.

She nodded, then took a step toward the door. I stopped her with a hand around her arm and tugged her back to me, not giving a damn if the other two saw. I offered one more short passionate kiss before pulling back to look into her eyes. "Be careful," I repeated.

Hera's tongue touched her lip, as if she missed my taste, and I forced myself to let her go and step away before I took her right there.

She turned away and left, a quickness in her steps that suggested her cheeks were bright red.

I twisted to find the other two no longer bickering, but instead staring at me with wide grins, as if they'd just gotten treated to the most amusing sight they'd ever seen.

I narrowed my eyes into a glare, then flipped them both off before storming back into the main area of the empty shop.

And I tried my hardest to ignore the laughter from behind me.

About the Author

Jayce Carter lives in Southern California with her husband and two spawns. She originally wanted to take over the world but realized that would require wearing pants. This led her to choosing writing, a completely pants-free occupation. She has a fear of heights yet rock climbs for fun and enjoys making up excuses for not going out and socializing.

Jayce loves to hear from readers. You can find her contact information, website details and author profile page at https://www.totallybound.com

Home of Erotic Romance

Sign up for our newsletter and find out about all our romance book releases, eBook sales and promotions, sneak peeks and FREE romance books!

www.ingramcontent.com/pod-product-compliance
Lightning Source LLC
Chambersburg PA
CBHW050600260626
47157CB00002B/650